The Wentworth attic was broken into many dormer spaces. The smaller rochambers—for the ser
aren't uneasy about b
Perry, the butler.

"Oh, no." But I loo
what about the little gable rooms, what about this one?"

"They're all open, I believe. No, not that one, Miss Miller. That one has been locked up for years." Perry looked uncomfortable, I thought, just for a moment—then properly bland. He disappeared down the servants' stair. Why had only one room been locked? I looked closely and saw that the plates on the door and doorframe were somewhat loose. The wood was old and fibrous.

I shouldn't do this, I told myself.

The door gave. When the dust settled and I could finally see, the room didn't look too promising. A low pallet bed. Bare walls. Nothing else.

Except for a small strongbox of dull metal at the foot of the cot . . .

★ ★ ★ ★ ★

"A lively, spunky detective with a dry sense of humor. Lamb writes well, evoking a bygone era through the eyes of her romantic but undeluded heroine."

Portsmouth, New Hampshire, Herald

CHAINS OF GOLD

Margaret Lamb

BALLANTINE BOOKS • NEW YORK

Library of Congress Catalog Card Number: 84-22853

ISBN 0-345-33280-6

This edition published by arrangement with St. Martin's Press

Manufactured in the United States of America

First Ballantine Books Edition: July 1986

For my mother, who likes puzzles

Contents

ONE

For me there were special ghosts on the staircase, known voices in the brown old rooms—presences that one would have liked, however, to call a little to account.

—HENRY.JAMES, ''The Sense of Newport''

PROLOGUE:
Pleasures and Palaces

I've always liked old houses and the stories that go with them. That's how I got involved with an old murder, through my job at *Pleasures and Palaces*.

You know the magazine: glossy full-color layouts of gilded old resorts, country houses we don't visit, exotic tours we'll never take. The history is well researched (by me), the architectural notes accurate and surprisingly technical, the prose spare and good. The magazine exists, of course, not to show the rich to themselves but to help the rest of us fantasize.

My own fantasy was that through *Pleasures and Palaces* I would get a privileged glimpse into other people's houses and lives—strip off the outer walls (more subtly, of course, than the wrecker's ball) and see the dramas, or at least the decor, within. In a year and a half I had had only a peek. There was the Park Avenue pad of a dowager devoted to spreading the message of a great ascetic Hindu mystic; in the library devoted to the Master, all of his works were *bound in calf*. There was the East Side chateau of a French countess, chock full of Impressionist masterpieces, with anti-Semitic French publications lying open on the ottoman before the fire. Mostly, though, I worked in the office, checking other people's facts.

So I told myself, that bright Monday morning in August, that I had to get up and go to work because I was lucky to have an interesting job in hard times. Oh, to be an idle heiress (I thought), even a poor one who had to idle in Coney Island. I just wanted to take the library's Edith Wharton omnibus out to the beach. But I had to put on my girdle, poetically speaking, and "go to business," as Grandma used to say.

I lay in bed and stared at the bare white wall with the square of sunlight trembling upon it: it seemed a living work of minimal art, bright on white. Beyond the little bedroom of the new law tenement, my tiny living room and kitchen were fresh and clean. There was not a single plumb line or right angle in the apartment. I had just moved in, at an outrageous rent.

I loved it. My friends who were, like me, four years past college, lived in Hoboken or Brooklyn or at home—or three to a one-bedroom in Manhattan. I lived alone in Manhattan!

But I couldn't get out of bed. Since the chain-snatching incident in the hall the week before, I'd had great difficulty getting up in the morning. I was frightened. I got anxiety attacks. And Dr. Geldohr, my shrink, was on vacation, so I couldn't tell him what had happened, that it wasn't all paranoia and fantasizing.

Brrrnng!

I had to get up to answer it.

"Hello, Penny? I thought you'd be gone already. Are you okay? What are you wearing to work today?"

"I'm fine, Mama." I put on my cheerful wide-awake animated self faster than makeup. I painted the picture:

silk blouse, linen skirt, all natural and tasteful. "And, of course, I'm wearing the gold chain you gave me for my birthday." Why did I have to gild the lily? I looked at myself in the mirror above the sink to check the ugly red line—like whiplash, but I couldn't sue—where the chain snatcher had pulled it right off.

"Good. Silk is good, especially if you're losing weight. Well, I have to go to work early. They're acquainting me with the new computer."

In the shower I noticed that I wasn't losing weight. Poor Mama. My mother was a crack executive secretary who did the boss's work. An energetic and very intelligent woman, she had, since she'd quit smoking, taken to borrowing romance novels from the other "girls" at work. She read them at top speed, flipping pages and muttering, "It's trash, trash."

"Then why don't you go back to mysteries?"

"Suddenly mysteries make me nervous, I don't know." Since my father died, she, too, had anxiety attacks; and we compared notes.

So she read romances and complained that they weren't real. All the same, she had faith I'd find romance at *Pleasures and Palaces*.

One cardboardy slice of toast. Black coffee like viscous rubber. Leaving the chain on the door, I unlocked, opened, peered out into the hallway. No one. It was a terrible habit I'd gotten into, even before the chain snatcher.

"Why do you want to live," my Uncle Sheldon had asked, "down there where *my* grandparents started out in 1901? Almost the very block—anyway, the Lower East Side."

"The East Village," my mother had tried to explain, defending me. "Now they're getting condominiums there too."

5

The East Village. I loved it, but now I was scared, having my own apartment in New York for the first time. From my window I had seen the Narcotics Squad lead a dope ring out of a basement factory in an old Federal-style house across the street.

Heading west as the tropical New York morning sun beat down on my head, I passed new co-ops and the crumbling brown building where Emma Goldman had published *Mother Earth* with Alexander Berkman, and from whence Berkman had sallied forth to shoot Henry Clay Frick during the Homestead Strike. As I walked, history rose up from the steaming city surfaces of tar and concrete, old scenes wavy with heat. I felt a pang—guilt, and the unrequited researcher's love for the graduate program I'd given up because I couldn't afford the outrageous tuition, and because there were no college teaching jobs anymore anyway. Besides, who would want a doctoral dissertation on Anarchists of the Deed, Kropotkin's apocalyptic disciples who had dreamed that the neatly timed bomb, or the assassin's single bullet, would bring down the structure of society? How quaint they seemed now, in an age and place when such deeds would only seem part of the pattern of random violence!

I passed the place where the Academy of Music had stood on Fourteenth Street. There the old Dutch- and English-descended landowning New York Society had kept the post—Civil War capitalists from renting the boxes. Now all was sleaze in transit. All the past aspires to the condition of music, that is, it vanishes into the air.

On to Union Square, where my grandfather had attended the big Communist rallies. Down into the subway, all sway and roar, which made sweating steerage passengers of us huddled, hurtling masses. Hanging on the overhead bar, I stared up at a cool blond couple cavorting on a yacht. It was a cigarette ad. No vacation for me this year, I thought; I owed Dr. Geldohr my vacation money.

Debouched to the innards of a glass-and-steel tower, I felt nervous again. To gain access to the elevators, we had to flash our IDs. People had been robbed at gunpoint in the gleaming white elevators in this heart of corporate America. Ascending, I felt my heart ascend to my throat. I couldn't breathe for a moment . . .

Pleasures and Palaces shared a floor with other H. H. W. publications. When the management of H. H. W. Enterprises had killed *Clio*, the dignified hardcover history monthly, I had been shuttled to *P&P*. Others had scattered to the Books Division, *Sportsweek*, *TV Topics*, *Celeb*, or other more vital organs of that vast and pulpy empire.

On my desk was a note: *Penny—Urgent—See Flora.*

Flora MacIsaac, editor of my section, sat in her windowed office amidst a swirl of tacked-up publishing schedules, issue schemes, color photos of Scottish castles and glass summer houses.

"You finished that piece about the brownstone debunker, didn't you, dear? How'd you like to go up to Newport for a week?"

"Me? Newport?" I couldn't afford a vacation, I owed my shrink a thousand dollars—and here was Newport, handed to me on a silver salver.

"Ward Dart needs some help with his story on the 'cottages.' Checking facts, making appointments. That kind of thing."

"Oh." Since the unspeakable Christmas party I had scarcely spoken to Ward Dart. He had followed me into the ladies' room on all fours and I had slammed the door on his head.

"He's staying with friends—you know Ward. The researcher we send will put up in a motel or—why not?—a

7

rather nice rooming house I used to stay at. It's about five days' work. Not a vacation, of course. But a change. It's cooler up there."

Flora crossed her arms and fixed me with her eagle eye. She was a plump, fortyish woman, cheerful but cynical-sounding, with flaming hair. Once she had been a fashion model, then—briefly—had run a modeling agency, which experience had made her feel, she said, like a madam. Flora claimed she had developed an interest in architecture and decorating only after she realized she no longer looked smashing in designer clothes.

When I had gone as a provisional to *Pleasures and Palaces* from the collapsing *Clio*, Flora had looked me over and barked, "My, you're green, aren't you?" When I allowed as much, she took me on. We got along fine.

"You can work with Ward, can't you." It wasn't really a question. "You can be spared at the moment, so I thought of you. Of course if you have appointments in the city this week—"

"Nothing I can't put off."

"Good. Call Ward."

I went back to my office and made the call to Newport.

"Penny? You'll come? Did Flora explain about my interview with Miss Wentworth? No? Well, I desperately need your fantastic memory, my dear. Miss Wentworth doesn't believe in tape recorders—she scarcely believes in electric lights. Who? What do you mean, 'Who?' She's the last of the fabulous Newport spinsters, about ninety-four, and no one has been able to get into that house to catalog the private apartments, though the place is open, of course, one day only during the season. And I'm simply awash in antiques; my story is now more a catalog than an article. You'll give some perspective, you have a good eye. Also, if you can figure some tasteful way of working in an angle on the murder—"

"I can come tomorrow," I said impatiently, expecting gratitude.

"Tomorrow, my God—today! You've got to come today. The audience with Miss Wentworth is set for this afternoon. Tea at Werthmere. It's easier to get an audience with the Pope than with Miss Wentworth."

"It's easy to get an audience with the Pope, isn't it?"

"You know what I mean. My old friend Dorcas De Heem—Dorcas Rivington De Heem Casamassima Crassis—you know, tankers, tobacco, and a chunk of the Bronx—is flying up at noon. Heliport to La Guardia. She's chartered a plane. She'll take you. No buts. Wouldn't you like to have a chat with the Debutante of the Year?"

"Which year?"

"Nineteen forty-eight."

"That was my mother's year."

"Oh? Where did she come out?"

"Brooklyn Savings Bank and New York Telephone."

"This is not just a favor to me, Penny. Don't think I'm critical, but a week in Newport will expand your horizons."

I told him I could be there that afternoon. At the very least, a week of sun would clear up my complexion. I might even forget Dr. Geldohr's desertion. Such were my thoughts.

Of Cottages and Crimes

From Union Square in the morning rush hour to Newport before teatime! The transition was physically so easy, imaginatively so difficult, that I felt as though I must have traveled through time as well as through space; all my week in Newport, that feeling was never to leave me.

For the first time in my twenty-six years, I flew in a small private plane. At first, whenever the pilot in front of me dipped a wing, I clutched at the fragile-looking frame of the cabin. If we went down, I thought, I'd at least have the posthumous fame of a share in the millionairess's obituary. Then, as Long Island and the Sound unfurled and the shapes on the map came true, I forgot my fears and marveled at the beauty of vistas at once vast and tiny.

Next to me in the four-seater sat my traveling companion, the heiress. During the hour-long trip she spoke scarcely a word but remained a mystery—turban-swathed, with dark glasses, leather complexion, heroic neck muscles. Clearly, she had never been under the obligation to make polite small talk with anyone. As the plane made a great racket, speech seemed superfluous anyhow. When we started to descend, I saw the famous "cottages" set out on neat patches of green, scalloped by frills of sand on one side.

An hour later, I had changed clothes, left my suitcase at Flora's rooming house, and was being driven along Ocean Drive by Ward Dart.

"Penny, dearest, you've saved my life. To be invited to tea by Miss Wentworth and not have a backup reporting system—because you have a fantastic memory, my dear, the brain cells of youth, and of course we can't take *notes*. Well, if she allows, we'll make this interview a little feature in the story: box it."

"I don't have a camera."

"Well, of course not. We're not going to take a picture of Miss Wentworth."

"Why not?"

"What a question! A lady only gets her name in the paper when she's born, married, and dies—three times, or, in Miss Wentworth's case, twice. She only agreed to speak to me for *Pleasures and Palaces* because of our story on the Queen Mother's houses. And, of course, because of my, uh, family connections."

"With the Queen Mother?"

"I take no note, child, of either sarcasm or flattery. At Werthmere, we concentrate on the building, the furniture. And the murder case, of course, if we can, discreetly."

"Murder? Who got killed?"

"Her father, the multimillionaire. I thought you were a historian. Miss Wentworth was only ten at the time."

"Oh . . . Wentworth. Sure. It happened here in Newport, didn't it?"

"In the folly on the lawn at Werthmere. Oh, look—

the De Heems built this cottage. Gilded Age Gothic, much more authentic in detail than the real thing. In Newport they tended not to mix styles in a single building, the way they did on Nob Hill, in Denver, or even on Fifth Avenue.''

Ward was a good guide for a tour of Newport: he was old family, yet literate. He capitalized on his entrée to write articles about old families and old houses, travel, antiques, even the classier sporting events in yachting, polo, and fox hunting. Now he was being entertaining. Sailor's sunburn over drinker's flush gave Ward the old-fashioned ''florid'' complexion. He had a voice to match, rich as the Limousin oak casks of the stuff he drank. Ward was a snob, but clever enough to know it and to offer up his obsession as an amusing special taste.

Now he sounded guilty. Apprehensive. What was it?

''Penny, my dear, I can't tell you how frightful it's been trying to get this article together. I told Flora, you are the only one who can read my handwriting and make sense of my scattered notes. And the extraordinary fact is, Miss Wentworth has the notion of giving out a commission, paying for a history of her family.''

''She wants you to be her hired writer?'' I laughed.

Ward was silent for the space of three stately cottages. ''She wants . . . someone to justify her sister. Lady Deake. She wants someone to write a riposte to some upstart.''

''What's the sister supposed to have done?''

''She is supposed,'' Ward said slowly, ''by people who are of course in no position to know anything at all, to have killed her father.''

''Really? In the folly?'' I'd heard of it as just an unsolved murder.

Ward told me more details. I didn't listen carefully. I

was beginning to suspect that Ward had a hidden agenda. He was serving me up this old murder mystery—just as he was including me in the invitation to tea at Werthmere—as a sop. Maybe he was having another of his famous writer's funks or blocks and wanted me to ghost his story without telling Flora. I'd seen enough around the office to know that Ward leaned on strong women when he felt pressure. Was I being upgraded from a young thing subjected to random occasions of sexual harassment to a strong woman subjected to appeals for help? It didn't matter all that much which I was. Either way, I'd had to rush up to rescue my gentleman writer, check his facts, and date his antique finds, all to get the "cottage" piece together for *Pleasures and Palaces*. The life of a lowly researcher!

At H. H. W. Publications (only a small part of H. H. W. Enterprises) almost all of the writers were still men. The researchers, who often did a lot of writing, were still "girls," at least to Ward, who ignored corrections to his sexist language. But he was clearly such a loser. . . .

"Look," I said, interrupting his disquisition on the Wentworth family. "That one's like Versailles. Maybe bigger."

At ground level, the cottages seemed, paradoxically, farther away than they had when viewed from the air. Now the houses were glimpsed through scrolly gates and thick privet hedges; they were hidden behind bulky gatehouses or over the rise of winding driveways.

There were Rhenish castles and Scottish keeps, Georgian façades and Renaissance palazzi, châteaux of all the Louis teens, from Musketeer XIII to Restoration XVIII. Successive styles of European residential and palace architecture had been recreated to veil the naked power of an age of steel and steam.

"If these places were in Europe, they'd have histories of crime behind each one," I said. "You know—here the Duc de Guise was assassinated from behind the arras, there Mary Stuart's second husband was done in by her third."

"That's what I'm saying, wench, we have crime aplenty in Newport. Here, of course, it's never political. But there's enough to satisfy your parlor-maid tabloid taste." Ward turned the wheel on the last convertible made in America, and a Venetian palace floated by. "This is Golconda, where the heir was found floating naked in the swimming pool, clutching a silk pillow that had belonged to the Marquis de Sade. Remember that last gatehouse, the one with the crenellations? The owner's wife and the gatekeeper were found shot dead in the little room up top of it. Never solved. And Dorcas De Heem's debutante party—she revived entertainments not seen since Caligula's last bash."

"I'm hungry," I said. "I missed lunch."

"It's just time for tea," said Ward. "And here we are."

He brought the sports car around a corner and stopped to treat me to yet another "cottage" view.

I saw a fierce stone silhouette set on the rise, against the sky. The spiked iron fence and almost treeless expanse of front lawn allowed a straight-on view of the house itself.

"This," said Ward, "is Werthmere."

And bleak it was, with mullions glaring in the afternoon sun. The old modest American Stick Style seemed to have petrified to some version of English Perpendicular. String-courses looked harsh as metal piping. Gables, chimneys, and crockets made a dragon-spine zigzag at the top. Still, the jumbled Victorian plan of the place softened the stiff right angles of the detail.

Werthmere. Scene of the famous Wentworth murder at the turn of the century. An unsolved murder—unless the tycoon had indeed been shot by his unhappy daughter. Not the daughter who had invited us to tea—not *the* Miss Wentworth, last of the famous Newport spinsters, but Lady—what was her name? Ward had told the story so quickly that I was somewhat confused.

A young man in Treasury green livery opened the Werthmere gate for us. We crunched along the pebbly drive. There were beeches and an avenue of elms at the sides of the estate. The front lawn, though, had only a few stone urns, empty and awry on their pedestals.

"Well?"

"I'm, uh, confused." I didn't want to admit I was impressed.

"Well, yes, the style of Werthmere is rather mixed. Miss Wentworth's mother did most of the building, except for the center hall, which was the old cottage of the fifties. Old Mrs. Wentworth was a social leader of the most ferocious stamp. I've heard that her husband—the murder victim—suggested she could build her castle cheaper and faster in cast iron. *She* didn't think it was funny. But the place does have a cast-iron air, doesn't it?"

"What's she like?"

"Miss Victoria Wentworth, you mean? As I said. Had a reputation as a wit in her younger days. Still has. Great stickler for punctuality. Tells a good story. Of course, I haven't seen her in years. She's the last, except for a great-nephew. It's a sad life, surviving everyone. Her father's murder, her brother's and nephew's sudden accidental deaths, her brother-in-law Lord Deake's murder in the thirties, her sister's life clouded with suspicion—What are you staring at? For God's sake, don't move."

"What, what?"

"Sit like a lady," Ward hissed, "and let him open the door for you. This isn't a New York cab you're in."

An elderly gentleman, surely an ambassador, was making a stately progress down the broad steps.

"Mr. Dart, sir," the man said.

At least, I thought, it's not "Mr. Ward, dear boy," et cetera.

"And Miss Miller," Ward said.

"Ah . . . yes, miss."

"How is Miss Wentworth today?"

"Quite well, sir, considering. She's amazing, you know."

"Ah, yes." It was as if they were talking about the weather. "I suppose summer makes quite a difference, with her arthritis."

"Ah, well, sir. It's a damp climate, even in summer."

We were ushered inside.

The hall had walnut paneling, all the way up. A carved single staircase started on the left wall, continued up on the right. The hall was so crowded with tapestry and display plate and paintings and armor and gladioli-stuffed vases that it looked small. Victorian Tudor. Shakespeare would have suffocated.

"One moment, please, sir, miss."

He left us standing before the cold marble fireplace. It must have worked, of course; but everything in the hall looked unworkable or unsittable.

"Don't be afraid of Perry."

"Is that his name?"

"Didn't you hear me say so?"

I was embarrassed. The butler had been introduced, or at least labeled, and I hadn't heard. Some democrat.

Perry reappeared. "If you'd care to come this way . . ."

"Oh, Perry," Ward said. "Could we. . . ? I've been

telling Miss Miller about the ballroom. She'll be cataloging some things there. . . ."

Perry led us to the right, through a half-open sliding door into one of the largest private rooms I had ever seen. The period effect was somewhat tempered by shapeless fringed chairs around the walls and heavily framed nineteenth-century narrative paintings.

"No electricity," Ward whispered. "It's still candlelit for parties. Candles make a lot of heat. They'd sweat like pigs."

White tapers bristled everywhere in chandeliers, wall brackets, and single silver candlesticks. The room was an enormous birthday cake for an old, old child. Looking up to admire the plaster ceiling frosting, I tripped and almost fell.

We passed through a drapery-framed doorway into a small gallery and then into a darker room. Before I could see clearly I heard the voice, piercing and as petulant as a child's:

"Don't take them through the ballroom, Perry. You make my visitors late. I know you'd rather be conductin' guided tours of Werthmere. But just wait 'til I'm dead, I mean to say."

The Second Last of
the Wentworths

The old lady sat in a straight-backed Jacobean arm-chair, her head cocked birdlike, assured and challeng-ing. She looked about to puff out her breast and sing. Her elbows, nose, and chin jutted out at jaunty angles; her long-sleeved dress, though, covered a plump body of shifting shape. She was rather like her chairs with the carved antique extremities and overstuffed upholstery.

While Ward was explaining that the ballroom tour was all his fault, not Perry's, I studied the butler. Somehow Perry's balding head, his look of intelligent discomfiture, reminded me of someone. Of whom? Someone I knew well, I was sure.

"Well, never mind," said Miss Wentworth. "In my day the butler kept us all in line, don't you know. But Perry is getting on in years, I'm afraid."

The mysterious resemblance deepened with Perry's distress. He seemed relieved when ordered to go out for the tea things.

"Well, now, child," Miss Wentworth said. Address-ing me. "You had a peek at the ballroom. Some people, you know, keep the state rooms under wraps. Dustcovers and closed doors. Well, if you've no one to do the dusting for you . . . The ballroom doors at Werthmere close only for a lying-in-state." She grinned smugly, perhaps anticipating her own.

Ward leaped in to start a story about his father's visit to Werthmere on one such sad occasion. Nodding and bobbling, Ward was so patently willing the old lady to remember him, to acknowledge his connection there—his invitations past and present—that I was embarrassed for him. And surprised.

"That was my mother's funeral," Miss Wentworth said. "I remember your father came. He went smash about then. Nineteen-thirty."

"Uh, yes," said Ward.

"Smash. Do they say that nowadays?" said Miss Wentworth. "Your mother was a . . ."

"A Cotton," Ward said.

"Yes. *They* went smash too." She said it with enormous satisfaction.

"And now I'm here to write about this beautiful house. And to help you in your researches," Ward suggested softly. "And Miss Miller, Penny Miller, is my assistant. We're both here, to serve you however we can."

The old lady cocked her head at each of us in turn, as if to let the honey pour first into one ear, then into the other.

What an awful old woman, I thought.

"A penny for your thoughts, young lady," Miss Wentworth said. "A penny! Ha, ha. Thinkin' about what an awful old woman I am?" I cowered. She turned her fierce eyes on Ward. "So, young man. D'you think you're the person to write the family history? The Wentworth story?"

Ward sat bolt upright, then slid carefully into a more

casual, yet still respectful, position. I wondered why he seemed so nervous about it. Surely he had no ambition to undertake a vanity history of the Wentworths? Surely he must realize he'd have to collaborate every inch of the way with the last survivor? No, she wasn't the last. Ward had mentioned a great-nephew. But she was the last from the Gilded Age, repository of the old family poisons in undiluted form.

I looked around at rows of leather-bound volumes rising to the coffered vaults of the ceiling. It looked like a noble old bank, but it was just the library. I had to admit that it impressed me, too—me with my used-up credit cards, my debts.

I tuned back in to Ward's pitch. He was talking with uncharacteristic modesty about his lack of qualifications.

"I have the enthusiasm, of course, dear Miss Wentworth, but not the scholarship. I don't have the trained scholarly mind that's so important in these matters. I can't shift and weigh." He shifted in his chair, looking sidelong from Miss Wentworth to me. "I think of myself as a mere catalyst, a bringer together of those who can do things properly."

"Well, I don't know. I've heard some of these historical scholars who say they know what they're doin'. Experts on my own time, our 'way of life,' don't you know. They make money for that. But I can't talk to 'em."

"Well, of course, there are such people," Ward said. "Specialists who can't feel at ease with . . . what they admire."

"What's your name, child?"

Miss Wentworth was staring at me.

"Miller."

"Yeomanry," said Miss Wentworth. "Decent stock." It was not a question.

"I'm—" I added "Jewish" but was drowned out by Miss Wentworth, who had not paused for a reply.

"My father always said that a lady could complete her education in her father's library. My father was a very responsible man. We had the best right here. There was never a game room in this house. This is the library. What have you studied, young lady? What have you done?"

"History," I chirped. "Art. I worked at *Clio*, the history magazine. Before the parent organization dropped it. Then I was moved to *Pleasures and Palaces*."

I answered without thinking. Old ladies asked such questions, just as I myself might ask a child, "What grade are you in?" Then, as I heard Ward go on about my fine scholarly background, I realized what was happening. I was being interviewed. For a preposterous job. Ward wanted the social credit of doing Miss Wentworth a favor, but not the bother and boredom of doing the work. Researching an old unsolved murder!

He had tricked me. I didn't want to object in front of the old lady. And if I told Ward no, he could make that an excuse for another teatime audience to say that the young person simply wouldn't do after all.

Perry entered just then with a massive tea tray. I was famished to the giggling point. I felt like eating all the bread and butter just to put Ward in a fit.

"Open the draperies, Perry, so they can see the view."

Late sunlight, massed silver, and bone china. The delicious effect of it all filled me right up to the brim. Perry, Miss Wentworth, and Ward all seemed to be winking in the sudden light. I suddenly realized that the butler's mysterious resemblance was to Henry James— the perfect butler!

"The sun is so beautiful on the tea tray," I said, tickled by my discovery.

"Why, my sister always used to say that," said Miss Wentworth. "Isn't that amazin'? Only my sister said it poetically, of course."

"Miss Miller—Penny—is also an author, in her modest way," Ward chimed in. "Not a poet, of course, like Lady Deake."

Not a poet, but Miss Wentworth was smiling at me—almost graciously—and asking me if I would pour the tea.

I poured with aplomb, lifting high the silver teapot and the cream pitcher, curling my wrist as I had been taught to do for a college production of *The Importance of Being Earnest*.

"Why, you pour just like my sister. She was so graceful."

"Two lumps, Miss Wentworth? Three?" I flourished the silver tongs. Look, Ma, no hands. There was no way that Miss Wentworth, or even Ward, would know that I was just a klutz, acting.

While we had tea, Miss Wentworth talked about her family, about Newport.

"It doesn't do to live in the past. That's not my way, as people know in this town. I make 'em move."

"You're looking well," Ward said. "I'd feel presumptuous asking if you're as well as you look. I'm a wreck myself."

"You don't live right. Probably drink too much. Like my brother. My nephew. Know how I know, eh? You don't take sugar in your tea. Get your sweet from drink." She nodded approvingly at me. Out of a need for instant social energy I had taken three lumps.

"Ah, Miss Wentworth," Ward said, flushing. "Your little tea-and-sugar test would condemn many sober Orientals."

"I don't know," said Miss Wentworth, "about the Orientals. At Werthmere. Living at Werthmere keeps me fit. Everyone knows what to do here. We don't have the cocktail hour. Since my grandfather built this house, it has been run on a regular routine. Lunch at one. Dinner at eight—since the wings were added.''

Miss Wentworth stood to point out the window. Standing, she was shorter than I would have thought; and older.

The three of us stood looking through diamond panes to terrace, greensward, and distant sea. The light now was fuzzing up a bit.

''With a staff one can't do otherwise but live in a regular punctual way,'' Ward said. ''It's important.''

''If my sister hadn't lived in Europe for all those years, I believe she would be alive today. I've been told the English and the French still don't have decent drainage. My grandfather put in the first improved modern bathrooms in Newport. And the first bathtub with plumbing. That was thought more a folly than the real folly out there.''

''Do you see the folly, Penny?'' Ward gave me a *significant look*. ''It's a Roman teahouse. One of the first of its kind in the country.''

I saw a round, conical-roofed structure near the horizon, against the sea. That must have been the site of the famous murder. With its circular shape and its columns, the Werthmere folly looked something like the Temple of Vesta in the Roman Forum. But at Werthmere, the Vestal was still in office, tending the sacred fire of father and family.

''It was built right near the Cliff Walk. After the trouble there, don't you know . . .''

My ears tingled. What would she say about the murder?

''. . . The trouble, I mean to say, over claimin' the Cliff Walk belonged to the City of Newport.''

''Oh, who said that?''

23

"The Supreme Court." Miss Wentworth sniffed. "After that, we built the tunnel. No need to make it easy for 'em, if they want to use the walk. Of course, our folly is no grand affair like Mrs. Belmont's Chinese pavilion. Wasn't meant to be."

Miss Wentworth led us away from the windows, toward a pineapple-legged table heaped with Victorian albums. She went through her historical comments clearly and complacently. Her step was surprisingly springy— toes out, like a librarian. But Miss Wentworth was a librarian with one subject.

"This house was first built in 1859 by my maternal grandfather. Then it was completely redone with both wings and the third floor in 1895. Werthmere is the only house in Newport which incorporates the bracketed style—done here in stone—with authentic English Perpendicular."

"That was a stroke of genius," Ward murmured. "Going back to the source, really."

"That was what Mr. Stanford White told my father. He said he wished he had designed it himself. Of course, I never knew Mr. White or that Fish crowd. No child was allowed to meet those people. But our cottage was original. Still is. And we did it while they were vander-building that monstrosity over yonder—'The Wreckers,' d'they call it? It looks like Grand Central Station. I mean to say, they ought to have a statue of the Commodore out front. My mother always kept in mind that Werthmere was a house for a family."

Miss Wentworth was opening albums on the table and pointing to pictures of the house at different stages. A fringed table lamp gave an inadequate light. As Miss Wentworth opened an architectural guide, a picture fluttered to the floor.

I picked up the picture.

"Yes, for a family," said Miss Wentworth.

The three of us peered at the photograph laid flat on the green baize tabletop.

It was a family portrait taken on the porch of the fatal Roman teahouse. My eyes were drawn first to the two commanding end figures: the tall beautiful blond girl with close-set eyes and a smallish well-knit man in middle age. The girl's nose and brow were by happy accident cast in the noble style thought most beautiful at that time. The man's graying van dyke, like his three-piece suit, had come into fashion again. The three middle figures—the mother, a boy of seventeen, and a girl about ten—were seated on a cast-iron bench. I saw my hostess's plain features in both the determined mother and the complacent child. Miss Victoria Wentworth's stubborn, placid endurance—was that the natural inheritance of a youngest child always petted, always waited on by others?

"Such character," Ward said.

"That was the last picture of all of us together."

This family portrait, I thought, represented an unsolved murder, an unhappy marriage of international fame, a hated social leader, a tragic accidental death—and how much more? My head spun with all that Ward had told me. How long could Miss Wentworth go on talking about her family and not mention any of this?

"My father was a wonderful man. He told me—and I was just a little girl—that I didn't ever have to marry if I didn't want to. He could support me, he said, and I could stay with him. It was the last thing he said to me." Miss Wentworth's voice quavered and then grew very strong. "I wish his enemies could have seen and heard that. He was so gentle and good to a little girl, as good as gold. And all of our people here loved him. They

25

stayed on here twenty, thirty years, as long as they could work.''

Miss Wentworth spoke fervently, her head lifted. I followed her eyes to the wall above the marble mantelpiece. A large oil portrait of the man with the van dyke beard hung there. The expression was lofty and cold. Wentworth looked like Lenin, I thought.

''He was a great man. It was those wicked wicked men who cut him down. Men of violence. Cut him down in his prime because they could not stand to see a man so big. The truth will come out some day. Now nasty people can publish lies about him—about his family— and the courts will not stop it. Do you know that? And now that nasty professor is writing a book about us. The judge tried to make a mock of us. Our good name does not matter. I want everyone to know the truth. A wonderful Christian man. A devoted family. My father, my mother, my sister, my brother, my grandfather—all the way back.''

She stopped. It was as if the audience had ended. Ward began to clear his throat in a thank-you-so-much overture.

''Now, young lady.'' Miss Wentworth was smiling again. ''Don't let an old woman frighten you. Oh, I only want someone to gather the family mementos, to date and gather the pieces. There's so much—journals, old diaries. I can't bear to read them myself, but someone should. And perhaps write something about the way people used to live. The family values. Character. 'The Golden Age,' they call it now.''

Despite myself, I was touched by this monstrous appeal. Miss Wentworth was crafty enough to try to cover up her obsession to some degree. But I wasn't fooled. The old bird didn't give a damn about the Gilded Age

and its imported loot. The message was: justify my
father, my family, let my gods live after me.

"It sounds interesting, but . . ."

"Oh, you take your time to think about it," Miss
Wentworth said. She touched a tapestried bellpull. "I
have made inquiries at the historical society, about suitable remuneration . . . humph . . . for a young scholar
or writer who might . . . humph . . . For a suitable
monograph or article they suggested, ummph, a thousand dollars. Well."

A thousand. That was exactly what I owed Dr. Geldohr
for trying to cure me of paranoia and fantasizing.

We left quickly, whisked away by Perry, who presented me with an illustrated pamphlet, *Architectural
History of Werthmere, Newport, R.I.*

"Miss Wentworth hopes this will interest you."

The abrupt dismissal both rankled and amused. I supposed that Miss Wentworth had been picking up people
and putting them firmly in their place—saying "stay
there" to abandoned dolls—for more than ninety years,
with minimum fret to herself.

I said nothing to Ward. I wanted to make him apologize for bringing me to Werthmere under false pretenses.
Ward, thank God, knew nothing about the thousand-
dollar shrinkage debt that made the offer tempting to
me.

At the Werthmere gate we had to wait for a fancy
European sports car and its occupant to enter first. The
pale young man with furrowed brow made three cau-
tious passes at the ample entry space before he passed
through.

I knew him. I had seen him before somewhere.

"Did you see that? A Daisy Six," Ward said.

I tried to remember where I had seen the young man.
Could I be imagining—again? It was a mark of my urban

paranoia to make connections where none existed. After all, the young man with the dog I had let into my apartment building last week, the one (the man, I mean) who had pushed me and snatched my gold chain in the hall—I thought I'd seen *him* before too, thought he was a peaceable tenant and neighbor.

But I really do know this young man, I thought. And we had quarreled about something important. What was it?

And what was his business at Werthmere?

Chains of Gold

Ward took me to dinner at a rambling tavern and soda shop with pleasantly fake Olde New England decor. Rosy-cheeked young men with short hair were addressing older men as "sir." The girls had blond pageboys, deep tans, white piqué dresses—and looked as though they had stepped daisy-fresh from a 1950s time capsule. Everywhere there were school blazers and red slacks. Ward explained that breton red was the yachtsman's favored color for slacks, that the boy who smiled and frowned at the same time was Countess somebody's grandson. . . .

Ward was being entertaining. He was apologetic about misrepresenting the purpose of the visit to Miss Wentworth.

"It's not a kind of vanity work, Penny, it isn't. And think of the entrée it gives you. . . ."

I stopped listening to him, for—trilling above Ward's deep voice—I heard a sound that chilled my blood. As ominous to me as the hound's bay to a Baskerville, it was a style of utterance I had not heard since my scholarship days at a Seven Sisters college. The voice was saying:

"And I said to the little man who ran the elevator ; . ."

It was the cold and unnatural lockjaw speech of the debutante. *Quel* accent! The result, no doubt, of some mysterious social paralysis that must eventually reach the brain.

"You suddenly look very tired," Ward was saying. "Newport is a bit overwhelming, I suppose, the first time. For someone who isn't accustomed to—all this."

We went out to his car.

"Penny, my dear, I can't tell you how frightful it's been trying to get this article together." Ward opened the door on the passenger side, saw me in, shut the door. As he lowered his bulk into the bucket seat on the driver's side, I watched in vague alarm. A man who'd had a coronary shouldn't drive a sports car. "I told them at the magazine, you are the only one who can read my handwriting and make sense of my scattered notes. These old ladies up here—and this article—will be the death of me. Compared to some of these Newport people, Gina was an angel. Oh, well . . ."

It was a bad sign when Ward started to bitch about his ex-wives. The manner that I had first thought of as slightly effeminate turned out to be merely Old Boy. One of his sides was a touching old-fashioned observance of Front Page punctilio regarding liquor and women. Sometimes it sorted oddly with his social self. In Ward, the relentless optimism of the womanizer seemed a kind of naïveté, a second youth.

"The trouble with Gina—and Courtney—was that they hadn't any work of their own, so they went to work on *me*. I should marry a working woman . . ."

Ostensibly shifting gears, he brushed my leg with his hand. I moved my leg.

"Oh, sorry, love. About the Wentworth, uh, project. Don't make a hasty decision. Read a few things first. The notorious muckraking article that Miss W. couldn't suppress. Fellow's supposed to be writing a book on it. And the sister's memoir—the sister who's supposed to have done the deed. Prosecution and defense. Here."

Brushing my knees, Ward fumbled in the glove compartment for the books he wanted to give me. We barely missed a landmark graveyard. On the narrow streets, horizontal boards were harsh in the headlights, the glass panes ghostly pure. Old houses.

"Here we are. Shall I come up for a minute, Pen?"

"No." My voice sounded very loud in the quiet driveway.

He put his hand on my neck. "You won't be afraid in that big old house? Alone?"

"What? It's full of summer boarders."

"Oh. I didn't see them when we took your bag up."

"Well, they're there. And I'm tired."

"You sounded," Ward said, "so eager on the phone. So eager to come up here." He sounded tired.

"I just wanted to get away."

"From everything, eh?" Rebuffed, Ward made no further hints. Maybe the toff side would be dominant as long as he was in Newport: *noblesse oblige*. At least I hoped so. Sometimes in New York, Ward thought he was a football player.

Walking up the porch steps, I looked back to see the little sports car leave the drive in a shiver of lilac leaves. Ward was staying at the guest house of a woman whose estate he was writing about.

The house I was to stay in for my Newport week was quite beautiful. A hundred years old with three stories and a belvedere, with large twin parlors on either side of the hallway. Oriental scatter rugs, shampooed threadbare, made little islands on the broad floorboards. The furniture was good, although much nicked.

Upstairs in bed in a tiny third-floor bedroom—originally a maid's room, I was sure—I remembered Ward's question: "You won't be afraid in that big old house? Alone?"

There was a scratching at the window. Only a tree, of course. But why was it moving on a windless night? No lights outside. I opened the window and let in a noise like a power station: if they could harness those crickets for electricity, the Eastern Power Grid would never break down.

Inside the house there was no sound at all. I might have been the only roomer. The only roomer still alive. (I had heard, earlier, shuffling noises and a repeated gargling or death rattle from the bathroom.) Now I remembered a recent best-seller in which a young woman was terrified at spending a night alone.

But I spent a lot of nights alone. What was wrong with me? Glancing again at the plain latch lock (which was, indeed, locked), I took the books Ward had given me, took my flask of bourbon from the dresser, and climbed back into bed.

The flask was a present from Ward, who was born too late for the Lost Generation. A peace offering at the airport.

First I glanced at the architectural pamphlet on Werthmere. I read of oriel windows and heraldic stained glass (for which Mrs. Wentworth, mother of the present mistress of Werthmere, had invented a family crest), acres of linenfold paneling. Each of Mrs. Wentworth's furniture-hunting expeditions of the nineties had been a heroic Rape of English Historic Seats. One whole Jacobean bedroom had been imported with, it was claimed, its ghost intact:

The ghost is now known as the "Newport Maid" by those who say they have seen her walking abroad at night in her white nightgown-shroud. But she—or her legend—is indigenous to Chillingsworth, the estate in England from which the bedroom was removed. The original Maid is said to have been a very reluctant bride in a state marriage of the early seventeenth century. James I, a wedding guest, is reputed to have entered the chamber next morning (as was his, to modern notions, distasteful custom) to satisfy himself that the marriage had been consummated. But the bride died soon after, in the same chamber, and the legend was born.

I dropped the pamphlet to the floor and read the titles Ward had given me: *Chains of Gold: A Memoir*, by Elizabeth, Lady Deake. "The Wentworth Case: A New Look at the Unsolved Murder," by Pierre Rose. This was an article in an American historical quarterly of radical leanings.

I decided to tackle the prosecution first.

Professor Rose was a New Left historian who saw H. H. Wentworth's murder in 1901 as the result of a patriarchal family system connected to capitalism. To me the article was more interesting for its summary of the circumstances and evocation of the Gilded Age than for its speculations. The multimillionaire industrialist had been shot dead in a pleasure pavilion on his estate. A burglar theory had been advanced at the time; but burglary—the professor wrote—seemed unlikely, as Werthmere had on that night been ringed by policemen and Pinkertons. The victim's daughter had a motive for murder in wanting to prevent her approaching marriage to Lord Deake. Possibly, wrote Pierre Rose,

Elizabeth Wentworth, in despair at his refusal to let her break the hated engagement, killed her father in the heat of the moment. The deed occurred, after all, at the reception that was to introduce the titled fiancé to Newport.

33

Why not just shoot the fiancé? I wondered. Or run away into the night, as did the distraught heroines of gothic novels.

The writer advanced Elizabeth Wentworth's later mental instability, her lifelong exile to England after the marriage had taken place, and her lasting estrangement from her mother as circumstantial evidence against her. Professor Rose also noted that Elizabeth Wentworth, in writing her memoirs many years after the event,

> does not dwell on, but almost completely avoids reference to, the tragedy. This seems all the more peculiar in that old people are more often likely to emphasize, and even to magnify, the great happenings of their day.

If his facts were right, the professor showed pretty conclusively that the surviving members of the family had done all they could to quash the police investigation. And they had been successful. The writer of the article had not had access to any private Wentworth papers, or to the actual police records, which had apparently been destroyed. Rose tried to connect Elizabeth Wentworth and the murder to the New Feminism.

> She was highly intelligent, neurasthenic—there is no question but that her poetry exhibits a strong flight from sex, as well as an equally strong compulsion to dwell on some crime from the past, "from the sea," as she puts it—and she felt deeply her political and social dependence as a woman. Did she, one wonders, ever make a desperate attempt to escape the Chains of Gold—however she could? When one reads between the lines, one may find that certain historians are actually saying, "So-and-so could not have done this, she was too much of a lady!" Nonsense. Even the stiffly correct Old Guard of New York were subject to blackmail—by a fashionable abortionist in a famous case; by Colonel Mann

of the spicy *Town Topics;* and by publishers of other scandal
sheets of the day. One such publisher, in fact, mentioned the
Wentworth murder, following the usual practice of printing
first the damaging allegation with spurious names, and then,
in the next paragraph, an innocuous story with the real
names of those involved in the scandal *au-dessus.* Aristocratic connoisseurs of such gossip could readily find out the
worst—if indeed they did not, in the small closed world of
McAllister's Four Hundred, have prior knowledge of it.

Rose quoted two passages published in "Mr. Gotham's
Gossip" in October 1901, offering the juxtaposed passages as indirect proof of the heiress's parricide:

Fashionable people have no end of problems. Pity the poor
householders who returned home to find their furnace tender done in with a poker by his own daughter, an upstairs
maid—and all because the gal didn't like the Irish footman
"Pa" and "Ma" had picked out for her to wed! There is a
moral lesson for all of us in this tale, if we can find it.

* * *

The season at Newport, which was to have been extended
so brilliantly in the *fêtes champêtres* and dinners planned by
Mrs. Wentworth and the late Mr. Wentworth, has come
sadly to an end. There is frost in the air, truly, after this.
The bereaved widow has now returned to New York with
Miss Wentworth and others of the family party; it is hoped
that their comforting attentions will do much to—not lessen
but assuage the grief of "a mother's heart."

The analogy was clever, I thought: Mr. Wentworth
too had tended "furnaces" in the famous Wentworth
Works near Pittsburgh. But Professor Rose's research
and methodology annoyed me; he sounded too much
like *Town Topics* himself.

I had another swig from the flask and opened Elizabeth Wentworth's little book, *Chains of Gold.* The Sargent portrait reproduced as the frontispiece showed a

willowly blonde with classical features and rather closely
set eyes. Melancholy.

For some reason I got out of bed and went to the
bureau to study my own pudding-face in the maid's
room mirror: a complexion of freckles and whey that
would never dissolve into a nice, rich, even debutante's
tan.

I was starting to identify with Elizabeth Wentworth.

Danger, girl, I cautioned myself. That promiscuous
rush to empathize had made me unreliable as a historian
(my favorite teacher had told me); in my women's studies history class I had identified all over the place. I was
too sloppy, Anywoman.

Careful, I thought. Elizabeth Wentworth had no doubt
been much like the debutante I had heard laughing at
supper.

I opened the book and read the heiress's poetry:

> *Speculation!*
> *So many points adazzle on the sea.*
> *There's sunlight for you,*
> *False as diamonds*
> *Headache-hard.*
>
> *Sink thy secrets*
> *Where chains of gold deep-buried work the waves.*
> *The depths are soundless:*
> *Scuttled chest over*
> *Anchored fist.*

Privately printed. Yet these slight poems tugged at
me. They had their own faint echo—a wash, a rhythm.
Surely I could not hear the sea from my room, so many
blocks away from the water's edge?

> *The engines invented by man*
> *For his pleasure, his pleasure,*

Chains of Gold

> *Boil up and race down*
> *To the sea, the sea,*
> *And the maid, the maid,*
> *The heart, the heart*
> *In the way*
> *Are knocked flat*
> *Together.*
>
> *Call them obstacles*
> *In his race.*
> *Call it an accident.*

I didn't need that poem interpreted. Elizabeth Wentworth probably hadn't read Freud. Poor Elizabeth, knocked flat. I thought of Dorcas De Heem, who could marry whomever she pleased and frequently did.

I turned to the murder. But no, it was not there—not, certainly, in the memoir section of *Chains of Gold:*

> Of the tragedy that ended that summer and my girlhood—and my life in America—everyone has heard enough. I kept a journal then, as girls did in those days. . . .

Elizabeth Wentworth quoted "portions" of the journal. One brief entry was dated a few days before the murder:

> This morn, Mama cried at me: "In this country to be a Beauty is not a career! Can you name one who has succeeded?" I was so dumb struck I could not think of anyone, beauty or not, what did I care. "No, you cannot," said Mama, "for in this country Beauty wears out with childbearing or the boredom of children in the nursery, no matter how rich the husband may be. Yes, children are boring. In Europe a woman can be influential in politics. She can change the course of a nation as she advises its leading men. And do so in her own salon—where she is mistress and need not put up with the public. When you are older, Elizabeth, you will understand. Do you think I like to be a Social

Leader here? It is only that America allows me nothing else. But look at yourself in the mirror, child. With your face and mind, and added to that what you bring from the family, you can go anywhere." Then I ran away; but Mama came after me. A maid in the hallway turned away, but Mama was still crying out—she does not see servants and is not embarrassed. She cried that she will scratch my face. I scratched it myself with my ring. But it healed.

In *Chains of Gold*, Elizabeth included this passage without comment. Then why had she quoted it? To damn her mother, perhaps. I turned more pages and found that in England the daughter had not led the brilliant political life the mother had planned for her. Great personages (including Elizabeth's hated husband) trailed their titles through the pages, but they might almost have been Mama's maids, their presence was so little noted. The writer was neurotic and noble-minded, and with all these personal and small-scale observations the memoir seemed a bit sentimental at bottom. Maybe it was impossible for the very rich to avoid the sentimental when they wrote; the bedrock was gold. But was that any worse than my fascination with my dreams?

My dreams! Again I thought of my debts, especially the thousand for shrinkage. And then—in that small room in the strange old house that creaked like a ship—I grew afraid, afraid. The sights of the day, the impressions of Werthmere, floated in my mind along with the details of my bedtime reading. And the pale young man at the Werthmere gate—where had I seen him before?

In another life, I told myself.

Bourbon gold, another life shimmered before me. I tried to reach it, to get away from myself and my fears. Would Dr. Geldohr object if a nice piece of fantasizing brought in his thousand dollars?

*   *   *

Picture Elizabeth Wentworth standing near the Pavilion, above the Cliff Walk, having just fled from the house in tears. Her long dress, white eyelet pattern over white, whips in the wind. Despite the foamy sleeves and sashed waist (she is terribly thin!), Elizabeth does manage a somewhat sailor-like look: it's in the unfocused eyes, as well as in the floppy white tie and wide collar extending over thin shoulders.

Even through the pearl gray sky the sun will burn her, she thinks. She hasn't a parasol or even a hat.

But never mind. Where can she go? Every day this week she has run from her mother's scathing tongue, her mother's shrewd eyes. Her mother's tantrums are like her old governess's fits, she heard someone say once—"except that Eugenie Wentworth always *aims* her fits, don't you know, makes 'em work for her. Why, it's a regular system of nervous hydraulics."

Elizabeth is just beginning to understand this application of pressures, this science of maneuvers. She hasn't understood it before, because she has lacked the need to know. Why does anyone care about Mrs. Astor's decline as a social leader, Mrs. Belmont's earlier Vanderbilt divorce, Mrs. Fish's levity? Many people *do* seem to care—and Eugenie Wentworth most of all. She sniffs a possible interregnum in the social succession. She is bringing up all her weapons—one of the most powerful, though innocent-appearing, being a marriageable daughter whose beauty has been noticed by all.

Elizabeth does not for the moment see the battle, only her own part in it. Many ambitious mothers like to have innocent daughters as foils. And the father whose progress in business is presented by the muckrakers in the harsh yellow light of melodrama—he is not likely to have newspapers in the house. The children are not taught their worth in their parents' terms but are left, as it were, to play on the floor of the giant nursery. How could they, growing up in out-of-scale palaces, be anything but dolls in a doll's house?

So Elizabeth paces above the Cliff Walk. She can descend if she wishes: There is no barbed wire, in those days of effective invisible barriers, to keep off the tourists. But she does not descend. She does not try to run away. She hasn't even later heiresses's option of eloping with an imposter with a bogus title or telling her full story to a sympathetic judge or even hitch-hiking out of town. The impostors of her day have real titles.

Fenced in by inexperience and her own real sense of propriety, Elizabeth cannot run farther than the edge of Papa's property. Beyond that is only the sea: the sea—always indescribable, mesmerizing, a drug for her now as it was once a tonic. If she cannot escape, she must find friends.

But who is there in all Werthmere, this pile of newly quarried stone, who will help her? She has so little to offer. Her friendship is not worth much. Her whole identity is based on her parents; classical features mask the rest, if there is any rest. The girls her own age—in the drawing room now, practicing a dance which the cotillion master, a silly gentleman, has devised for them—they are not her friends. There is too much jealousy: for Lord Deake, the fiancé she met briefly in Gibraltar last year and again in Carribua over Christmas, is a connection of the late Queen. He is not an English duke, not a Continental rince (so many girls since Anna Gould have married *them*); but some of Victoria's numerous descendants did marry ''mere English,'' and so Lord

Deake has a royal connection. After so many years of intensive transatlantic title-for-share swapping, he is the best that any sensible mother can hope for. And the young man himself is rather handsome, with large prominent "speaking" eyes. No wonder if, when Elizabeth looks downcast, her more worldly peers consider her affected. They do not know how insipid his conversation is; they have not heard the rumors of his dissolute life. She cannot look for succor to the dancers in the drawing room.

Where, then, can she find help? John, her secret fiancé, decamped when her new—but not valid!—engagement was announced to the newspapers by her mother. John, whom she has loved and trusted so completely—John who alone has read her poetry—is opening a brokerage house in San Francisco, across the Great Divide.

But how? Why? Elizabeth knows that her fiancé's family, old Dutch, have been genteelly losing money for a hundred years or so. Are they at last waking up like old Rip Van Winkle and hustling with the rest of the country? Where does the financial backing for John's Western venture come from? Elizabeth suspects but cannot bear to think that he has been bought off.

The waves neither deny her suspicions nor confirm them. They crash and send up spray. In the ebb pause Elizabeth hears the ballroom piano, a sharp little rill of music. Crash of chords on rock. What a waste! Between breakers she imagines that she can hear her mother screaming from the windows. That is unlikely: the lawns stretch down such a long distance from house to cliff edge, and the wind is wrong besides. But Elizabeth always hears her mother's voice, here at Werthmere or in the château in New York or in the funny old-fashioned mansion climbing up and downhill out where the Wentworth money is scooped up and smelted. In New York there isn't even a lawn or garden to escape to—only the endless triumphal procession of carriages that is Fifth Avenue.

If she could escape that voice and listen to the voice in her ear! But how can she escape? In her eighteen years Elizabeth has never walked along a public street alone. She has been chaperoned around the world and has seen it only as an opera setting. She has never had an acquaintance who wasn't approved first; the girls she knows lead lives as circumscribed as hers. (It sometimes works the other way around: some children weren't allowed to play with her on Bailey's Beach because her Papa was so *firm* in business.) Almost all of Newport will be coming to the reception for Lord Deake in two days' time.

Two days! The screaming voice from the open casements is driving her mad. To whom can she turn? She turns and sees her brother pointing out to another young man the little rises and rolls on the lawns that will be, she supposes, marks in his obstacle race.

No, Hallie is no help. He is a year younger, silly in a way, though he has more worldly knowledge than she does. He is, besides, terrified of their mother—all the more terrified of making a scene because he thinks it unmanly to be openly humiliated by her. He has been on his best behavior the last few days, too. Mama is blackmailing him in some new way, no doubt. And Victoria, little Tory? A slow-seeming sly child. She can only turn to Tory as a last resort, and then only to employ her as some sort of unwitting messenger.

The only hope is Papa, who will be arriving in the afternoon. He has not visited the family in months. He is always working in the fields of his labor, overseeing

many projects, or visiting New York only to see his
Wall Street people. He relaxes on his yacht, the *Empress Eugénie*. The rest of the family have not set foot
on the yacht since returning from Carribua. What a fight
there was then, when she said she would not marry
Lord Deaks. Mama screaming and throwing the Oriental
pillows and brass trays—all the beautiful things they had
picked up on their world tour—and finally smashing the
multicolored glowing globe of an Indian lamp! Tory was
seasick. She herself was crying.

And when they disembarked, without Papa, Mama
announced the engagement.

But Papa hasn't seriously agreed to it, has he? Elizabeth asks herself. He is her last hope.

> Cold marble, salt sea
> Cold face and washed eyes
> Who would believe in the force behind the façade?
>
> Cold granite, salt sea
> Not "I dreamt" but "I dwelt"
> In marble halls with the parquet crumbling like waves.
>
> The cold stone sea
> Home.

She lingers a while and looks out at the sea. Her
mother is calling her. She has heard of old sailors who
always hear waves, even when they move far from the
tumultuous source. They can never escape.

> The sailor who hates the sound of the sea
> And tries so hard to escape it, to run
> To shelter inland; he finds there is none.
> For his ears have hardened to shells that whisper
> It's done, it's done
> She's won, she's won . . .

Only a sketch of what she means. She is always starting poems and is always interrupted before she can finish anything to her satisfaction. The only person who ever encouraged her, who liked her poems, was Miss Long, the old governess.

Forget, forget the poetry. Her mother's voice commands her.

Old Murders

For some reason I woke up with the desire to call my mother. But first I lay still to gather the wreckage of my dreams. A ghost in a long white dress rippled across the lawn before the brightly lit house. House and grass foundered. The ghost became a sailboat, scudding away.

I went downstairs to the hall pay phone. I didn't want to wait until evening to tell my mother about having worn the new dress to tea at Werthmere. *I* wasn't impressed, but my mother would be thrilled.

Mother sighed, long distance. When I left town, she was down.

"Well, Ma. Hello? Are you going to tell Aunt Brenda I'm hobnobbing with the Social Register up here?"

"Oh, you know Brenda, dear. When I tell Aunt Brenda about the wonderful places you go and the important people you meet on your job . . . she thinks I'm making up stories because you're twenty-six and not married."

I spent the morning sorting Ward's notes and matching them with the photographs. Later a photographer would come up from the magazine for the final shots. I tried to suggest various outlines or approaches to the article, while Ward fretted and fumed. But I kept thinking about Elizabeth Wentworth. Ward let me off for the afternoon so I could read more about the murder.

"But no promises," I said, going off to the famous private library.

I passed under fog-laden trees, along sedate streets. The atmosphere of Newport assisted reverie. In New York some furtive twerp was always trying to mooch in on solitary wanderings.

The library arose out of the fog, a sturdy Doric temple in a tidy park. Inside there were portraits, ample spaces.

"May I help you, miss?" A smooth face, another butler.

"No, thank you. I'll just look around first."

"Oh, but the library is private. Restricted to members."

I felt my mother's hoity-toitiest Bendel's expression freezing on my face.

"Oh. I see. Miss Wentworth suggested—there are some family papers here . . . but I'm sure it's no matter."

"Oh, yes, yes. Would you be so good . . ."

Waiting, I realized that, if admitted, I would be committed to the Wentworth project.

"It's quite all right. Miss Twitchett will show you the Wentworth collection."

I looked through elaborately printed rag-paper genealogies of Wentworths and Ritcheys, good yeoman stock who worked hard and married hard-working ambitious spouses of Christian principles and the best Scottish and English ancestry. It was teleological history, with Victoria Wentworth as the end product of all this boring toiling and begetting and amassing.

I went to the room where the old newspaper files were kept. These old papers were bound in large volumes; they weren't grainy ghosts on microfilm. There was only one other browser amidst the newspaper stacks, a young man who kept whistling "Blow the Man Down" in an irritatingly wobbly rendition.

Passing a table, I was riveted by an open volume of *The New York Times:*

LORD DEAKE MURDERED
ON CARRIBUA ESTATE

Ex-HUSBAND OF HEIRESS
FOUND STABBED IN BED

January 10, 1930—This small island was shocked yesterday by the news that Lord Deake, whose family holdings in Carribua date from Royal patents, had been found brutally murdered in his bed.

It is reported that Lord Deake's body was discovered by his butler. A manservant, finding his Lordship's bedroom locked in the morning, reported to the butler, who opened the door with a household key. The body is said to have been mutilated by a machete, of a type used locally to cut cane. The walls were spattered with blood.

Commissioner Sir Cyril Rattan-Roger, a close friend of the victim, has refused all comment. Newsmen are trying to get information from the natives, who learn everything from a special drum code for which the island has long been famous.

Lord Deake, who was 52, has most recently been noted for his attempt to start a railroad on the island. The venture did not fare well, and Carriburail had been in receivership. Since leaving England about ten years ago, Lord Deake has been noted for his more successful efforts in raising Aristo-hounds and registering the breed. On the island he was known for his lively hospitality and mercurial disposition.

The title is now extinct. Lord Deake's marriage to the former Elizabeth Wentworth, the American heiress, was dissolved in 1920.

I had read briefly of the Deake murder in the memoir and the "Wentworth Case" article. But why should volume 1930 of *The New York Times* be open to that page? A clue? A warning? Had I done it myself, unconsciously?

Stop it, I told myself: you *want* to be paranoid, you think it's cute, making crazy connections. It's not. It's just accident.

"Uh . . . I was looking at this." The whisper-whistler, a lanky young man, was hovering over me. He seemed to be claiming 1930 and the Deake murder.

I moved away. He seemed to have a strange look in his eyes. Perhaps it was only that one lens of his glasses had a spider-web crack.

I dragged down the heavy 1901 folio volume of a local newspaper and turned the sheets with trembling fingers.

A TABLEAU ON 'PROGRESS'
WILL GREET LORD DEAKE

NEWPORT EVENT PLANNED TO PRECEDE
APPROACHING DEAKE-WENTWORTH NUPTIALS

Mrs. H. H. Wentworth has planned a program of tableaux vivants on the subject of American Progress in the Nineteenth Century, for the entertainment of guests at the reception Mr. and Mrs. Wentworth will hold next week to honor Lord Deake.

Lord Deake is expected to arrive this weekend on the *Boadicea,* a steam yacht owned by friends. This will be his first visit to the city with which the family of his future bride has had so long and distinguished an association. Mr. H. H. Wentworth will pay one of his rare visits to Newport on this occasion.

The marriage of Miss Elizabeth Wentworth and Rufus Reginald Lord Deake will take place in New York the first week of November.

Mrs. Wentworth and the noted American artist Barbizon Peale Schmitt are planning a patriotic program of tableaux

vivants on Niagara, Electricity, The Driving of the Golden
Spike, The Great Divide, and others, to be performed by a
select group of young ladies, in the Werthmere ballroom.
Mourning for President McKinley will be reflected in a tableau of Indian Maidens Lamenting the Fallen Chief, authen-
tically devised by Mr. Will VanMeer, noted cotillion leader.

Young Mr. Hall Wentworth is in charge of an obstacle
race to be run earlier the same afternoon on the Werthmere
grounds. It is noted that this race, unlike others of recent
memory, will stress the same theme of American Progress.
Young Mr. Wentworth has recently purchased two American "bubbles" from the Stanley factory in Newburyport.

As Lord Deake will not have the time to make any "Grand
Tour" of America before the couple embark for England,
the tableaux vivants will afford him a brief "parlor view" of
our heritage, an informant noted. A fireworks display will
help give the English visitor the full flavor of our American
traditions.

I turned pages. The creep with the spider glasses was
still whistling. Now it was "Yes, We Have No Ba-
nanas," *largo*. I tried to concentrate on the long-ago
murder.

MR. WENTWORTH MURDERED
DURING TABLEAUX VIVANTS

DREADFUL CRIME SHOCKS NEWPORT
BUT KILLER LEAVES FEW CLUES
BURGLARY THE APPARENT MOTIVE

Mr. H. H. Wentworth was murdered by an unknown
assailant last evening at the family summer cottage, Werthmere. The terrible event occurred during a reception for
Lord Deake that was to be the high event of the social
season.

The police are refusing to comment to the press. But one
source in the household has predicted to a reporter that
startling disclosures will be made shortly.

Although no information is being given the public, we have learned that the crime occurred in the summer teahouse, a pavilion in the Pompeiian style near the Cliff Walk. While guests were being entertained in the ballroom by a glittering tableau vivant on the Great Divide, Mr. Wentworth apparently went to the Pompeiian Pavilion. Mrs. Wentworth, missing him some time later, found him expired on the floor of the teahouse, which is decorated with frescoes in the Roman style. He had been shot.

The murder weapon has not been found as yet, we have been informed by a source inside the house. An inventory of classical and Egyptian items, brought back by Mrs. Wentworth after her trip to the Mediterranean and kept on display in the Pavilion, is being made. But no item has been reported as missing.

It is surmised that the burglar did not deem the antique objects valuable, or that he was intent on obtaining ready cash. Mr. Wentworth rarely carried money on his person, so it is doubtful that the robber was satisfied to any degree.

The police are continuing their inquiries, along with the private detectives from the Pinkerton agency on the scene for the reception. Through her secretary Mrs. Wentworth has made a plea to the public to furnish any clue, any observation, no matter how distantly related to the tragedy it may at first seem to be. We, in our turn, ask our readers to assist, if possible, a distinguished neighbor and patroness in a time of sorrow.

Reporters and investigators all seemed to be looking resolutely in any direction but that of Werthmere itself. Further study of the same local newspaper revealed only more expressions of regret. Newport piously deplored the arrest—two days later—of a New York newspaperman on the grounds of Werthmere. He had come up from the Cliff Walk to snoop.

The gun was never found. The investigation slowed in the wake of the Wentworth survivors' removal to New York, the hurried Deake—Wentworth wedding, and—as I read between the lines—the widow's iron determina-

tion to show a united family front. The shock of the
murder was soon succeeded in the press by the greater
public indignation at the marriage settlement—shares,
ore mountains, foundries—made over to Lord Deake.

"Oh. You have 1901?"

I jumped. It was the whistler again. I gave him a dirty
look, then regretted it. Surely, unless the law of aver-
ages had broken down, he couldn't want all the same
volumes I did. It was a kind of molestation. A library
prowler in what (at my magazine) would be the morgue.

I went to the New York newspaper obituaries, which
were less cautiously pious and more informative about
H. H. Wentworth. I had remembered Wentworth vaguely
as one of the minor robber barons. This was correct: he
had been not a Napoleon but a Ney, a field marshal of
Morgan's and Carnegie's. He was one of those who had
emerged from the panic of '93 stronger than ever. Wentworth had kept the faith when reformers began to dis-
pute the right of the great industrialists to shoot strikers
and to give special rates to big customers. He had stood
in the front lines while the giants retreated to art collect-
ing, salmon fishing, and philanthropy—a man of courage
who had charged with his Pinkertons.

The whistler was hovering again. After *my* volume!

I stepped backward, away from him. He had an odd,
obsessional look, and he was rocking back and forth on
his feet in a way that (I had read somewhere) was a sign
of mental disturbance.

"Why don't you just get lost?" I said. "This is my
file. I got it first. I know your kind, and I'm not interested in playing games with you."

He looked shocked, all right. He looked around the
newspaper room. I realized that the two of us were still
alone there, and that there was no one in the next room
either. No sound.

He looked down at me carefully, squinting behind his cracked lens. Pretending I was some kind of insect whose presence he had just noticed, he said, "My kind, love, is called 'scholar.' At worst. And your kind, whatever it is, is *not* Newport."

I slammed the volume shut and hurriedly left the newspaper file room.

Safely ensconced in another section of the library, I spent an interesting two hours with biographies, studies of the period, and H. H. Wentworth's journal, which Miss Wentworth herself had asked be made available to me. The murder victim had written of himself in the third person, in a crabbed style:

> Mr. L. the Standard Oil lawyer came to see Mr. W. Agreement may be possible. Mr. W. did not indicate this, but sought to draw out Mr. L.
> Of 8 men in the room, 6 were directors or presidents of companies. We discussed the panic and the overcapitalization of companies, viz., Villard and others. What of the Public? someone asked. Mr. W. was of a mind to recall to them Mr. W. H. Vanderbilt's sentiment regarding the Public. Mr. W. noted he was the calmest person in the room, as in other crises. The Unions may win, but only if the men called to manage business and capital in this country are not morally fit to outweigh labor—one to a hundred, or to a thousand if need be, or to whatever odds they bring against us.

Only with his family did he drop the third person:

> Weakness everywhere. It is important to form character at the earliest age. Habits of frugality, command, honesty. The youngest has this. Regina Victoria. So serious for a child. She too watches the household. Sees. Will have a mind for business. If she had been the boy . . .

I flipped to the last entry, made the day before the murder.

> *Mr. W. amused himself by watching the movements of the servants in their duties. In almost all cases, their routines are as wasteful of time and energy, and as inviting to idleness, as are the routines of Society. A possibility here for experiment and planning. But there is no one who wants it done; the ladies here being as eager as the Amalgamated Agitators to enlist large numbers of Laborers under their banners, and sometimes as little eager to see them at actual productive work.*

Did Wentworth believe in work? I wondered. Or in the moral tests to which he could submit himself through work? What kind of man would write in his *Biograph. of Notables* entry "Occupation: Capitalist"? A man whose faith was Social Darwinism.

Too much reading had given me a headache. I left the library, walking outside into the sunlight with a firm, purposeful stride, picturing old H. H. . . . .

H. H. Wentworth enters his office at Coalville with a firm purposeful stride, though his brow is as white as dead McKinley's. He goes to the window and looks out over man-made smoke and fire. His own. The little knot of strikers has dispersed. He himself has just been among them, persuading the men. They are good enough men, when led by a man who can lead. Why do they want to be led by men who talk destruction and call it "reason"?

Reason, I'll reason you, Wentworth thinks. If I am one man against a million, I must have strength equal to one million. If I have one million times as many dollars as you do, I must be that much stronger. I must be steel. To be steel, I go through the fire, again and again. Do you think it is given us for our pleasure?

He frowns, reminded of Newport, that pleasure dome. Tomorrow he must go there. Eugenie will not let him stay at the Works. Doesn't she understand? Like W. H. Vanderbilt in '77 or Frick in '93, he has had the courage to cut wages and fire hundreds. Eugenie would of course see the practical benefits, as do the lesser partners, but not the enormous faith required—the fatigues of his paternal vigilance.

No one sees the spiritual exertion. One must not make the least misstep. How many weaker men has he seen ruined, damned?

Still, Newport . . . He will see his family. The children. With the children, at least, all can be made to go well.

Fatherhood brings out the tenderest feelings he has known. Yet it is important that these feelings not be expressed in ways that would soften the children. Their characters must be formed so that they will be equal to their destiny—the destiny that his struggle has won for them. So he himself, in the strict code of his time, cannot declare his love, except in ways that will set the example; give a moral lesson. Life is a struggle from which one wrests—character and rewards. As the rewards will come anyway to the children, developing their characters is all the more important. Yet duty leaves him so little time. Later, when they are grown, perhaps when he himself is dead, they will understand this stern, unspoken love, the noblest sort—paternal love. It will be engraved in their characters. His legacy. The children!

He thinks of his youngest, little Victoria, so serious and so devoted to him. She should have been a boy.

Wentworth goes to the personal drawer in the double desk and takes out his special charitable checkbook with his children's pictures engraved on them. He goes through his eleemosynary correspondence and writes checks quickly.

At one letter he frowns. The widow of a dead competitor from long ago; she had made scenes and gone to the newspapers, she had held off selling for a long time. Not enough customers could afford to buy the products, especially during the financial crises: that was the real truth of her husband's ruination. Other producers fail during panics, but Wentworth rides them out. The capitalist faith requires a mental discipline that must be constantly kept up: in the present instance . . . he drops the widow's letter into the waste basket. Where honor and duty are concerned, no quarter can be given.

Wentworth lapses into reverie. That is, the secret bookkeeper-dance goes on in his head. He sees all the separate Works operations, the separate sources of materials, and he tries to make men and great machines dance—in his head—faster and faster, to fewer notes. How?

For me, two mysteries deepened. If Wentworth and his colleagues always held the line on wages, Who did they think would buy the increased products from all their capital investment? And could a man of Wentworth's character, who seemed to despise Society, have insisted that his daughter marry for social reasons? Was he a man who never retracted, even in private matters? Had he died because he was a domestic stand-patter?

"Watch out, stupid! Nearly killed you."

I was suddenly sitting in the gutter, outside the library gate.

"Glasses. Where's my glasses?" A familiar voice. The young man was groping in the gutter.

Reconstructing the immediate past, I realized that I had almost been run over by a car on the avenue—while

I was daydreaming—and that the young man had pulled me out of the way.

The young man was the one I had met in the newspaper files.

Then I saw that the car that had almost hit me was the Daisy Six I'd seen at Werthmere gate the previous day. Now the Daisy was stopped at a light a block away. From behind, I could see the towhead of the driver, the man I knew from somewhere.

Where?

The Cliff Walk

"You walked right out against the light," my savior said, complaining.

I had to do it. I went over to him and thanked him. Shakily.

"Okay, okay. I'm relieved." He spit on his dusty glasses and wiped them with a dirty handkerchief. "I was afraid you'd haul off and slug me."

"Slug you! Why?"

"Well . . . you walked out in the way of that car with such a determined stride. As if you meant to be run over."

"Oh, no. I was daydreaming, I guess."

"Well, that's a relief. Let me buy you a drink or something."

"No, let *me* buy *you* one."

I was walking along with the whistler, buoyed up by his bobbing energy. Outside in the late sun he looked less sinister than he had in the newspaper file room. He was about my age, tall and very thin. The splintered lens in his glasses made him appear to be winking. He was

wearing old corduroy pants and an Irish fisherman's
sweater festooned with unraveled loops. As he walked,
the loops bounced like poofs on a clown costume.

"My name is Penny Miller."

"Pierre," he said. "Pierre Rose."

I stopped dead. "Oh, no!" I should have guessed.

"What's wrong?" Pierre Rose asked. "Somehow I
knew you'd get mad. But what'd I do to you?"

"It's not what you've done to me. It's what you've
done to Elizabeth Wentworth."

Pierre Rose stopped. "Oh, that's great. Am I notorious in Newport now?" As I frowned, he laughed. "Hey—
you're not—are you?—Miss Wentworth's latest archi-
vist?"

"What do you mean?"

"Every year Miss Victoria Wentworth pays some poor
graduate student or librarian a small retainer to write
a—a scholarly, accurate whitewash of some degenerate
relative or other. Occasionally the wastrel brother or
nephew. Sometimes the mother, who was a bitch on
wheels. Usually the father, because I"—and he laughed
—"I am the archfiend, working to bring down the House
of Wentworth. But her slavey-researchers always give
up. She doesn't pay enough."

"Well, I've gotten interested in Elizabeth. You didn't
have to work quite so hard to bring her down. It's not
fair. And it's not thorough or scholarly either. You swing
wild."

We had reached a little tavern. Over the beer steins,
Pierre asked, "How long have you been working to
rehabilitate Elizabeth Wentworth?"

"Since last night." Why not be honest? I told him
what I thought.

"It sounds as if you're concentrating on the murder.

I'm really doing a straight study of the old man. It's a Ph.D. dissertation, but I know I can publish it. I have a contract. I've found a lot of new business dirt on him. But I've dug up a few things that might interest you. I was just looking up the accounts of the murders again, because of my new information." He thought the 1930 Deake murder might be connected too.

"All this is still very confusing to me," I said. "I haven't even visited the scene of the crime."

I meant it as a joke, but he stood up. "Let's go. You mean the Pompeiian Pavilion?"

"But I think it's too late to go to Werthmere now."

"We won't go by way of Werthmere. We'll go by the Cliff Walk, which is public property. It's dark enough now. I always go to Werthmere that way. She doesn't invite *me* to tea, you know."

I objected, but Pierre's bouncing energy and his obsession were infectious. I hurried along after him on what was—I realized more and more clearly—a long hike. By the time I was ready to protest we had reached the neighborhood where the gates of great estates glittered like harps in the sunset. As we walked along, we exchanged biographies. Pierre was a history teacher at Stone Grass College in Vermont.

"It's experimental. They ski and meditate a lot. So I started to write articles. Summers, I do my thesis on old H. H."

"But you're all wrong about Elizabeth Wentworth. If you knew—" I hesitated; I had been about to say "her."

We paused to admire a mansion so fancy that the façade looked like a rococo interior.

"Wow. That's the kind of place that caused the Revolution."

"But not here," Pierre said. "Not in Newport. No

revolution here. When the Grand Duke of Russia came to Newport, he said he'd never seen such luxury back home. But this 'cottage' has an interesting private history. The couple who owned it shot each other one night in the thirties. Each claimed to have heard a burglar.''

''But how could each . . . ?''

''Separate bedrooms. Separate shotguns. I forget which one died. No inquiry about the death. It's only the divorces that go to court. . . . Now here's a mansion that's just a shell now. No, we can't see it. All overgrown. The big debutante party a few years back where the kids wrecked the place. They hushed up the rape cases, but not, of course, the fire. Oh, we should get bicycles one day and go all along Ocean Drive! There's an estate where the lawn slopes at such an angle—forty degrees or more—that the gardeners and big lawnmowers have to be lashed to trees so they won't plunge into the waves. One gardener did drown. Mower rope tangled around his neck. The lady who owned the place at the time had a succession of gardeners. And vice versa. *She* later fell off her yacht and was drowned, swept overboard in a great calm. Her poor husband was so broken up over it, the formal inquiry was conducted without him. Although he was the only witness, the only other one on board.''

I thought of the Wentworth daughter, the dead daughter now accused of parricide. Perhaps, after all, she *had* killed her father. Society seemed to be a locked-room crime case where nobody was ill-bred enough to spring a denouement, though everybody knew who-done-it.

We came down on a path between estates to an arm of the sea. The water was gray and sparkling. Seagulls whirled and cried.

''This is the Cliff Walk. But you've been here before?''

"Never," I said.

The Cliff Walk was wonderfully varied. I walked with Pierre high above waves that dashed on massed rock or leapt over rough sand. Some stretches of cliff were supported by stone breastworks. Then the walk would descend in narrow stairs to take a lower path where there were no cliffs. On the heights, tough knots of shrubbery sometimes obscured the view down to the sea.

But the view inland! One at a time the great cottages appeared. As we worked our way around the long scallops and points of the Cliff Walk, each mansion presented profile, full view, far wing. It was like seeing one gothic novel cover next to another—and another. With so many great houses competing, the cumulative effect was slightly comic, no matter how impressively the waves dashed against the foot of the cliff.

Money, said the Breakers, *money*. The Breakers was like a great railroad station lifted up by a silly giant and set down far from its arteries, its masses of people, the proportionate life and communal use that could have given it true grandeur. *Money*, said a French castle authentic if only it had been smaller.

"That's a girls' school now," Pierre said. "But look."

He was pointing. Squatting atop a tunneled arch in the path ahead of us was a small-columned round building with a coolie-hat roof.

Pierre clambered up toward the barbed wire. I followed.

"Wave to your swell friends," said Pierre.

Far away at the crest of the rise of the crewcut lawn, Werthmere rested rather crankily on its harsh right angles. Even in fog the Perpendicular wall and roof ornamentation had a drainpipey nineteenth-century look. The Werthmere lawn was more steeply pitched than the others, and the cliffs were highest there.

On the barbed wire near the Pompeiian Pavilion was a sign: DANGER PRIVATE FALLING DOWN TRESPASSERS PROSECUTED KEEP OUT.

"If they were smart, they'd just write 'Rats,' " Pierre said. "Anyway, there's no visiting charge this way."

Should I go after him? I had a flash of fear: entombment under the folly, which might fall in; my name then linked in death with this idiot I'd just met, with his views of the Wentworth Mystery.

Pierre was already climbing ahead of me, testing a slack section of barbed wire. I scrambled up after him. The vulnerable cliffside turf was full of clammy life that came off in my hands. Wildflowers quivered. My legs felt weak.

"Why did they use barbed wire? Cheap, cheap." Pierre carelessly wiped his hands on his chest. Streaks of blood appeared on the raveled festoons of the Irish fisherman's sweater. He looked quite mad.

He gave me a hand up.

"Heave ho! My God, girl, you weigh a ton."

"One hundred and thirty pounds," I said, subtracting five.

"That's right. Don't be ashamed to mention it. Enjoy your fat. Now, isn't it cute? A little Grant's Tomb."

That was why the Pompeiian Pavilion had such a familiar look to it. The column-circle and peaked-hat roof were a replica of the top layer of Grant's Tomb, only squashed a bit.

I looked fearfully up across the lawn, but the second last of the Wentworths did not seem to be glaring at us through the mullions. No Henry James butler came sprinting across the grass. It was misty. The light was fading. We interlopers would not be seen.

Busy Pierre was opening the folly door, a fasces-barred gate. I went up the steps, under the portico, and in after him.

"Keep the door open. There's no light."

Pierre climbed up on a stone bench and opened the shutters of a large high window opposite the door. The window had no bars or glass; probably so that it could let in a little more light and air from outside. For a pleasure dome, the place was rather dark and funereal.

The inside diameter was about eighteen feet. I peered around at flaking Roman-style frescoes of maidens walking and running away through green grass. Bare feet and flowers stood out sharply against the stained greenish walls.

"That bench there is an Etruscan sarcophagus."

The bench looked like an old-fashioned bathtub supported by a swarm of sinister bulbous-muscled little boys. The marble cover was the seat.

"Flesh-eater. That's what *sarcophagus* means." Pierre lounged with one leg over the end of the bench. Thin and sepulchral in the gloom, he really did look as if the stone was eating him away. "Now . . . look around you."

"It's not used now," I said. But I sensed a presence.

"Old H. H. and his missus stashed their Greek, Roman, and Egyptian loot here in the folly. Now . . . set the scene of the murder. Imagine . . . Egyptian gods on pillars. The beaked lead Horus over here. Ra in stone. In cabinets along the walls, tiny scarabs, obsidian lips—yum, yum"—and Pierre Rose smacked his own lips—"and painted wooden eyes. The antique oil lamp lies tipped on the floor. The tripod is tipped over"—and Pierre arose and came toward me; I was shaking—"tipped over, with one leg in the air. Guttering fires run along little streams of the oil—"

"No, stop!" I couldn't take it. He stood before me, this stranger with flashing eyes behind cracked glasses, flailing his arms as he spoke. What was it with him? Ideological violence against the friends and hirelings of the rich? Sex crimes? Simple murder in historical settings?

"Yes, picture it—the oil fires merging with a trickle of blood—"

"No, no, I can picture, I can picture—no!" And somehow I was wrestling with him; we were locked in some sort of combat. And then suddenly he lay on the floor at my feet, his limbs awry.

"No. Pierre?" I thought confusedly of the secret pressure points through which someone can be killed. Had I hit on one accidentally, like the Lost Chord?

"That's great," Pierre said from the floor. "You really get into the spirit of it. That's just how it happened. I'm the dead man. And you're—Elizabeth Wentworth."

"No, I didn't do it. I didn't kill him!"

In the silence I realized that I had screamed it. Pierre sat up and stared at me.

"I . . . my parents used to tell me I'd be the death of them," I stammered. "My father died—heart attack— just after I broke my engagement. To a doctor." I sat down on the bench and laughed. Pierre came over to sit beside me. "But it's not that. No psychological crap to do with me. It's Elizabeth Wentworth. She was too passive. She lived like under water her whole life. A prisoner. Even her poetry was passive. She wouldn't have been free enough to strike out like you or me, like a modern person. Besides, the father is the wrong victim."

"Shall we go back?" he said. He looked embarrassed. "I'm sorry. Sometimes in my classes I have my students act out the historical possibilities."

"No." I was determined to snap out of it. "You told

me you had some new information. Against Elizabeth Wentworth.''

"Can I trust you?"

"If it's damaging to Elizabeth . . . I won't tell a soul."

We laughed. Pierre fished in his pants pocket and brought out a sheaf of papers. "My secret is, I've located the missing police records. The interviews with the Wentworth family."

"Oh? Where?"

"Where they were is still my secret, for the time being."

"You stole them from the library."

"No! That would be a capital crime—one of the few. I only took them there so I could compare notes. I have a lousy memory."

He passed me the photocopies. Spencerian script. I stood up on the sarcophagus-bench to read by the fading light that came in at the little window. After the murder, the police chief had interviewed everyone in the library— everyone except Elizabeth Wentworth, who had been sedated and sent to bed before his arrival. Mrs. Wentworth, very lucid and self-possessed, had explained that her husband had been shot by a burglar.

I looked at the Pavilion floor. There he had lain, said the police report, face down but partly turned over, "in an awkward manner." As the police report had it: "He had been shot at close range with a revolver, in the chest and neck. He had been dead for a few hours, and must have died instantly. The murder weapon was not in the summerhouse and has not been discovered." The report went on to corroborative statements from Pinkertons and police doctors, interviews the same night with family and servants.

I squinted at the interviews. They were written out

like playscripts with the speakers' names at the margin. Reading to myself, I could not help but see the scene spring to life.

"My husband," Eugenie Wentworth says (bravely forbearing to glance at his portrait over the library mantel), "my husband had been watching the entertainment. But he went out for a cigar. Where the ballroom adjoins the conservatory. I did not see him leave the ballroom but was told so by my son, who saw him go out. In a few minutes, seeing that our guests were well disposed, and somewhat fatigued myself, I decided to join Mr. Wentworth on the grounds. There were lights on the terrace, but I did not see him. There was a light in the Pompeiian Pavilion—we kept an oil lamp there, an antique, but it is used—and I went in that direction. I heard a shot. I went in and discovered my poor husband."

The police stenographer works with bowed head, perhaps in awe of the splendid surroundings. The poor chief is obliged to speak:

"Was anyone else in the Pavilion?"

"No."

"Did you see anyone, Mrs. Wentworth? Anyone near the Pavilion, on the lawn, or coming from the Cliff Walk?"

"No. But I could not see distinctly." Outside the windows now, the Werthmere grounds are dark.

"But there was a light in the summerhouse?"

"I saw it," says Mrs. Wentworth, "as I crossed the lawn. But the light flickered. My poor husband—in his last effort, his agony—must have upset it, for the light almost went out. I saw nothing until I saw him. The next thing I saw was my daughter Elizabeth."

How long is the pause? If the police chief waits over-long to speak, his words may seem more ominous than he perhaps intends them to be.

"And where was she?"

"Why, there. At the door. I mean coming from the house."

"So she was the second one to come on the scene."

"Yes. Very soon after me."

"A minute or two after? Mrs. Wentworth?"

"Poor child," says the mother. "She is in a state of nervous prostration—could scarcely speak. I doubt she saw anything. I am confused myself. The light was so bad . . . I have a feeling that perhaps . . ."

"Yes, Mrs. Wentworth?"

"Perhaps I saw someone go over the cliff. But I am not sure. I am too ill to answer more questions tonight."

Mrs. Wentworth breaks down imperiously. The questioning procedure has become an audience. The chief is dismissed, and yet—

He does not leave. Eugenie Wentworth "takes exception"—yet the police chief, a mere native, insists on sitting up all night at the bedside of the drugged Elizabeth. He may sit stiffly at the bedside of the sleeping maiden or—if that seems indelicate—perhaps he paces near the bedroom door, receiving whispered communications from his minions: the doctor probing the great industrialist's corpse; the constables busy interviewing the servants. For the first time, Eugenie Wentworth is not mistress of the house she built. She is not allowed to enter her daughter's room. No one is, all night.

The chief and his monkish clerk wait up in the Newport Maid Room. No ghost emerges from the linenfold panel-ing, but in the morning the sleeping beauty wakes to give her statement to the police.

"I had been in the Niagara tableau," says Elizabeth, "and I felt very hot and faint. I went out to the terrace. I saw a light in the Pavilion and went toward it. I looked in. There was Papa."

"Then you were the discoverer of your father's . . . of your father?"

"If . . . yes."

"Did you see anyone else?"

Is Elizabeth shrinking under covers? Has a maid, at least, been allowed in, with a dressing gown?

"I . . . no. I saw someone going over the cliff."

"Who?"

"No one. I don't know. A woman. It was too dark to see."

"You saw no one else?" the police chief asks.

"No. Only—my mother, of course. She came. Oh, it's so disgusting. That's all I know. I can't think anymore."

"It's too dark to read," Pierre said. "Want to go back?"

"Yes." I got down from the window.

We left the Pavilion. Pierre descended first and helped me down to the Cliff Walk. I could hear the waves, calm and secretive, below us. I was full of a nameless dread. What was it?

"You see it," Pierre said. "You see what's wrong."

"Yes."

"Both mother and daughter claim to have discovered the body first."

"Maybe the mother did it. What did the others say?"

Strangely, Pierre didn't turn district attorney on me. Maybe he could feel (pedant though he was) that I was in no mood. As we walked slowly up a public path between estates and along a broad avenue, he told me

68

more testimony. I took in only pieces of it. Lord Deake had been surrounded by people all evening as he sat with stiff upper lip through all the tableaux and scenes of American Progress. Hallie, the seventeen-year-old Wentworth heir, just kept saying (according to the police record) that he'd like to kill the bastard: as the record delicately put it, "I'd like to kill the b-blank. My God, if I could do something. I wish I could kill the b-blank." Both bridegroom and heir seemed impossible as suspects, having alibis.

I felt curiously depressed.

"I wish I could cheer you up. Let's have a beer. A hamburger."

Across the table from Pierre in a coffee shop, I said to him, "You feel responsible for me because you saved me from being run over."

"Is that it? Never mind. Here's something on the human-interest side. Testimony of two servants." He read: "Mary S.: 'I can't say right now, but you will be hearing soon. There will be a break. Put that down. Will it be in the newspapers?' And another servant, Mary M., says: 'I didn't see nothing. I was helping in the kitchen the whole time. Ask cook. You leave me be. Why do people always come nosing around? I ain't done nothing.' You see. The two opposite classic servant reactions. One hints darkly at what she might know. The other insists on her innocence."

"Uh-uh."

But I was not interested in either talk or food. My depression was related to the past, but it was the present I could not bear. Too much fantasizing again? I liked Pierre, but at the moment I wanted to be alone. So I buried myself in the onionskin notes, reading the police follow-up.

"Hey, listen to this. You know that servant with the suspicions, the dark hints? She died two days after the murder."

"It sounds promising," said Pierre. "But it was an accident."

"Suspicious. But it's just a footnote. 'Died—accident.' The date. No more."

"Almost as many laborers died building Werthmere as died building the Brooklyn Bridge. Servants died like flies."

"So Society done it. Killed servants, I mean."

"What the police record doesn't add," said Pierre, "is that Mrs. Wentworth gave the diamonds from her ballgown to the Newport Police Widows' and Orphans' Fund. Although no such fund existed."

"A bribe?"

I was outraged. My depression evaporated in indignation. Pierre suggested that I try to find out more through the household records at Werthmere. Servants, maids, and the like. I agreed this was a good idea. Then Pierre started to talk about Wentworth, Carnegie, and Frick, and about the way things were still being run. Oh, God, I thought: he's going to turn out to be one of those people who say that one percent own ninety-eight percent of America. Instead of the real figure of two percent of consumer units owning forty percent or whatever. One of those pop radicals so careless because maybe secretly they don't think the country is bad enough as it is.

But I liked him. I would overlook his sloppy thinking. And it would be fun to prove—if I could—that Elizabeth Wentworth hadn't killed her father.

When I got back, I found a note on the telephone stand. Ward had called. I called him back. He had wanted to take me to dinner, but I hadn't gotten back, and so forth. And now he was torn because he had a sailing invitation for day after next.

"Take it," I said. "And I'll do some sleuthing."

"That's a love," Ward said. "And we won't tell *Pleasures and Palaces* that you're—we're—moonlighting."

That night I dreamed I was a scullery maid at Werthmere, and a laundress, cleaning blood off all the china, silver, and linen, washing everything undersea, and it was all somehow in a poem by Elizabeth Wentworth.

Management and Labor

All the next day, Wednesday, I was the perfect secretary: retyping Ward's revised notes and interviews, checking facts on furniture styles (in the library, where I failed to see Pierre), and revisiting, along with Ward, three houses he was using in his story.

"It's so fatiguing," Ward complained at dinner. "One has to be so *nice* to these people. And I was invited to go sailing tomorrow. . . ." It was on his conscience.

"So go. We can call Werthmere and ask if I can catalog the Newport Maid Room furniture and everything else over there. You wouldn't have to worry; there are so many catalogs and monographs to go through, after all."

"Mmmm . . . and maybe you could get Miss Wentworth to say, 'I remember when Mama told me about the ghost.' Or reminiscences of Tennis Week. You know. And of course"—Ward smiled—"you'll solve the murder mystery."

"No promises."

On the morn I rose happy as a tweeny maid on her

Thursday off. How often did the servants at Werthmere of old get a day off? Never mind. Walking along the great avenue, I was plunged in a dream of an autumn week at the beginning of the century. The inscription on the Werthmere gate glittered in my mind only after I had passed through. What was the Latin of it? *"Unde in . . ."* In my memory the iron scrollwork letters formed something like "Unearned Incrementum." I would have to check on it. Another time.

I half expected that, as in a fairy tale, my hostess would be invisible, that *objects* and secret volumes would magically appear before me. I followed the butler up the great staircase and along a wide corridor and into the Newport Maid Room. There sat Miss Wentworth, deep in flowered crewel-work cushions, before a fire. The birdlike slant of the head and shrewd spoiled-child expression were even more marked than before: Perhaps because of illness or fatigue?

Miss Wentworth took my hand and gripped it tightly for a moment.

"Well, young lady—don't stare. I always have a fire when it rains. Even in summer."

I looked from the fireplace to the windows. The sun shone through the mullions, diamond-bright.

"Yes, look out at the view. . . . When I was a child I used to creep out of bed at night and look out there, out toward the water, to see the Newport Maid. The ghost, don't you know. Saw her too, more'n once. My room was next door, and this was my sister's room then."

The famous ghost chamber was a disappointment. It had been changed to a sitting room with lots of cheery chintz-upholstered chairs, plumply and frankly no-style. The imported wainscoting and black walnut Jacobean four-poster (partially hidden behind a flowered screen) looked innocent enough by daylight.

"No, child, I didn't sleep last night. And I thought of you coming, and of so many old childish records and books. Strangers'll be readin' them someday, I thought. Oh, no, they won't says I, not while I have my fire. And then I thought of you again." With a cane she poked at a pile of stiff marble-paper covers and dog-eared leather. A volume fell to the floor in a cloud of dust, and I hurried to pick it up.

"Miss Wentworth, you mustn't."

"You see, you value the things. Why not look through 'em? I can't read 'em. My poor brother's old diaries, my mother . . . I can't bear to crack 'em open." She drew herself up, twitched the upswinging Celtic eyebrows inherited from old H. H. "I mean to say, I don't live in the past. But lately someone gave me a book I was readin' in when I want to sleep. Queen Victoria's family, just their own letters and journals, don't you know, but they show what the times were like. The Golden Age. Standards. The family virtues. A few people might be interested still in those things."

"So you would like me to look through these records, too, with an eye toward . . ."

"Oh, just look through 'em." She waved the cane.

Plainly the audience was over. That was all right; I could check the Newport Maid Room for Ward's article another day.

"I'll be pleased to." I looked at the stamped gold coat of arms on a leather-bound volume as I gathered up the books. A scallop-patterned shield. " '*Et Undas Requiescere,*' " I read aloud.

" 'And to stop the waves,' " said Miss Wentworth. "I didn't learn the Latin, it wasn't considered necessary for a lady. We're descended from King Canute, don't you know, in the female line."

At the door I turned. "Miss Wentworth—"

"Oh, Perry will speak to you about a retainer."

I flushed. I really felt like a hireling. The governess in plain merino. "It's not that. I wondered if there might be staff records available. Household accounts, the day-to-day scheduling of events in a house this size, when the family was in residence. For the period when your father—I mean, it's difficult to get a sense of the life, even a sense of proportion, without knowing something about the staff. Perhaps servants even left private records."

I felt like a fool. But Miss Wentworth nodded.

"Like John Brown."

"Who?"

"John Brown. He was a Scottish attendant of Queen Victoria. He wrote his recollections of her."

"Oh."

I must have smiled, because Miss Wentworth added: "I believe they were quite appropriate. The recollections." She pushed a buzzer set into the fireplace mantel.

Perry came to usher me into the library.

"There will be a check tomorrow," he said. "A retainer of two hundred dollars, if that is agreeable. With the rest to follow, if a suitable work results."

"Thank you, Perry. Would you convey my thanks to Miss Wentworth." Convey, yet. Was it proper to thank Miss Wentworth, to acknowledge the passing of money?

Alone in the Werthmere library, I was too exhilarated by a glamorous vision of myself to settle down to work at once. I imagined myself in the library for hours, reading by the fire, climbing a graceful sliding library stair to find an old family record that would reveal the secrets of the Wentworths. ("Just put the sherry there, near my chair, Perry." "Very good, miss. It's a pleasure to see the library really used, miss, if I may say so.

Miss Elizabeth—Lady Deake—loved to sit here for hours and read in the rain. Just like you, miss.")

It was beginning to rain. I pressed my nose against the leaded panes. Below the terrace the grass shivered, dragon green. Where a section of frontage fell away toward the sea, I could see the waves break into foam on the rocks beyond barbed wire.

With H. H. Wentworth, great apostle of efficiency and the work ethic, staring down at me from the shadows above the fireplace, I turned to my work.

I felt suddenly helpless before so much faded script. In one journal the dust between mottled pages was so old that it had turned green. Daily life came down to this, in the end. I began to shiver, realizing that I was alone in the library, perhaps alone in that part of the house.

To calm my nerves, I began to read. First I read at random in Mrs. Wentworth's journal, her social secretary's book, seventeen-year-old Hallie's diary, and the ten-year-old Victoria's ruled book. Little Tory's handwriting was large and unformed:

> *One of the maids left today. Brigit is the maid who left. Hallie is in Covintry. They never tell me what happens.*

The next entry was dated two days before the murder. I decided to organize the otherwise hopeless research by reading first every reference in each private source to one particular day—say, two days before the murder, the day of Mr. Wentworth's arrival.

I began with Victoria, the child who was now my employer:

> *Since my Papa is here I will write more, since it is more important because he is here.*

When Papa came, Papa and Mama were in the library. Then Hallie went in. I could not hear. Lizzy cried again.

Papa came. I asked him why Brigit left. He did not hear me. I said, "I know the names of all the servants. No one else in our family does." But he did not listen.

We looked at pictures in the ballroom. I asked Papa if I will have to marry and go away and live in England like poor Lizzy. Papa said, Your Mama is a determint woman. You will be like her. Yes, I said I think so, because I will stay with you. He did not look at me right away. Then he said, Victoria, if you do not want to get married you do not have to, you can live as you wish. I can support you. I said I will always live at home and take care of him.

In the laundry there were 2 maids. New from this summer only, but I know their names, Big Mary and Skinny Mary. They do not care or bother about me. They were talking about Brigit and lie. It has its uses said Skinny Mary. Then they told me to go away. The servants are just like grownups, they do not want to talk when a child is there.

Victoria's brother was less communicative, except on the subject of the obstacle race and the cars—"bubbles" —entered in it. There was one mysterious personal entry in Hallie Wentworth's diary:

Mama still angry about B. B. went away two days ago. M. told P.—she is so angry she even spoke her threats to him.

Who was B.? The young man's mother wasn't saying either. Along with copious notes on the order of tableaux vivants entries (Spirits of Steam, Steel & Oil to follow the Golden Spike), Mrs. Wentworth had recorded her displeasure with both of her older children:

Spoke to Hallie about the latest incident. *The automobile was given him on condition that he stop that. "Oh, Mama, then you must give me a Mercedes like yours." Slapped him. If Mr. W. had been by my side all these years, the*

*children would not flout me at every turn. Told Mr. W.
about the girl. Told him I could have killed her—I am so
helpless, everyone crosses me—and just then Jr. came in for
his "few words" from father. I hope Hallie heard what I
said. He should know what suffering he causes his mother.*

*Spoke to E. this morn. She is hysterical again but will be
grateful later. Told her what to expect from men. Told her of
H. Even hinted at my own sufferings as a wife. Illustrated
with letters from her friend, which I had acquired. She
wept. But strictness is necessary with a daughter, a woman's freedom being dependent on knowledge of the worst in
men.*

What a philosophy! I wondered if Miss Wentworth's
single state was due as much to Mama's views as to
Papa's promise.

The wind riffled the grass on the great lawn; the rain
washed out ever more clues to the past. For an hour I
had been reading, telling myself that every casual noise
meant—nothing. Now, behind me, a door creaked. I
jumped and turned around.

"Oh—it's you!" I said.

"Yes? Have we met?"

He came slowly toward me. Young, but with mummy-
smooth features, antique crewcut, spectacles cased in
translucent flesh-tinted frames.

"You almost ran over me two days ago. On Bellevue
Avenue."

The young mummy blanched.. "Oh, God . . . not
again."

"Don't look so worried. It was my fault, a witness
said so. Do I look like the type to sue, just because you
drive a fancy car?"

"Oh . . ." He groaned. "They often try to sue me."
He sat down in a Louis XIII chair across the immense
desk from me.

Then I remembered where I had seen him before. In New York.

"I know you," I said. "Management and Labor."

"Pardon?"

"Negotiating the last union contract at H. H. W. publications. I was a labor rep from *Clio*, the history magazine. Your side promised not to kill *Clio*, but you did. You sat opposite me at the table. You were—"

"Management," he said. He had kept just that smile all during the negotiating period. The smile had seemed to me a great asset in labor bargaining—though it must be a disadvantage in personal life, supposing he had any.

"You were a director of the parent company. So young. Such negotiations!"

Both sides had been locked up together with a city negotiator. First, cheery greetings. "How's everything in Greenwich?" (Where Management lived.) "Fine, fine. How's everything in the Village?" (Where Labor lived.) Then long hours of melodramatic, even operatic performance: indignation to outrage with all the whistle-stops in between. I had not said much at these meetings; I had been too angry with the lush who was head of my local. And this incredible young-old man—this director of companies, who was rumored to have had a heart attack at twenty-five—sat opposite me during these arias and *winked* at me. Flirting like a foxy grandpa.

"I'm Penny Miller."

I reached my hand across the table. We shook, firmly.

"Quint Wentworth."

"Oh, my God. Of course."

Of course I had heard the name before. H. H. W. Enterprises—I had been working for the Wentworths all along, through a maze of interlocking companies. Or anyway, the Wentworths still owned a piece of *Plea-*

sures and Palaces. And this was the last of the Wentworths.

I knew from my researches that H. H. Wentworth V
(therefore Quintus, or "Quint") was posthumous: his
father had died in a car crash on the way to a horse race,
and the pregnant chorus-girl mother had gone to court to
prove the legality of the marriage against contention
of—could it be Miss Wentworth? Or had there been a
custody struggle between the playgirl mother and Miss
Wentworth?

"Uh . . . I'm sorry. It's just the name." I felt I must
explain my long stare. The murdered industrialist had
been Quint's great-grandfather, the Second. Grandfather
and father had both died in auto accidents.

He seemed embarrassed too. "I came up to see my
great-aunt." Was he winking? Was it a tick?

"Of course." I was putting my books in a pile. "I'm
finished here. I'm doing some research for Miss Wentworth. You can have the library to yourself."

"Oh, don't . . ." He was standing too. He made a
feeble gesture. "I just came in here looking for someone
to talk to." He giggled. "The Curse of the Wentworths."

Was he feebleminded? No, during the contract talks
he had made some astute points.

"I'm sorry, but I'm working now. Research. I have to
go." I know me place, and I hope you know yours:
maybe that was sometimes a polite way for the maid to
avoid telling the young master that he was a bore.

Secrets of the Attic

I left the library by the door through which Quint Wentworth had entered. I found myself in a corridor leading to the terrace door on my right, and back to the great hall on my left. Opposite the library was the dining room, with casements looking out to the sea.

I hurried back to the hallway, past the stairs and into another corridor to the left of the front door. The service offices were that way, I knew—past the dining room and ground-floor sitting rooms.

A parlor maid flattened herself against the wall as I passed. I remembered having read that Mrs. Wentworth had required servants to freeze—and so become invisible—if she accidentally encountered them in the house.

Perry was sitting in the butler's pantry. It looked quite comfortable, with ledgers and papers on an old desk.

"Ah, yes, miss? Miss Wentworth suggested you might want to look at the old household accounts, from her father's time. And what personal records there might be among them."

"Yes, if you have time now."

"Oh, I have time." He stood up, creaking. "Here, we'll take the back stair."

"I haven't seen this part of the house before."

"Here we are, you see: butler's pantry, laundry, and kitchen on the sea-side—like the dining room and library." The kitchen was cavernous yet comfortable-looking. "The stairs are over here. . . ."

Perry led me up a narrow back stairs. At each floor the stairway was pitched more steeply, with many turns.

"Too fast for you, miss?"

"No, no."

The precipitous stairs did not open onto each floor but were separated from the halls by doors at each landing. I rarely had claustrophobia, but the sealed-off service staircase made me uncomfortable.

"This is the attic." Perry found the key on a large chain. "It's kept locked because no one has been up here for years. Since so much of the house is closed now, we use other space for storage." He opened the door and we climbed a few more stairs into the attic.

The Werthmere attic was broken into many dormer spaces with the roof descending to the corners like a tent. Corners were crowded with boxes and furniture. I moved to the center of the long confused space; only under the peak of the roof did I feel easy about standing upright.

"There's such a narrow space to turn around in. What are all the doors for?"

"The smaller gables are divided into little chambers."

"Rooms? What for?"

Perry hesitated. Was some family skeleton about to rattle?

"Why, for the servants in the old days. None of these rooms has been used, of course, since the thirties. Many of the current staff have homes in Newport. And it would be too costly to heat the attic now.''

"Was it ever heated?" I asked. Perry smiled. To be fair, Werthmere had rarely been open in the winter in the old days.

"The staff is much reduced in size from what it was, of course.''

"Much reduced?"

"I wasn't always here, miss. You'll have the advantage of me when you've read the household books. I know that the stableboys and gardeners lived over there, in the stables.''

"There are so many gables. Not much space.''

"I do know," Perry said, "that the late Mrs. Wentworth did not want a full attic. You see, the Breakers had to put on an extra story to house the staff, and that was regarded as hurting the proportions of the cottage. Mrs. Wentworth wanted this story to appear to be mere attic.''

"So the servants had to crawl along to their rooms.''

"No, no—they only had to stoop occasionally.''

"Are there books up here? Records?"

"There seem to be some old records, including some taken from the Fifth Avenue house when it was torn down. Everything that was judged important has been given to the historical collection of the library, of course.'' He went up two steps and pushed open a door to one of the gabled rooms. "This room seems to have been kept as a place for storing books and personal mementos.''

"Of the family?" I peered in: a little chamber with a pallet bed and stacks of books.

"Oh, no. Of the staff.''

"And they left their things here?"

"I suppose so, miss. Or perhaps . . . some of them died here.''

"Died?"

"I only mean, people who had been in service with the family for many years. No one would have wanted to dispose of their personal belongings, you see."

"But their families?"

"Well . . . many people in service in the old days didn't have close ties. Cooks, butlers—very often they weren't married. For people in service, it was very difficult to earn a living—to establish a family—until recently. Do you think you can manage?"

"Me?" I had a confused impression that he was asking me about my own financial management, inquiring paternally into my affairs. Could I earn a living without going into service? I wondered.

"I mean . . . you aren't uneasy at being left alone in the attic? Excuse me, Miss Miller."

"Oh, no." But I looked fearfully around at the stacks of old paintings, the shadowed rows of porcelain basins, ewers, and chamberpots. "No . . . But what about the other little gable rooms. What about this one?"

"They're all open, I believe. No, not that one. That one has been locked for years."

"Oh? Why?"

Perry looked uncomfortable, I thought—just for a moment—then properly bland. Perhaps I wasn't supposed to ask questions. "I don't really know. I suppose now it is simply not worth the bother to open it." The locked room had a barricade of antique bicycles, bedsteads, and chests before its narrow door.

"Could I look in?"

"I suppose the key is lost."

"I'm sorry, Perry. I just supposed . . . that you knew everything about Werthmere."

To my surprise, Perry started to laugh. Was he blushing? "Oh, my goodness, no. When I first came here, there were rumors of a . . ."

"A . . .?"

"A ghost."

"Oh." I was disappointed. Did he expect me to believe that? Scratch a ghost and there's some real source of discontent, even evil, beneath the scary story.

"Not that I believed it, even as a boy. That was just before the War."

"The Second World War?"

"Miss Miller." He looked pained. "I was born just after the Great War."

"Oh, of course. What kind of ghost?" I asked, eager to humor him.

"One of the servants. An accidental death. Right around the time . . ."

"Of . . . ?"

"I don't know. Servants were very superstitious, of course. People then didn't take to new ways. New things."

"Who was the servant?"

"I don't know. A woman."

"Where did she die? Here, in the attic?"

"That's all I know. Only one thing more, miss: if you wouldn't mind, when you come down, please use the stairs we came up by. The other way leads to the family's private quarters.

"Of course." Family! So far as I knew, there were only two left. Unless a mad relative was locked up somewhere in one of the bedrooms. . . .

Perry disappeared down the servants' stair. Alone in the silence, I turned to my work. The disorder of the attic was distracting. There were satinwood dressers and tapestried chests with neat labels—twenty-five of them,

at least—oases of Orientalia and sports equipment, pyra-
mids of gilt picture frames laid out flat. Miss Wentworth
appeared to be a compulsive saver in the heroic mold of
the Collier brothers.

In the heavy, dust-laden stillness of the attic, I sat
amidst this past that had never been discarded. I went to
work making a brief catalog of the records in the little
room that Perry had pointed out. Few of the records
seemed sufficiently interesting to warrant a good read.
The old household records were there, with expenses
for soap, starch, wine; with wages paid and reasons for
dismissal; all written in brown ink in a Spencerian hand.
There were records of tennis games played at the Casino.
Boxes of letters—none of them to or from Wentworths.
School notebooks, however, were in the handwriting of
the Wentworth children—Elizabeth Eugenie, Harold Hall,
Regina Victoria—with comments by a governess.

I flipped through and catalogued everything. Then I
stood up, stretched, and ducked into the other tiny gable
rooms. I made quick inventories of whatever record
books were in the other rooms.

All but one. Why, I wondered, had only one room
been locked? None of my business, perhaps; but then
again, whose business was it, after all these years, if not
mine? Servants had not been allowed to lock their rooms
in the heyday of Werthmere.

The barricade of metal-barred bedsteads looked as
formidable as a succession of little jails: square-cornered
French brass, homely pipe-shaped brass, Calder-curved
cast iron—they were all heavy and hard to move. I
pressed up against a large tricycle—had grown-ups rid-
den such machines?—and saw that the plates on door
and doorframe, where the hasp of the padlock ran through
two spuds, were somewhat loose. The wood was old
and fibrous, soft pine for the servants.

I shouldn't do this, I told myself.

But I couldn't resist. Trying to make as little noise as possible—for the entire attic was as noiseless as a sealed tomb—I pushed aside the heavy bedsteads and moved aside the tricycle. It didn't take me long at all.

I opened my purse, took out my nail file, and started to work on the screws that attached one plate to the door frame. It was easy.

The worst they could do was fire me from my job as researcher or archival assistant to Miss Wentworth—or whatever I was.

The plate came free. I tried to open the door. It was locked—either bolted, I thought, or locked at the keyhole.

No, stupid, I told myself, how can it be bolted from inside? Not unless someone is still in there.

Exasperated at my own stupidity, I shook the door. A bicycle fell down behind me, and an imposing brass sceptre—the corner of a bedstead—knocked heavily against the wood of the narrow door. The door gave. I pressed through. As I entered the little cell, the metal plate from the rotted jamb fell on my foot.

"Damn!" I said aloud.

I hobbled into the little room and started to sneeze so hard I couldn't see at first. The dust of the past seemed to spring to life at my forced entry. I sprang to the low window but couldn't budge it. For a minute I just stood and sneezed. There were motes in my tears. The risen dust writhed in my hair like a living creature.

When I could finally see, the locked room didn't look too rewarding. A low pallet bed. Bare walls. A room five feet by nine. Nothing else.

Except for a small strongbox of dull metal at the foot of the cot.

I knelt above the strongbox. It was secured with a

leather strap. Under the crumbling strap was a discolored piece of paper with the legend in script: *Hold—M. Smith—Paterson.* I undid the strap and opened up the box. Inside was an envelope of old photographs, vintage 1900, I guessed, and a stiff black notebook with the label, ACCOUNTS. I glanced at the photographs: large groups of people posed before the side of a house. Most of the people wore livery or maid's uniforms. They squinted in the sun. All long dead.

I opened ACCOUNTS and was at once immersed:

> *I have thought whether it is right to keep this record. Only as a footnote to the other. Because I sense so strongly the evil at Werthmere. I have lain awake all night and wondered if it is right to write this. It is right, for I do it for You. All for You. I want You to understand. I have doubts, even nightmares. Is it right? I ask myself—for I dare not ask others. I am so cut off from all who can inspire and comfort. I need uplifting words and cannot hear them. The other record is of the Deed, Faith, and great words. This must be only my own thoughts and hopes. It is right. For the great Life—Paradise. We must build in the hearts of men. We must establish a kingdom of God.*

The writer went on a while in this vein of mystic generalization. The writing dipped and slanted and was sometimes difficult to follow.

> *. . . the Agency where I submitted the testimonial of my former service. They looked at me hard, as if they supposed me to be an impostor. I am not. I have worked. These Agencies are impostors. Often the people sent out from them are spies. Watch.*

So people were paranoid then, too, I thought. Watch, indeed! The writer was evidently a domestic servant. Names and places were initialed or abbreviated, but the

writer kept reminding herself (for I instantly assumed
the diarist was a woman) of inspiring moments from her
past. Much of this past was apparently connected with
New York City. There were references to Third Avenue, Fourteenth Street, rare days off.

> *At last I have been able to see G.____again. To hear that
> voice! She is not beautiful, not now at least, but for what
> she says she is beautiful. All hearers were uplifted—this is
> truth—and the faith that I have wanted! She gives and
> gives. This is what I want. It is what I wish I could do. And
> her relationship with those who are uplifted—and who uplift
> her in their turn—that is what I want with You.*
>
> *All this will not be understood. I understand it myself as I
> recall her words. Dare I approach her later—or never?*

In her new post the diarist described the employer's
family with great care. I was rather surprised that someone in service in that day should be so interested in the
upper classes. I had always supposed that servants really cared as little about masters as masters did about
servants.

> *The children are named after Queens and Royalty. Yet
> they are put back by their Mother. Their spirits are broken
> as—it seems to me—mine never was.*
>
> *Now we are at N. All is different. The sun and sea are so
> beautiful. I want to run out, run to the cliff edge to see all
> that, but am kept working from dawn to dark. At night I
> scarcely have strength to put pen to paper; but duty—and a
> sense of high excitement, I must confess—keep me going.*
>
> *I sense the presence of evil, of unspeakable wickedness,
> very strongly. Here—where people come to play!*
>
> *The daughter. Is she eighteen? I must not speak to her,
> not try to help her, for in a sense she is a willing prisoner.
> And yet another poor girl upstairs. Poor Bridget. Lye. Quickly
> done. I thought she would die.*
>
> *My employers and their friends: they can see neither the*

beauty nor the evil. The money gilds every creature, so that none can breathe. All are asleep now and I write as I wrote in the loft at home. Only one child in this house. She never cries. I think of the little ones at home—I say your names. So many of us! Such life! I will never have any. O my children—Do not think of that. I will always be with our little ones. Our life is given us—mine is given me—for them. A sister for sisters and brothers—

So far from home, from love. Since I came to this country, I have been able to hear—things. So clearly. The priest who was after touching my brow and saying I was marked. For vocation? My prayers, then.

It's the same sea here as at home. A strange land. On the other side of the same sea, they stand on the cliffs and look. For them the dawn is coming while they look West to me in the darkness here. O my brothers and sisters! I do have my children! I feel taken along with you. And with the many people in New York—I do not fear them now—no more fear. I pray.

I used to think of starving myself. To the death. As the people did in the old times.

She must be Irish, I thought. Religious. Terribly lonely. Anorexic—but in those days they would not have put a name to that, or to the yearnings that isolation and (I assumed) sexual deprivation brought to a sensitive religious nature. How many had crossed the ocean and bound themselves to lonely toil, sending money back, perhaps sending for the others to come?

The evil is as strong as the fog. They speak of ghosts. Spectres. A spectre haunting this place. They are right.

A custom here: Mistress insists, if a servant is about but not needed directly by one of them, the servant must pretend not to be there—when they pass by. We turn to the wall and go all stiff. To be summoned is another thing. Then you must be visible. Butler, Cook, and the sour French maid are not with us "invisibles" in this. We are mere ghosts.

If we could be seen. We shall be seen. When? Fas a Bealàc! When we are heard. I will speak of this Evil. I will

*not be silenced. They are planning a play. They are always
playing.*

*I am so lonely, yet have faith. The recent Event speaks
to me—to Us. A miracle. It does not matter if I never
hear G.____ again. What a dawn we shall see together.
What a paradise!*

I flipped through the diary. There were about fifty
pages altogether. I was intrigued by notes on the household routine at Werthmere—it had to be Werthmere, of
that I had no doubt. Toward the end, dates appeared in
the journal. The writer of the ACCOUNTS had been on the
staff at Werthmere during the summer that ended in H.
H. Wentworth's murder!

So there was a witness—at least to the larger round of
life at Werthmere. Someone unconnected with the family ambitions and plots, someone who might somehow
tell—what? She hinted that she knew something.

But as I read on, I realized that this witness was a
very imperfect one. The narrator seemed sometimes
moved to religious ecstasy; at other times she was com-
pelled by a strange anger. Even if she had seen something, her angle of vision might be too odd. Suppose you
have a possible witness to a murder—and the witness is
too wrapped up in her own gothic dream of "evil" to
notice real goings on?

I flipped back and forth in the book, half hoping that
the figure of the servant girl would form and move
through the stiff pages, like the people in those old
parlor decks that anticipated motion pictures. The entry
for two days before the murder was more detailed, more
concrete, than most:

*The little one followed me about today, watching. She
wanted to play in the laundry, but we sent her away. She*

*has been sent away by everyone, she said, and will make the
servants mind when she is mistress of Werthmere. "No, you
will marry well, like your sister." "No, no, I will not."*

*Upstairs, in my new duties, I was nearby to Miss W.'s
room. The Mistress was screaming at her—opened the door
to leave but stayed a while so, with the door open, and
screamed some more. About the marriage. About the
brother—so they know—poor Bridget! The father too—his
affairs with servants, so she tells the daughter. Then Mrs.
comes out and I freeze to the wall. Mrs. passes by me, her
skirt brushing me, but did not see me or did not care. I went
in to change the linen for Miss. I knew I should not, but
could not help from going in. Miss W. was very white. She
watched me from the dressing table mirror, her back to me.
Then she said, "You are not the maid who has been doing
my room. Where is the other?" She questioned me closely
about B.'s illness and used the word "disgusting." I was
angry, and I spoke out. And when she spoke against B., I
hinted at her own case; which might lose me my place. I
spoke out of anger but in sympathy too: toward her as well.*

*Mr. W. arrived in the afternoon. I have not yet seen him.
There is a scullery maid who has worked three years and
has never seen him and seldom Mrs.*

*I am so weary I can scarcely lift the pen. I hear the
voices. G.____and others. Luminous eyes and words. Other
voices in languages I do not know. I want to rest. The gates
of paradise. Open them, we are knocking—*

I was beginning to feel weary myself. I was very dirty
too, with all the dust I had displaced.

I choked back a scream. What was that? Dry claws on
dust. Only a mouse running across the floor.

I slipped the maid's journal into my bag and left the
stifling cell. I closed the door to the locked room carefully behind me and set the bicycle across it. Probably
no one would notice that the locked room had been
opened. I moved the bedsteads an inch at a time, a bit
jittery at the thought that they might collapse in a heap
together, a jangle of horrid harps. My head ached from
reading the faded script in the close little place.

The main part of the attic was darker now, the west light diffused in motes of dust. I groped my way along the furniture. Boards creaked. I felt something moving and furry near my fingers and I suddenly stepped backward. A thing caught at my hair. I turned quickly, putting my hand out to hit, and knocked over a screen. The body of a woman in maid's uniform fell heavily to the floor, landing with a sickening thud.

I screamed and tried to run. I fell into an unguarded short stairway and tumbled down. I kept screaming and pounded on the door I ran up against at the bottom of the stair. Locked! Then someone was pounding and shouting on the other side. The door opened. I tumbled into a man's arms.

"Hullo? What's wrong? What is it?"

"A body—there's a body up there."

As I turned blindly to lead the man up to the attic, I realized he was Quint Wentworth.

"Oh, no. Ghosts. Where?"

"Yes—a maid. No ghost. Real. Dead." I pointed. I thought I was marvelously under control.

Wentworth brushed past me. He went to the body and started to kick it.

"Don't. No!"

"It's a dummy," he said. "Didn't you know?"

"Why?"

I stood above the life-sized figure and now saw quite clearly that it was cloth, stuffed with some compact material so that the head had made the deadly *thunk*. Wentworth turned the body over, and I gasped: the face had no features, only an ugly brownish stain like old blood running down it. The details of lace on the real apron and cap, the real uniform with buttons, made the dummy obscenely horrible.

"Why . . . ?"

"Obstacle races," said Wentworth, calmly pushing it with his foot. "When they first had cars in Newport, they used to take them out on the lawns and have obstacle races. Just for sport. There's another one." He nodded toward a wicker perambulator.

I peered into the perambulator and saw a dummy baby.

"They tried to hit the dummies with the cars?"

"A long time ago. My grandfather was interested in the sport."

We looked at each other. I realized that I was all dusty and mussed.

"I've just been doing some of my research up here. On the family."

"Oh? Of course." Perhaps he was too much of a gentleman even to speculate on what I might be doing up there.

"I have to go now." I turned blindly, toward the back stairs.

"This way."

"No, I have to go the other way. Perry . . . Oh, what does it matter?" Feeling like an idiot—and yet afraid of running into Perry or Miss Wentworth—I let the last of the Wentworths escort me downstairs the front way, like Quality.

"I'll get Raymond. No; on second thought, may I drive you?"

I was surprised. This frail, practically extinct creature stood smiling and blinking at me. "Why, thank you—"

I was about to say "no" when he gently suggested, "Quint." As if I'd forgotten his name.

"Quint," I repeated.

"Oh, jolly. But it's still raining. Here."

He foraged in a Chinese vase umbrella stand, took out and opened a large black umbrella—in the hall.

"Oh! That's bad luck." We both started to giggle.

"The curse of the Wentworths," he said. "It's cleared a bit."

The wind had died down although it was still raining. We walked sedately along the drive, under the great umbrella as under the Wentworth cloud. It looked like Great-Aunt Tory's umbrella: the horn handle might have been carved from mammoth tusk.

The chauffeur opened the convertible door for me. Quint went around to the driver's seat. Ignoring Raymond's gestures, he put the car into reverse, and we shot backwards out of the garage and onto the front lawn. A crumbling stone urn behind us rocked gently and crashed into the low-slung trunk—or was the engine back there? But the urn was hardly our main concern.

"Put up the top," I shouted. Rain was coming down my neck.

Quint thrust the umbrella into my hand. Had he started the car while still holding the umbrella over his head? We went forward, jolted, just missed hitting the gate, and careened along the avenue, the umbrella dipping rakishly into the view of the road before us.

"Watch it, you caught my eye!" Quint yelled in a high agonized voice.

He was still trying to bring up the roof.

"Forget the top and drive!" I yelled. "No, no—left. Right—here. Stop—stoplight."

After the stoplight, Quint recovered sufficiently to creep along without further directions from me. Puddles spit against the low underbelly of the car. Quint stopped for fully half a minute at each cross street, then shot out halfway through the crossing to stop and peer again, while I held the umbrella over his head. I was getting soaked.

"This is a custom Müller-Matta Daisy Six," said Quint. "I hate cars. It's from my great-aunt. She wants to be the last of the Wentworths. She wants me to crack up. Sorry about the trouble at the start. I have more accidents in reverse; I don't know why."

I reached over to touch a button on the dashboard. Slowly the dark cloth of the convertible roof crept up to cover us, collapsing the umbrella in the crush of its advance.

With me calling the turns, we made our way, slowly and a little more surely. To my surprise, Quint seemed relieved to have me take charge. He relaxed enough for small talk.

"Were you at Miss Porter's? Radcliffe?"

"No—hey, watch out!"

We talked about our undergraduate days. Quint had hated Harvard, which he said had fallen on evil days. I assumed he meant radicals, the student strikes of a few years back, before he'd been there. But no.

"That too, of course. But it goes back to the theology. Unitarians. They've been so far out on a limb for a hundred and fifty years, you know." He confessed his real wish. If it had been possible, if it hadn't been for the family duties, he would have taken orders. "As it is . . ." The speedometer crept up to twenty-five.

I could see him as a bishop. "Yes, I can see that."

"I'm especially interested in eschatology. That's—"

"The four last things. Yes."

His face lit up. "Of course. Are you—high?"

"What?" Maybe he was taking something.

"High church."

"Christ, no. I'm Jewish."

Quint laughed, "heh," as if to acknowledge a bad joke. The car swerved, almost into a Farewell Street graveyard.

Finally we arrived at the house where I was staying. Our entrance left the old lilac bushes atremble.

"Well, thanks for the ride." My legs shook under me.

"My pleasure." He winked and smiled. "Bit nervous, you know. Ulcer last year. Health."

I thanked him again. He looked as if he wanted to say more, but instead he blushed and roared off again, almost knocking me over.

A strange one, I thought. The curse of the Wentworths. Atavist Club at Harvard, no doubt: a premature little old man. And he got his flirtatious kinks right out of the twenties, somehow. Frightened to death. The curse of the Wentworths.

Ward was sulky because the rain had ruined his sailing party. He had sat with his friends on the great goldplater in the marina, just drinking and getting seasick from the swell.

To cheer him, I had dinner with him and brought along the maid's diary. I showed him the purloined journal only after swearing him to secrecy.

"Isn't it odd," Ward said. He read: " 'The piercing liquid eyes, even from the stage—the voice—but most especially the words. I have heard and seen many, but none like G_____. It is all very clear.' How strangely they wrote then! A religious fanatic, with God as the audience. And lover? All this seems so sexual now, doesn't it, this sort of religion. And it comes from Werthmere?"

"Those are the interesting bits."

"Servants are rarely so articulate. It's strange."

"They don't let on that they're smart."

"Still, how is it going to help you in your work for Miss Wentworth? You are going on with that, aren't you?"

"If I can. The magazine wants me back in New York next week, I suppose?" It would be nice to wangle an extra week in Newport, I thought.

"Well . . . I don't know what I'll do without you. I can't do all this work myself." Ward turned to his lobster Newburgh. Over coffee he referred to the maid's journal again. "I don't see, really, how this glimpse below stairs is going to help. Oh, I know your mind. I'm every bit as vulgar. 'What did the upstairs maid—or the tweeny or scullery or whatever—know that was driving her mad? What was the strange love that drove her to Werthmere? The obsession with Evil . . .' And so forth."

When I got back to the house, I found a telephone message: Pierre's name and number. I was eager to speak to him, but to my great disappointment he thought the diary I'd found was "women's magazine stuff."

"But, Pierre—"

"Sure, it's good to do social history and get the servants' views. But this journal is obviously the work of a paranoid-schizophrenic—or a sex-starved, unbalanced young woman—"

"Aha! Like Elizabeth Wentworth? Is that why you fastened on Elizabeth as the killer? What's wrong with being paranoid? Or having a rich fantasy life?"

"Calm down, Penny. I only mean that the worthwhile questions are the logical ones. One: what did Mrs. Wentworth tell Elizabeth two days before the murder that so impressed and disgusted her? Two: why did she keep the police away from Elizabeth? Three—"

"Four, five, six! I can count, you know. What you've got against Elizabeth and this servant is that they're women, thus, irrational creatures." I was shouting into the hall telephone. I was surprised to be so hurt at Pierre Rose's pooh-poohing my discovery. "No, don't say that, it's sissified, being sorry. I have to hang up now, Pierre. My woman's intuition is starting to solve the Wentworth mystery."

TWO

They say she died of a broken heart
(I tell the tale as 'twas told to me);
But her spirit lives, and her soul is part
Of this sad old house by the sea.

. . . And ever since then, when the clock
    strikes two,
She walks unbidden from room to room,
And the air is filled that she passes through
With a subtle, sad perfume.

—BRET HARTE, "A Newport Romance"

Two Days Before the Crime

I went up to my little slant-roofed maid's room, flopped down on the bed, and thought. That night the darkness and the branches scratching on the window could not disturb me. I didn't even feel like getting up again to lock the door.

A sort of dark clot was forming on the imaginative matrix of my brain. Creative work seemed like playing in a squash court: it's all closed in, and every shot you make has to return somehow. The thinker thinks within the invisible web of the obsession. Paranoid, huh? Only connect.

Fantasy! My shrink was always saying I should deal with the here-and-now—wherever *that* is. If I only had the confidence to write down my fantasies, I thought, I could be a writer. All these free movies that flicker through my brain pan!

Questions to ponder. What did Mrs. Wentworth tell Elizabeth two days before the murder that so impressed—and disgusted—her?

Was the locked room connected with the crime?

Who was Bridget, and what happened to her?

What about the servant who died two days after the murder?

Had the servant who kept the diary known something? Could the murder, despite appearances, have been plotted in advance?

Why did Mrs. Wentworth eschew the English conquest that she had been planning as her next move after the wedding? Did either daughter or mother know something about the other that made them avoid each other for the rest of their lives?

No, no, I told myself. Too many questions at once. Concentrate on one day at a time. The day of the victim's arrival at Werthmere—two days before he was murdered. If it could be recreated from a patchwork of diaries, police reports and newspaper accounts, what would it be?

"Do you want to be promoted upstairs, then?" the big blond woman up to her elbows in a zinc tub is saying to a thin dark one who brings her more sheets and other night linen.

"Someone must do it, now Bridget is gone." The thin woman drops her burden—all white, slept in only once; but the sheets must be ironed again.

"Let them pay someone, then. It's the missus sent the girl away. If it's a permanent place you're after, I can tell you you're daft. Another week here, and they're back in the city. There's the opery, the horse show and all. And the wedding, don't forget. Herself will get someone cheaper, and right off the boat."

"We are only for the season," says the thin servant. She stands on tiptoe to look out the window, straining to see the sea, thinking her own strange thoughts. The little ones. She almost cries. So much beauty she cannot reach—

"Let her find others, by God. To be in service with this one, it's like changing the guard at Buckingham Palace. Even Cook and Butler go, it they can get a character."

"Shush." Mary is always quick to sense the presence of a child.

The child of the house stands in the doorway, frowning. The little girl knows she is not welcome in the laundry, but she also knows that these servants—unlike Cook and the butler—haven't the right to send her away. (Mama is busy yelling at the new secretary, who keeps dropping notes and is almost in tears.) Lizzy is sulking outside, as she always does, and Hallie is busy with the automobiles. Even the dancers are boring to watch after a while, and old Mr. VanMeer—just like an old lady! —makes her giggle, she doesn't know why, as he shows them the steps.

"What are you doing?" the child asks.

"Working."

" 'Working, miss,' " the child corrects her.

"Working—miss." The big woman rubs her anger out on the scrubboard.

"Miss Victoria," the little girl says.

"Don't touch that," says the thin servant. "There's lye there."

"What's lye for?" Tory asks.

"It has many uses. Too many for little girls to know. It's dangerous."

"One thing it's used for," says the other one, "is to bleach clothes."

"What's 'to bleach'?"

"To whiten. To take out the spots and stains and make clean."

"Then it's like to christen, isn't it?"

The thin dark woman stops with a pail in her hand and laughs sharply. "Yes. Poor Brid—"

The big one slaps the skinny one across the face. The skinny one stares, the soapy foam across her mouth.

"Don't say what will make you sorry," says the big blonde.

"I don't like white," the child continues. "My sister always wears white. I don't like white because brides wear it. The Newport Maid wears white. I saw the Newport Maid this summer. Two times. Going across the lawn."

They are too busy. The child goes away. Perhaps when Papa arrives he will talk to her.

Eugenie Wentworth is greatly vexed. Her daughter is trying to thwart her. Her son, of whom she asks so little—it is enough that he is male, he has the name—insists on his automobile race. She would have canceled the race except that Deake wrote back expressing interest. And her husband—he is the great unknown amiable enough in their secret estrangement, but possibly grown stubborn since the Christmas quarrel on the *Empress Eugénie*. What Mrs. Wentworth knows beyond argument is that she has had to be both father and mother to her children; they may show the forms of love and loyalty to *him*, but they owe the substance to *her*.

In her larger sphere as a social leader Mrs. Wentworth is cruelly taxed. The Fates have no more consideration than her family. She wants to introduce Lord Deake at Newport, where the best people from Philadelphia and the South—families who have known her Ritcheys, if not her husband's more lately arrived Wentworths, for generations—will be at their cottages. The setting is romantic; there is room for ample effects. Mrs. Wentworth is a Belasco of these amateurs, and rightly sees the house, especially since its enlargement and rechristening, as a stage setting. When her daughter Elizabeth leans languidly against the balustrade of the terrace, twining her fingers among the honeysuckle, the proud mother wants Society to admire the effect; perhaps she even wants the *New York Herald* to admire it and pass it along to the larger public. But in this instance Deake cannot arrive before September; rather late, but let that pass. Late in the season may be best, considering the delicacy of the operation, for that means less time *for anything to go wrong* before the wedding in November.

And then—a tragic national embarrassment. The President is shot by a madman. Impossible to stay above it. Mr. Wentworth has dipped his fingers into the rich oil of Ohio politics these many years. He has been a friend of the anointed—indeed, a maker of Presidents, if he wanted to stoop to the smaller arena of official government.

In the week that President McKinley lingers, dying always amid optimistic medical reports, Mrs. Wentworth languishes over her decision. Should she go ahead with her plans for a ball, with the entertainment of quadrilles to be danced by the guests? There is the ever popular Hobby Horse—such a success at the Whitneys' at New Year's; poor old Ward McAllister's Mother Goose Quadrille, almost a classic by now. Should she scale down her campaign of entertainment? Luckily, the hostess has planned tableaux vivants that have elements of the patriotic as well as of the picturesque. The frivolous quadrilles are canceled. Mr. VanMeer is in the ballroom at this very moment, turning the Indian Maidens' Love Ballet into a sedate and proper Lament for a Fallen Chief. One of the most fashionable artists (and a Westerner, for novelty), Barbizon Peale Schmitt himself is arranging the tableaux.

No two-hour cotillion can, in the circumstances, follow this sober and informative entertainment. The supper is still on—one must eat—but even this repast is in mourning, as it were: not with black and purple swags replacing the festoons; but with an accompaniment of patriotic fireworks like a funereal cannon. Mrs. Wentworth has the operational thrift of the born administrator: in a twinkling the wedding feast furnishes forth the funeral bakèd meats.

So the reception will be in the best taste, even helpful to assuage the pain of loss by stressing—to guests and to the nation—the stability of business, the breadth and greatness of the country.

Still, Mrs. Wentworth must tread softly. The press has not been sympathetic lately to such efforts. The Bradley-Martins meant, through their grand costume ball four years back, to give employment to American seamstresses and restaurant workers, to lift them from the depression then idling millions. The press, however, was witheringly sarcastic and the Bradley-Martins moved to England. Also, the newspapers have been suggesting that the sun should set on transatlantic marriages; the press does not understand that each such dynastic marriage is different.

The word from her husband in the fields of labor strife has been generally supportive, yet laconic:

> *For the President's death: as Mr. Morgan and Sir Thomas Lipton have postponed their race for a week or two, I suggest you take in canvas in some similar fashion. I must know if my presence is required absolutely for the affair you plan. There is some business out here which may reach the molten state; unlike a fancy-dress ball, it may not be put off by the host.*

But Harold is coming. She has seen to that, by writing back about urgent family matters.

Her daughter Elizabeth drifts past the terrace, no weight or purpose to her. The mother, up to her ears in invitation lists, is furious at this public parading of idle unhappiness.

"Elizabeth. What are you doing out there?"

The girl enters through the French doors of the dining room. "Yes, Mama?"

"What are you doing out there? You'll catch cold in the wind."

"Why not?"

"Why not?!"

"Catch cold and die," Elizabeth murmurs, gliding past, behind the bulky Louis XIII dining chairs.

"Elizabeth! What did you say?"

"A line from a poem."

She slips out and tries to escape—to the library, to the ballroom—but she cannot. Her mother bustles after her, trailing a train of wrath.

"Elizabeth—"

"Shh! Mr. VanMeer—"

It's no use. In a crowd one finds no sanctuary from Mrs. Wentworth's domestic fits. One of Mrs. Wentworth's strengths is that she is beyond shame. Her intensity is such that, in the heat of the moment, no small part of her stands aside to look on and perhaps feel foolish. She does not hesitate to make public quarrel in the presence of inferiors. She is never wrong, never remembers being wrong; and the proof of it is that she gets her way.

"Elizabeth! Come here."

The piano falters and stops. The carpenters at work on the gallows-like stage at one end of the ballroom—stop. The artist stares at his draperies. The Indian Maidens freeze in their tragic positions. The cotillion leader looks for inspiration to the decks of gilt-framed pictures. Elizabeth would like to sink through the floor.

"Go on, dear Mr. VanMeer," says Mrs. Wentworth. "Young ladies—you look lovely."

One by one, the girls curtsy, or bow, straggling and embarrassed. This is enough of public victory and humiliation, respectively, for mother and daughter. The daughter smiles desperately and goes out. The mother smiles magnanimously and follows her.

Elizabeth crosses the hall and goes up the stairs, thinking, But if I go into the church and say no, I will win, won't I? But if I can't speak now—to the girls in the ballroom—how will I ever say no then?

She runs quickly up the carpeted stairway. Her mother treads slowly, unperturbed, rehearsing the scene in her mind. With Mrs. Wentworth, anger is a prod to action. Her victims are generally those whom anger paralyses. She has brought up her children to be this second type: that is, well-behaved.

I won't, I won't, Elizabeth thinks, walking quickly along the corridor. I'll say no at the church—but why couldn't I say it downstairs? It would create a terrific scandal to make a scene downstairs—all the girls would tell their mothers. But no, she'd only lock me up. I'll wait for the tableaux vivants—I'll say it from the stage. No, first I'll tell Papa.

Her mother's step is heavy, close behind her. Elizabeth ducks into the bedroom where seamstresses are at work on her Niagara costume and on the curtain for the stage. The little gray women look up, surprised, from their clouds of white tulle, waves of gold brocade.

Say it, say it, say it—

"Good morning, Miss Wentworth."

"Good morning, Miss Wentworth."

They hold up an empty dress.

"It's lovely," Elizabeth says, in her mother's voice.

Her mother stands in the bedroom doorway and smiles at the charming scene. Elizabeth feels the cloth and reluctantly leaves these women bent over their work.

Once Elizabeth gains her own room, her mother steps in quickly, shuts the door, and leans against it.

"I am working only in your interest," Mrs. Wentworth says in a new confiding voice that surprises the daughter. It's as if she were to say, "Quick, I'm a spy who's been on your side all along—but I have only this one minute to speak."

Elizabeth walks nervously near her dressing table, picking up and putting down toilet articles and knick-knacks. Against the polished oak wainscoting the birds-eye "bamboo" furniture looks surprisingly light; it's her choice—she couldn't sleep in the Jacobean four-poster with the pedigreed ghost. The truth is, she had started to "make up" poetry to keep awake and fend off the ghost, in early adolescence. But how can she fend off her mother?

"I know my interests," Elizabeth says.

"My dear, how can you? A woman's interests are always relative to a man's. You know nothing of men—so how can you know what your interests are and will be?"

"I cannot love Lord Deake."

"My dear, he does not expect it. In his family, no one has married for love in four or five centuries. The children of great houses marry for duty."

"Duty! Money, I'm sure. And a title."

"Oh, my poor child," says the mother, seating herself on the bed. "The penny papers talk about money and a 'title.' People from Chicago or Colorado may marry for such reasons. Or decayed 'princes' from the continent— they will do anything. But our sort must think of duty."

111

"Mama! No more, please."

"Yes. It's right that you hear. The best families in Europe—in England especially—and the people who have become leaders here know that the only safety is in helping one another."

"Safety? Oh, Mama, who can hurt us? You make me laugh while I'm crying!"

The mother, strangely, controls her temper this time. "I am talking seriously to you, as one woman to another. There are many people in the world who are against us, against the stability and order of our life. People will want what you have. With this marriage both families are happier; it is right for *us*."

"Oh, Mama. Don't talk about politics. What you do best is—giving parties, building houses."

"I am building houses."

"Mama, these political arrangements aren't for us women," says Elizabeth. She is covering her ears. Her mother pulls the daughter's hands away.

"When you are Lady Deake you won't have to shout. With your face and mind and what you bring from the family, you can go anywhere. You will have a brilliant career."

"I don't want a career."

"You will, you will. Do you think beauty lasts? There is nothing for an intelligent woman except her career."

"For me, there's love."

"For you! And John de Feenste? John de Feenste had a love affair with Dolly Farren, you know, and it didn't end while he was paying his attentions to you."

"*No!* I don't believe you. You would have told me before."

"I wanted to spare you. Now I see you aren't a child. You need reasons. I am giving you reasons to last a lifetime."

"I don't believe it. Why would he?"

"Why?" Mrs. Wentworth's cheeks are hectic with triumphant anger. "Why? Because men are like that. They are beasts—and the only way to deal with them is to get the mastery of them. . . ."

"I believe it only of this man you want me to marry. *He* is a beast. I heard that he had to take a cure for some—disease."

"So he is cured. A gentleman, at least. Not like the Emperor Franz Joseph, who gave his disease to the Empress Elisabeth. And Lord Deake is not like your brother, whose disgusting conduct has just led to a second dismissal of a servant here. Not—"

"No. I don't believe it."

"Don't be a child. You see what I have to face. What can I tell your brother? At least I can tell you: The only freedom you have is in marrying where much of your fortune will be secured to you—and where you will have a sphere of operation to suit your talents. Women like us have more freedom in an aristocratic society than in a republic. In England a social leader is a political leader as well. Now dry your tears. When your father comes, I must speak to him about this business of Hallie's. So don't bother Papa with your little—tempest."

"I can't believe Papa wants me to be unhappy."

"Papa! Men! Do you think he is better than all the others?"

"No—"

Mrs. Wentworth has opened the door, stands ready to leave. But Elizabeth runs out, at this monstrous suggestion. Out the window the sea dazzles and slops in the sky. She must get away.

Her mother follows her into the hall. Her mother keeps talking, although a maid carrying linen passes them. The maid stops, frozen, turns to the wall.

"If I am cruel, it is only to make you understand. After establishing yourself in a way that assures you some dignity, the next most important thing is to keep certain matters secret. Childbirth is nothing compared to these other pains we women must suffer."

Mrs. Wentworth goes to her own room. Elizabeth returns to hers and flings herself down on the bed. Out the window the sea reflects the shattered day, and the conical roof of the Pavilion pokes into the marble-hard sky.

Her mother enters again to put a small jewel case on Elizabeth's bed, then retreats, her tread steady as ever.

Elizabeth flings the case to the floor. It opens and letters spill out. Elizabeth picks them up. From a woman to a man: to John de Feenste, from Dolly Farren. But it hardly matters now. Her mother has bribed some servant for the letters—but that does not matter either.

There is a knock at the door: only a maid, who enters with a pile of folded sheets.

"What are you doing? You are told to do that when you won't disturb anyone."

"I'm sorry, miss. I'm new upstairs." But the new maid looks around with naked curiosity. Dark-haired, even thinner than Elizabeth.

Elizabeth stares at her. "You're not the one. What happened to her?"

The maid turns to go. "I'm sorry, miss."

"No—stay." Elizabeth runs across the room, closes the door, and leans against it as her mother had done. "The maid who did these rooms—and my brother's— where is she?"

Thin Mary is not frightened. She is more curious now about the girl than about the room with its ceiling frescoes and carvings. Perhaps the servant glances out to the effervescent seascape for a reminder of her mysteri-

ous, strengthening love; the passion she confides to her
diary.

"What happened to the other maid? I don't know her
name. It was to do with my brother, wasn't it? What
happened?"

"Oh, miss . . ."

"Is it true? They met—the Pavilion. At night." Everyone, it seems, knows more than she herself does.
"What happened? Was she going to have a baby?"

"Not now, miss," says the maid. Her face is sad,
exhausted. "She won't have a baby now."

"No?"

"She almost died." The face is full of misery. "We
tried to help her," she whispers. "Upstairs. But, Bridget
is gone now, miss. Don't worry about her. Though she'll
get no recommendation for a place. And she's sick still."

"How old are you?"

"Twenty-six, miss."

Elizabeth stares at the worn, pained face. A beautiful
brow—she sees now that the wrinkles show suffering,
not age. This woman's problems would sink her.

"Well, so that is why the other one is gone," Elizabeth says. "But why didn't she take care of herself?"

"Well, miss, look at yourself. There is something you
do not want to do, and you cannot take care of yourself,
either.

The maid goes out. Elizabeth realizes that by being so
candid she has put herself in a servant's power. Scandal
sheets bribe these people to tell secrets of the great
families they serve.

Lost in the contemplation of her own indiscretion, her
moment of reaching out, Elizabeth forgets the crime that
is being done to her. To maintain silence—that is
everything.

* * *

Mr. Wentworth arrives in the afternoon. He slips in. He does not care for ceremony, has perhaps never cared much for the harsh stone castle his wife has raised around her family's old bracketed cottage. He greets his wife, who tells him the news: his son's escapade with a servant, Lord Deake's scheduled arrival, the plans for the reception.

"And Elizabeth?"

A shadow crosses the mother's face. "Ah. She was so happy . . . until yesterday. It's so odd: some women are almost different people at . . . certain times. She was always sensitive, so it is not entirely surprising. But it's best not to talk to her for a few days."

Thus warned, the industrialist scrupulously avoids his elder daughter as he would a woman in purdah. She notes his aversion and believes her mother has reported to him her reluctance to marry Lord Deake.

"Papa, I need your advice—"

"Oh, not today, Lizzy. I am so buried under work."

He requisitions the library and works as if under siege. He *is* under siege: out in the West, where the great strike at the Works has become a small war that threatens to spread. And at Newport, by his wife. He treats Mrs. Wentworth as a prime minister would the eccentric monarch he serves. Five years ago, after his activities in the Sound Money campaign, Mr. Wentworth decided that his wife's tantrums must be dealt with exactly as Mr. McKinley dealt with Ida McKinley's epileptic fits. When the language remains that of romantic chivalry, the domestic facts can be ignored by the busy warrior. Still, Mr. Wentworth sometimes wishes he could just throw a handkerchief across Eugenie's face to calm her down—as the lamented President occasionally did for his wife at state dinners, with no embarrassment to either party.

"Don't speak to Elizabeth. Not now. She is hysterical. Next week. But you must speak to your son."

"What can I say?"

"*What?* You are his father. I can't speak of such
matters."

"You dismissed the servant?"

"Yes. I had to do it directly." Mrs. Wentworth is a
woman who prides herself on speaking only to a butler
or housekeeper, never to the lower orders of servants.
"I gave her some money—not wages, but something—
which I'm sure she considers a bribe. And I was thinking, 'Oh, I wish I could kill you—' " Her voice rises.

"Hush, Eugenie—"

And the son is entering on cue: perhaps mother and
son plan their collisions for maximum mutual embarrassment.

Then Mrs. Wentworth is gone, leaving father and son
enveloped in a horrid intimacy. What can the father say
to the son? Can any generation gap be greater than that
between the man who has made millions and the one
who has only to spend them? Mr. Wentworth is well
aware of having come on the scene at the high classical
moment for American business; he cannot cherish the
national dream that his son shall outstrip him. That is
impossible. What does he want, then, of Hallie? A sober
stewardship? Some men he knows with similar responsi-
bilities have called the seventeen-year-old namesake into
the library to offer a choice: infinite wealth and work in
the firm; or idleness and mere riches. A surprising number of sons choose the latter.

Paternal duty requires that the father express shock
and anger at the son's affair with a servant. In truth, he
is much more depressed and wearied by the son's sins of
omission. As he says the proper righteous things, the

father thinks what a loss it is that his only son will never be a partner.

After sternness on one side and penitence on the other, they turn with immense mutual relief to a discussion of the planned festivities.

"You won't believe, Pap, how the Stanley starts up: accelerates to sixty in fourteen seconds flat."

After the son leaves, the father sits alone in the library. He generally likes his solitude . . . but not today. He yearns to return to the field, to lead the moral struggle against men who would withhold their labor *when work is given to them*. Even now, while he sits in Newport in enforced idleness, men are being arrested—perhaps being killed. Without him, his lieutenants falter. Only he can bring the agitators first to their knees and then to their senses.

The industrialist rises and walks about. How monstrous and heavy the marble pillars seem with their green-veined clouds! What gloomy weather they make in the house. The master enters the ballroom, where a wooden stage stands finished but still nude of drapery.

A little figure comes hesitantly across the ballroom floor to him. Mr. Wentworth has entirely forgotten his third child. Newport is not built for children; sometimes when there are many guests, the ten-year-old and her nanny are actually bundled off up to the servants' quarters.

His impulse is to go to the child, take her up, hug and reassure her that the clouds will pass. No—he would only frighten her. Besides, that is not the proper expression of his feeling for the children. But on this visit, he will spend more time with Tory, and with Hallie and Elizabeth, too.

He does not stoop. He holds in his tenderness.

"Papa, why did Bridget have to go away?"

"Hmmm . . . your Mama sees to the servants, Victoria. It is not for you to bother about."

"I know all the servants' names, but you do not. Papa, when I grow up, will I have to marry and go away like poor Lizzie?"

The father looks down at the child with her pronounced, unpretty features, her brow as strong as his. He makes her the promise that she will never forget.

The family, united, sit over a silent jellied dinner. They are spied upon by footmen. That night perhaps little Victoria looks out for the ghost on the lawn. But certainly the ghost is not there.

Fog

Friday was my last workday with Ward, for even the idle rich keep the weekend sacred and do not want the journalist-immortalizers of their property mingling with their guests. I spent part of the day, pleasantly enough, in a garden with huge animal-shaped shrubs and a famous maze. The maze really worked—I became lost in it. The gardener was eager to talk to someone about the dying art of topiary. Craning my neck to see a densely leafy dinosaur's neck disappearing in heavy fog from the sea, I filled in the missing head with fantasy.

I imagined Elizabeth, Hallie, and little Victoria walking peacefully past the Casino in the fog. Or (the day suddenly sunny in my mind) Elizabeth taking a parasol to the water's edge while bathing—never alone, for a lady always had an escort or even a hired bodyguard at Bailey's Beach. As mere moving portraits, these old actors would take their own pace. But then the events of long ago began to present themselves in the toy theater of my mind, first frozen in a series of tableaux vivants. Then my pictures would start to move. . . . The cards would flip faster and the figures assume a crude frenetic life. When the gestures of the actors seemed too crude, then I would put aside that version of a scene.

Sometimes, for example, on the day of her husband's arrival in Newport, Mrs. Wentworth goes for her usual drive along Bellevue Avenue. She waves and bows to acqaintances at their first encounter, merely bows her head in acknowledgment at the second, looks straight ahead to the eight ears of the horses at the third, and actually turns her head away (as does her neighbor, with perfect amiability) at the fourth. The world is so small. Speak of the Four Hundred! One finds so *many* people only in Gotham, and only after the horse show at the Garden. Now, Newport is almost empty—or would be, if many had not lingered for the Deake reception. Some people have already gone to the Berkshires or up the Hudson. The ocean is not the best place to see leaves, they say, though the great elms above the avenue arch and meet in the only true high American Gothic.

Or perhaps Mrs. Wentworth takes out her little Mercedes automobile—for she is one of the first among the new autonobility—and drives out well swathed in veiling, bowing less formally when she passes other cottage dwellers. This year the Newport horses, almost as sophisticated as their owners, are not so likely to shy as they were last season or the season before: they are getting used to these ghost-drawn carriages.

However she is driven along in the face of her world, Mrs. Wentworth is driven. She must work off her high feelings. How can she persuade her daughter that her proper sphere of activity is the political? And that only by becoming Lady Deake can she enter the world where clever women rule through influence? Mrs. Wentworth herself should be a director of companies.

Perhaps she speaks to Elizabeth more kindly the next

day, representing them both as pawns in a cruel game, dynastic necessity. Perhaps she can explain the game with the addict's fervor, or perhaps she can trace the pathos of her own life. Or perhaps not. Mrs. Wentworth is more likely to press her attack on men, their natural nastiness and, consequently, their use—to the woman who refuses to give in to despair—as levers in a world of masses and powers. What might the mother not insinuate, to keep Elizabeth from the three men who might help her, from father, brother, and former fiancé?

Traces of the mother's campaign appear in the daughter's memoir. Could an interpretation of events—of the murder night itself—support speculation that that fierce struggle ended in murder?

And the others in the drama: Does Tory laugh with the laundresses—do they let her help? Does Nanny join in games with the only child at Werthmere? Does the dark-haired maid imagine her brothers and sisters at play in the great rooms? Is there ever laughter in the house? Or are the actors always like their pictures—posed? Certainly the Wentworths still hold to the custom, fast giving way, of calling friends "Mr." and "Mrs." or "Miss" in public.

I ran many scenes backwards and forwards in my head, in slow and fast motion, but one I could never imagine was Lord Deake's arrival. I knew from the newspaper stories that he came up with Wentworth friends on a yacht from Carribua, that the yacht dropped anchor in Newport harbor. But it was beyond me to imagine what sort of reception he had in the family. I saw the servants assembled in the great hall. I caught a flickering picture of Lord Deake and Elizabeth Wentworth disappearing down a leafy avenue. Were the real conversations so banal as to be impossible to imagine?

In memoirs and in newspapers, Deake was always

described as being outwardly correct and pale in youth and florid in later life. Perhaps the Wentworth marriage settlement put the roses in his cheeks or gave him more scope for his dissipations.

I abandoned my attempts to sketch the day of Lord Deake's arrival. I myself had a crowded schedule for the weekend that would round out my week in Newport.

Pierre called Friday evening.

"I want to apologize for being so sneery."

"That's all right."

"Well . . . I'd like to apologize in person," he said. (Still, he didn't ask me how my research into the mystery was faring.) We decided to take a walking tour of the old colonial port the next day, when the buildings would be open.

Later in the evening I got another call. Quint Wentworth.

"It's vitally important. Can't talk now."

"Well . . . does it have to do with my research?"

"Yes," said Quint, "and no."

Had he been drinking? I agreed to go to dinner with him Saturday night.

As soon as I hung up, Ward called to announce that as a special treat he would take me to dinner at an exclusive club of which he was a member. I told him I had a previous engagement for Saturday night.

"In Newport? With whom?"

"That's me own business, sir."

"You're here to assist me," said Ward, not quite joking.

"Even the maid gets a day off now and then. Even at Werthmere."

In the morning, I found Pierre sitting on the porch. We wandered down to the old port, past a noble brick building with Ionic pilasters, and out onto Long Wharf. Pierre pointed out streets behind the wharf where old houses had been lovingly restored. After the fossilized grandeur of Werthmere, wooden frames looked light and clean as bones. Here were skeletons with nothing to hide, I thought.

"About 1740 this was a bigger port than Boston or New York," Pierre said.

A scrap of history and a date, spoken over water, always have the effect of old movies on me. Tears danced in my eyes, and through them I saw the old Newport: a delicate scrimshaw of church spires and honest artisans' homes. The sailing ships shimmered, the Quaker merchants exchanged the pure silver *thees* and *thous*.

"Architecture really does reflect the values of a time, doesn't it?" I said. "I mean, look at the fake effects with genuine marble the robber barons got in their cottages compared to the houses of even the *rich* people who lived in Newport in earlier times. Honest merchants, but pretty well off. Miss Wentworth had a maternal ancestor who had seventy ships at once right here in Newport Harbor."

"That guy?" Pierre hooted. "He made his pile in the slave trade. He had a beautiful house over there—with an underground tunnel from the pier, so that he could bring in the 'cargo' by night."

"Oh." The vision of white dancing boats vanished. I had forgotten the source of the Ritchey fortune. Their good taste had been sustained by human slavery. If they had lacked ostentation, perhaps it was because they had had something they were conscious of having to hide. Unlike the robber barons, whose consciences were clear.

"Before the Revolution," Pierre began.

"What? What revolution?"

"The American Revolution. Remember, we had one. Before the Revolution, as I was trying to say, the negro slaves of Newport had a once-a-year festival all their own. Every June. They elected a governor. Had games, wrestling, jumping. Dancing in the evening. But you're hung up on the Wentworth connections. Too high-falutin to go bicycling with me. I'm just a winter boy."

Pierre turned and started to bob his way back along the Long Wharf. I followed him.

"What's a winter boy?"

"A winter boy is a native. See, I know the language. I used to go out with a debutante, and she said I was a winter boy."

"Was that her debutante year?"

"No. Later."

"Did she come out here?"

"Here, there, and everywhere."

"Did she like it?"

"She said it was like being a whore for a year."

"Yeah, sure. How'd she know."

"Oh, I think she tried that too, for a while. She was a wild one. No she's a housewife. Or a divorcée. One of those."

"Do you have a bicycle?"

"I rent," Pierre said.

"Were you thinking of going any place in particular?"

"Wherever you want. We could go out to a beach."

"I'd like," I said, thinking of the maid who had died two days after the murder, "to visit a cemetery."

We were walking on a street that had a little grave-yard full of old lozenge-shaped stones with round angel heads and wings hunched over inscriptions.

"Look, there's one of Mrs. Wentworth's Ritcheys," said Pierre.

"Can't be. They're all in the vault."

"At the bank?"

The tombstone read, in noble but close-spaced Roman letters:

OCEANA
SERVING MAID
TO MR. HOSEA
R I T C H E Y
FEB^{RY E} Y 3 1766

"See," said Pierre. "A slave."

"How can you tell?"

"She didn't have a Christian name. They could have more fun naming slaves. Like with naming dogs. You forget that in the North in the eighteenth century a lot of people had slaves."

"I'm looking for a serving maid's grave," I said. "But from somewhat later."

"Are you still on that?" Pierre said. He put his hand over mine on the graveyard fence. "Is that what you're thinking about?"

"Maybe because I'm paranoid-schizophrenic. Like Elizabeth Wentworth. And the maid who died."

"All right. Maybe I was wrong. It could be interesting."

"It is. There's something definitely strange about the whole thing," I said. "I've been looking at things logically. The journal ends just before Mary Smith died. And she died two days after the murder."

"What do you think you'd find in a cemetery, Penny? There wouldn't be a stone. You'd find out more from city records. But not on a Saturday. What do you want?"

I stared at the gull-white sky. I was confused.

"I don't know what I want. I guess I want some face-to-face confrontation."

"With a ghost?"

"I wish I could find out how she died."

"You don't think you're overdoing this personal history stuff?"

"She was young," I said.

Why was I so emotional? What was there in that diary that I felt so close to? I was identifying with hysterical women again. No—with the lives of the obscure. With Mary Smith.

"If you want to talk face-to-face with a sort of ghost," Pierre said, "I think I can arrange it. If that's what you need at the moment. There is someone I want you to meet, anyway. Down on Thames Street."

Pierre took my hand and we walked back toward the harbor. We entered a low-built old warehouse, a sort of antique slum. The place was a bar. It was so spare and spartan as to be immediately recognizable as a neighborhood old men's club rather than the public tavern it legally was.

"Penny, meet Gramps. Gramps used to work at Werthmere, among other swell places. Pantry boy, stableboy, and all."

Gramps was a skinny, frail-looking but jaunty old man. His dark eyes snapped as he waggled his white beard and shook a long finger at Pierre.

"Now, sonny, I didn't work for them. Pack o' murderers over there. I was a fisherman."

Something in his features looked familiar. Why did I have the feeling that I'd seen the old man before? A week in Newport, shrinkless in the sea air, and I was losing my grip on reality.

"Now, Gramps, you know that you worked at Werthmere." Pierre slid into the booth so that the old party couldn't escape. He nodded in my direction and stage-whispered: "She's a reporter."

"Oh, that's all right then," said the old fellow. He

winked at me. "Press? Newspapers? I did work over
there. I worked at more 'n a few of them houses. During
the Season. Summer. That's now. They guv you five
dollars extra if you let 'em put cornstarch in yer hair for
a party. And wear them cutoff George Washington knickers. Five dollars more a month." He looked about to
speak again, then wet his lips. He'd gone dry. He looked
speakingly at Pierre. "Beer?"

"How many so far?"

"One. But it spilt some."

Each of us had a beer. The old man went into what
was evidently a well-worn routine about the night of H.
H. Wentworth's murder. He had been a pantry boy in
his early teens then, only a summer recruit.

"Oh, but I wanted to be a stableboy and look after the
fine horses they had. Come a big party, there'd be a
hunnert 'n more 'n the stables, all prancin' an' pawin'.
But there I was tied to the house: 'little blaggard,' footman called me, on account of my dark hair. Layin' out
things ready, runnin' to the kitchen. Cook an' butler
screamin' at me. It was like a battle. When I went over
to France in the trenches, it minded me of one of them
big Newport dinners. In the War yer scared of dyin'. In
the kitchen, yer scared—you don't know of what. But
even Cook is scared and yellin'. . . ."

"But that time, when there was the murder . . ."

"Oh, yessiree, I told that story many a time. Then I
was tickled that I worked in the house. We had it all
over the stableboys then. The police wasn't near as
interested in the stableboys as in us. *They* was way off
with the horses, and not likely to see the things I seen."

"What did you see?" I asked.

"Mmm, well, now . . . I didn't see so much. Runnin'
back 'n forth like a chicken, fetchin'. But then the police
come back later to ask me more questions. See, they

was a woman—a maid—that died, got run over by one of the automobiles."

"When did that happen?"

"Two, three days after the big man was shot."

"What happened?" I asked.

"Far as I know, it just bolted out and down the lawn. She was going down there."

"Which maid?"

"I didn't know which. You couldn't imagine the people they had working at Werthmere. . . ."

"Wasn't there an inquiry?" I asked.

"An inquiry? No. A servant in the house . . ."

I realized then that this man was in his late nineties. If he was confused, he had reason. Or perhaps *I* was confused, for the old man patiently explained, "See, this was a servant. And not permanent. Not a local. A foreigner. There were accidents with servants all the time. When they built Werthmere, there were some killed. Italian laborers. It was a hard life." Gramps went through his litany of servants and their movements on the night of the murder. He had seen nothing of the Wentworths and their guests, who might have been on another planet.

"But the day before *he* died, I seen *him*. Seen him clear as day comin' out in the kitchen with a gold stopwatch. We all stopped work and then we worked so fast we couldn't get nothing done. He looked right at you, deep. That's the only time I seen the deceased. 'Deceased'! They're all deceased now. The missus was different; she never looked at you at all. . . .Some of this I recall, but some is what the older ones said. Now it's hard to tell one from t'other."

I wanted to buy the ex-pantry boy another beer, but Pierre signaled no. Whn I inquired about Mary Smith, "the skinny one," the old fellow couldn't remember at all.

"No, not at all. There was so many of 'em. So many maids. They looked pretty, the young 'uns, in the white aprons standin' up starched out." He sketched wings above my shoulders. It was like a kind of blessing. "I'll remember *you*, though. Good of this young fella here to bring you around. Didn't know he'd have the sense t'know what I like."

"All right, that's enough. See you, Grandpa."

Out on the street I said, "You're right. There's nothing to be learned from interviewing survivors. They fantasize as much as I do. But I like him. . . . I was surprised though, you calling him 'Grandpa.' "

"Oh? why?"

"It sounds so patronizing."

"Huh? But he *is* my Grandpa. Great, in fact. My mother's grandfather." Pierre laughed. "People even say I look like him."

As we walked to the bicycle rental shop, Pierre talked about his family. The old man lived with Pierre's widowed mother, who dropped the old man off four mornings a week on her way to work and picked him up on the way back; Gramps could be with his cronies, and the bartender had strict instructions for a two-stein limit.

"It's been rough. I always wanted my mother to quit working at the naval base, and now it's closed down. The biggest employer in the area. Now, all this is welfare blight." Pierre waved his hand at the square before Old Colony House. "Newport's only industry used to be the defense of our Atlantic shores. My mother was civil service, though, so now she works for the income tax. But it was rough for the town."

"Isn't Social Newport an industry?" I asked.

"Are you kidding? The big cottages used to have twenty-four servants, but they mostly brought their own staff. And they paid lousy. Grandpa never got a pension

from the Wentworths and the rest, for thirty summers'
work. Thank God for the First World War and veterans
benefits. Well, here we are. Four-speed bike? Girl's?''

We pedaled along side by side, very slowly through
the old streets crowded with holiday traffic; then in
single file, leaving old Newport.

Pedaling, I thought about the Wentworths. Perhaps I
could try to find doctors' records. A doctor had been
called for the maid who died.

We rode for miles, out to a region of sandy pools and
crossroads so bleak they looked like little airfield run-
ways. There were vistas, near but unapproachable through
the fog and marshy land, of modest developments of
small one-family frame houses. The houses were identi-
cal in shape but painted in various Easter egg colors.

Pierre stopped. "It ain't Bailey's Beach," he joked,
panting.

He was pointing to a narrow strip of clean beach
fringed by tall grass. We were all alone on the beach.
The grass and the sea were disappearing into the fog.

I looked at the water and thought of Elizabeth Wentworth's poems:

> *Cold is the sea, and cold is the marble house,*
> *Standing in ruins, a tomb for living souls,*
> *Cold is the house, and cold is the marble sea,*
> *Over the folly the green-veined granite rolls.*

"Penny for your thoughts. Ha, ha."
"Last night I memorized some stuff by Elizabeth Wentworth. Do you know 'The Mermaid's Wedding'?'' I
walked on the sand and recited:

> *"A table was set for the feast of the guests,*
> *Another was set with their gifts all of gold.*

131

*The bride set the guests at the board laid with gifts
To feast with their eyes while the viands grew cold.*

*" 'We cannot eat plate,' all the guests did cry out.
'I cannot breathe dust,' was the mermaid's reply.
She toasted with water—while the guests toasted wine:
'I cannot love power, the air is too dry.'*

*"The mermaid stepped out of her scales called a dress
And walked on the terrace and ran down the lawn
And dived in the ocean and danced under water
And never returned tho' they searched until dawn."*

"I like the sentiment," Pierre said. "The sentiment, at least. What you don't see is that I think Elizabeth Wentworth was right."

"Right? How?"

"To strike a blow for progress. Against the patriarchy! But I'm freezing."

"You don't strike a blow for progress by killing on impulse, in despair," I said, moving away. "I have to get back."

"Oh. Why?"

"Quint Wentworth called. He said he has something important to tell me. I can't afford not to find out what it is. What if I write something brilliant—or even find out about the murder—and get Great-Aunt Victoria's thousand dollars?"

"Okay, suit yourself. Nobody's won her brass ring yet. But maybe later? Could I come over to your place?"

"No, not tonight . . ."

"On the job all night, eh? For your thousand dollars."

"Listen—"

"Nah." He waved a hand, dismissing the fog. "Listening isn't what I want to do. And investigating isn't what you want to do. You traipse around sniffing into this and that, taking impressions."

"Listen—"

"Probably recreating historical moments, Virginia Woolf—style."

"What are you—jealous?"

"You won't face the real evidence. Your friend Elizabeth Wentworth attempted one murder a few hours before her father was killed. You never mention that."

"Oh . . ." What was it? I'd forgotten.

"The problem with you—"

"Don't bother to tell me!" I yelled.

"—Is that you have very big value conflicts. You— wait!—you work for this glossy magazine, *Pleasures and Palaces,* and you know it's not serious—either for you or for the readers. But it *is* serious, in a way. You can't admire the houses without thinking about what they represent. These aren't fairy castles made from nothing. Not sand castles." He scooped up sand and threw it to the wind.

"I *do* think about it. Do you get this preachy with your students? You must be pretty dull in the classroom."

"And now this Wentworth twerp. What a transparent story he's giving you. Are you really interested in this guy?"

"I'm just going to dinner. He wants to talk." I was trying to be patient, but I was very angry.

"Talk! I'd like to talk, too. Can I call late tonight?"

"Sure. I expect to be home early. Why not?"

We pedaled back into Newport. I was fatigued. Pierre had to keep stopping to wait for me to catch up.

When we reached my rooming house, Quint was already there. He was sitting in the Daisy Six next to the newly shredded shrubbery.

"Oh, I'm sorry. We got lost."

"I'm early," Quint said.

"Quint . . . uh, Pierre." I pretended to be the casual

type, as if I couldn't be bothered with last names. Luckily Quint didn't seem to recognize Pierre as the archenemy of all the Wentworths. Quint spent only a couple of weeks a year at Newport, no doubt out of duty and prudence; he might not be very interested in his great-aunt's crusade.

I had to go upstairs to take a shower and change my clothes. I hated to leave Quint to Pierre's tender mercies, but what could I do?

As I left the two men, Pierre was leaning over the car and saying to Quint, "Isn't this model supposed to be very dangerous? I'm surprised they're still importing them. . . ." And Pierre started kicking the tires.

Up in my little room, I realized that I didn't want to listen to Quint, I wanted to argue with Pierre. What had he said about another attempted murder? I hurriedly flipped through the pages of Pierre's article on the Wentworth case.

> And it is a matter of record, in the published reminiscences of at least two Newport contemporaries, that Elizabeth Wentworth was so nervous on the day of the murder as to be involved in a "dangerous accident during the obstacle race." Lord Deake was "much shaken by the incident"—in which he was involved. From the "dangerous accident" we can at least assume that Elizabeth Wentworth was in a dangerous mood that day. . . .

I skimmed the details of the incident and decided that all my original feelings about Pierre had been correct. Even if he was right about the automobile race, it didn't mean that Elizabeth had killed her father.

When I got outside again, all fresh and ladylike, I found Quint alone. He was pale from his bout with the muckraker, but properly noncommittal—to my relief. He opened the car door for me.

"I wanted to tell you," he said, "my theory about Great-Grandfather's murder. But shall we eat first?" He inched into the quiet street and looked both ways. It was a one-way street. "This is a somewhat upsetting errand, and I have a delicate stomach."

"Yes, of course. I'm starved." Too late, I realized that ladies didn't admit to being starved.

"Good. I'm glad you're starved." He winked and smiled. "I can have only clams with milk. Milk is good for me. But you have whatever you like."

We were out in the traffic. Quint's demonstration of hysterical caution on wheels made my stomach churn.

Don't think about it, I told myself. I shut my eyes and tried to think about something else, about the obstacle race on the day of H. H. Wentworth's murder. . . .

Bubbles

At the end of the terrace at one side of the house, a great tent has been set up, striped in what Mrs. Wentworth has decided are going to be the heraldic Wentworth colors. Maids and footmen are already setting up tables for tea in the tent, the Pompeiian Pavilion being too small to accommodate the crowd. The footmen wear long trousers and unpowdered hair, for this is to be a self-consciously republican and modern event. The ladies seem to float along the greensward in their light layered dresses—or skim, buoyed by a full rigging of fantastically flowered, feathered, and beribboned hats. It is the pure gold of the season, Indian summer, as Mrs. Wentworth is remarking to Lord Deake. She seems to drift on his arm; in actuality she takes in every detail of the guests' arrival, the race preparations, the bustle in the tea tent.

"In this country, of course, the Season is winter. So cold and dreadful in New York—we must have balls to keep warm. Not like London, where the Season is at its height in midsummer."

"Yes," Lord Deake says doubtfully, as if he has never heard of London.

Perhaps he finds more to interest him in the arrangements for the race. At intervals on the great lawn sloping down toward the cliff, flags on tall poles have been set into the ground as markers. Other obstacles are stuffed dummy figures: a nursemaid in "real" uniform and apron wheeling a wicker baby carriage; a dog; a deer; a farmer with a wheelbarrow; a housemaid; a policeman. These life-size figures—some borrowed from those who have hosted similar famous events held at Newport these last two years—are to be avoided by the drivers as they ride a slalom on the green and pleasant lawn.

Under the great elms at the kitchen end of the house, the automobiles are lined up. These pioneer cars are so different in appearance to one another that each might almost belong to a different species of machine: a Renault two-seater with escargot horn; an open Panhard et Levasseur with the seat high as a coach seat; a tall Daimler with its carriage top folded back; a long beautiful Mercedes with front wheels larger than the back ones; and three American "steamer" models, two from the new Stanley factory.

A modest and limited slate of starters, for the emphasis today is on science and progress, and on the American possibilities in the new sport that Europe has dominated. The newspapers have been instructed that entertainment is not the main purpose of the Wentworth obstacle race: the publicity that results is free promotion for the new industry, especially for the domestic entries. Nevertheless, the lady co-pilots have festooned the entering cars with blue hydrangeas, ribbons, and "favors" such as gloves.

Mrs. Wentworth sees that Lord Deake is mesmerized

by the bug-eyed battery of automobile lamps. She graciously frees him and goes to greet other guests and to arrange the spectators on the terrace.

So far, the weather is beautiful; so far, her husband, son, and daughter are behaving themselves. Elizabeth stands pale and picturesque near a stone urn; she has not been acting peculiar, thank heaven. No—at the present moment the mother is more concerned about her son. Hallie has been stopped twice for reckless driving this summer, and fined once by the Newport police. In his mad tours around the countryside he has somehow provoked farmers to throw rocks at his car. In one incident he was threatened with a horsewhip by an old lady angry about her flower garden. In another, Hallie reportedly drew a revolver. Once to her knowledge he came home with straw all over his clothes and the automobile upholstery; another time, it was wet sand. Hallie does not want to go to Harvard next year, or to Yale either. He has in mind some scheme about producing his beloved machine in great numbers. Useless to tell him that plan is like breeding polo ponies for the masses. The American people will, in general, never buy "bubbles." How many will ever have the time and money—and the expanse of greensward—to indulge in obstacle races?

Deake gravitates toward his future brother-in-law. Young Wentworth is explaining to other "bubblers" the salient superior points of his new steam model.

"Talk all you like about your Red Devils, your White Ghosts. This is the automobile of the century. Accelerates from zero to sixty in fourteen seconds—"

"Oh, I say, Wentworth."

"Yes, Wentworth, I grant you that. You build up steam with the emergency brake on. Let her out and you can go as fast as you like—but she comes apart, like the

Wonderful One-Horse Shay. The wheels and structure won't take the strain.''

"They'll be made to."

"Who will make them to?"

"Perhaps I will." He is a tall young man in a boater, searching the crowd for his father. Isn't his father going to watch the race?

"I say, Wentworth, what's that?"

Around the corner, bell clanging, comes a horse-drawn red fire engine.

"Oh, no! I say, this is too much. She couldn't have. Not for an obstacle race on our own lawn. Mother? Did you . . . ?"

The young man goes off in search of his mother.

The other young men laugh heartily. It is true: Mrs. Wentworth has called the fire department to stand by in case the steamers explode. The Stanley, this new American model—of which two hundred had flooded the country last year—has a dangerous reputation. Poor Hallie thinks the car is much maligned. His friends argue about whether the water tank under the floorboards of the Stanley can possibly burst during a run.

"Last week I saw the fuel burner flood on Hallie. Kerosene, you know. Smoke and flame enough for a real 'red Devil.' "

"No, no, Dart. The front compartment is quite separate with my bubble there's no danger," Hallie insists.

"There was to that farmer and his haycart."

They laugh again. But Hallie Wentworth wrings a compromise from his mother: the fire engine will retreat to the Werthmere stables, ready to dash forward if anything "should go wrong."

Lord Deake is charmed by the simple American bubbles—"almost like perambulators." He wants every detail explained. Hallie is eager to help, begins to think

Deake may not be such a dull fellow after all. The wonderful machine is shown to be almost as simple as a box camera: no clutch, no gears.

"You can go just as fast backwards as forwards."

"Yes, Hallie did that last week on Bellevue Avenue— greeted people goin' away from 'em." The friend chortles.

The distinguished English visitor is persuaded to sit in one of the American steam models. He calls out so excitedly—"What's this? What d'ya call it?"—and sits so proudly on the tufted seat, he looks like a boy on his first pony. The ladies and the spectators on the terrace turn to look. It's the first symptom of personality Lord Deake has shown. The noble visitor is happy; his joy is a benefice to all; they are all richer. Mrs. Wentworth glides closer, smiling, and draws Elizabeth in her wake.

"Oh, it's so simple, I almost feel I could . . ."

"Yes, you must. Dear Lord Deake must be in the race. Here is a 'bubble' free. If Hallie can show you how it runs—"

"Oh, he has. It's quite simple. I have automobiles, of course, but this is so charming—but is this one really free?"

Mrs. Wentworth nods, taking herself and a Southern cousin out of the race.

"Yes, yes, it will be a wonderful boost to the people who make 'em, you know," says Hallie. "A wonderful, generous gesture of you, Lor—uh, Reginald—to join us."

"But I must . . . very well. But only if Miss Wentworth will accompany me."

Elizabeth shrinks away. "Oh, no. I don't care for automobiles."

"Forgive me. It was reckless to ask. I shall not race. I may not be a good driver of this machine."

Lord Deake climbs out of the machine. Consternation.

Elizabeth feels faint as she often does when in the public eye. In this momentary swoon a vision comes to her, as often happens. She steps forward, determined.

"Oh, but I do want to be in the race. Please. I have changed my mind. I am only nervous by habit."

She all but takes her fiancé's hand. An electric moment! It's the first flush of public spontaneity seen in the engaged couple.

"It's settled, then. You are my co-pilot."

So she is. The spectators settle themselves on the terrace. The judges spot themselves at strategic spots—on the Pavilion portico, near obstacles, and near the hedge at the far ("finish-line") end of the Werthmere property. One boy in knickers straddles a forked tree behind the starting line. The entrants draw positions by number. A famous old sportsman holds a revolver loaded with blanks—Hallie's revolver—and a red bandana handkerchief. Several spectators have stop watches. The knights of the tourney and their chosen ladies (some seated beside and some behind the driver, depending on the car) line up behind the couple who have picked number one out of a straw boater.

The shot is fired. The first automobile shoots itself downhill, hydrangeas tearing, makes the first two S turns around obstacles without mishap, then slams into the wicker perambulator and sends the dummy nursemaid flying, cap in air. There are other mishaps before the end, which is a well-executed turn before a stand of little saplings. As the automobile snorts up the hill again along the hedge, there are cheers from the terrace. The dummies are replaced.

Then the next entry makes the tour, and the next. The lifesize cloth obstacles raise laughter—and a thrill of fear?—as, struck, they fly up. The obstacles are carefully replaced for the next run.

Young Wentworth is next. He has forgotten for the moment the Bridget trouble, the farmers with rocks. Hallie's official young lady waves a bouquet of asters and wild grasses. The shot is fired. The car is impelled forward in a smooth gliding motion that seems too graceful to be compatible with so much speed. The bubble skims over the pleasant green landscape, dances in elegant parabolas around the flags and play-dead obstacles, rolls in a constant opulent curving flow that in later times will come to be associated with films and aerial acrobatics but now—to the man who controls this new power— must seem a true dream. How quickly people have accustomed themselves to the new sensation of speed! The rich in their enforced idleness are as ready to embrace innovations in sport as their acquisitive elders were to seize on new frontiers for work. Young Wentworth comes to the end of the course and the cheers go up. The parasols flutter.

His time is fantastic. It's true—recorded, pinned, and held up for display in silver stop watches. Hallie Wentworth and the young lady roll sedately up again toward the great cottage. Hallie sees the signature of his accomplishment on the pastoral scene—with flags and doll bodies unscathed, untouched by the steamer in its headlong career.

The golden world. His father wordlessly shakes his hand and presses his own silver stop watch into that hand. It is the happiest moment of young Wentworth's life. Now he knows: the secret of life is to open the throttle. Like the Spaniards who drink from the gourd without swallowing, he will go on and on. . . .

Hallie's thoughts continue through the next run and the next. The petroleum-fueled and electric bubbles dart forward in starts, stitch their way across the greensward— which is beginning to look like no-man's-land, but it can all be replanted next week, despite the chief gardener's dire prediction that grass takes years to grow back properly. (Mrs. Wentworth, who has built two castles in two years each, is incredulous at the English belief that two hundred years goes into a good lawn. Progress does not play on such fields.)

Elizabeth Wentworth's private thoughts, like her brother's, continue through the next runs, as flags fall and bodies fly. She sits with her fiancé and smiles. She is curiously exhilarated with her first sense of public power. Is this feeling a part of her mother's argument? Her destiny linked with a man, in an engine of the future.

She feels the mechanical pulse of the machine. Its throbbing bounces the bubble and its passengers, shakes the heads off the daisies twined around the frame. Her fiancé smiles. What does he say that she can catch, below the cheers and roaring engine?

"Your eyes are like the blue flowers."

Is that what he is saying? Elizabeth looks nervously away toward the house, her own room, and thinks of Tennyson.

> *Many a night from yonder ivied casement, ere I went to rest,*
> *Did I look on great Orion sloping slowly to the West.*

But her room looks East. Sitting in the machine, she wants some thought to counter that noisy power, the banal remark, the strong kerosene smell and pallid smugness—some manufacture of her own. But Tennyson, her old English governess's safe favorite, runs on on his own course:

> *As the husband is, the wife is; thou art mated with a clown,*
> *And the grossness of his nature will have weight to drag*
>   *thee down.*

143

What can she do?

She is not to have her own thoughts, even now—especially now, and perhaps nevermore, according to the poet.

They are at the starting place, building up steam. Elizabeth too gives in to exaltation. She sees the revolver pointing at the sky, she sees the shudder but does not hear the crack.

They are off, in a noisy rush of steam, almost flying along, high, dragging a dummy, charging a bamboo flagpole to cheers and laughter and the steady hiss of steam. For the first time she sees in her husband-to-be the stamp of concentrated thought. Is he like this when he pays attention? When he makes love?

Elizabeth's high feeling is one of intimate, exalted loathing. Her mother's recent words are a goad, a whip lashing her forward to the finish as she reaches to control the machine—as she struggles with her astonished partner—*she steers!* The bubble veers, it accelerates still more, off the course and headed now straight down toward the cliff over the ocean! Silence, and then a shriek. But with a strength rare to him Deake wrests control from her. The steamer veers again and is catapulted—hung up!—on the quivering little stand of saplings.

There is a moment of dreadful silence on the scene.

"I told you fellows!" young Wentworth shouts, ecstatic, from the heights of the terrace, his voice cracking. "You can climb trees with 'em. Deake wanted to show us, I guess. Good man!"

All are relieved to agree. This is the social tone to take. Once again, and for what reasons he does not fully comprehend, the young heir to Werthmere is the man of the hour. His friends surge over the broken lawn to pick the daring couple off the trees. When they are helped out, the light bubble is buoyed up a moment by the supple saplings as they spring back.

Mrs. Wentworth announces tea at once. Her son remonstrates with her.

"But Mother, we can't end it just for a little toss like that. Donald and Mrs. Stackers have still to go. Hang it, in France they've had regular road races for years, and even people being killed doesn't stop 'em from finding out who's fastest."

Everyone assures young Wentworth that he is the fastest. All except the diehard young bubblers move off toward the vast tent. Lord Deake seems to have lost his enthusiasm for bubbles. He retreats behind a tea cup. His smile is fixed. Miss Wentworth is still pale and shaken, as befits a young lady. Mr. Wentworth, who perhaps missed the last little flurry, emerges from the library to take tea (to be introduced to Society by his wife, as newspaper wags like to put it). This is the sort of rough course on which Mrs. Wentworth, gliding noiselessly on her own endless supply of steam, operates superbly; she avoids all obstacles while appearing not to notice their presence.

"Why are you smiling?" Quint asked. "Because I said you're a good listener?"

"Oh . . . not that." I tried to look mysterious rather than mystified. I was dimly aware of having heard Quint talking over an excellent dinner. What was his subject? His inherited collection of antique cars. I had been drinking quite a lot of wine; the waiter was again at my elbow, pouring. Brimming with ideas, with pictures, I stared at the bubbles winking in my wine goblet.

"But you *are* a good listener. Most people keep interrupting."

"Well, I . . ."

"Don't apologize. I'm so sick of hearing people give me psychological interpretations of my whole life."

"Well . . ." I proceeded cautiously. "It's my business. Listening, I mean. And remembering. I memorized some of your Great-Aunt Elizabeth's poems." I quoted:

> *"When the bubbles of the future trail their trace upon the earth,*
> *Shall the ocean stanch its power and man's ancient bed of birth?*
> *They are harnessing and branding and smashing up each dream*
> *And driving women to their deaths with juggernauts of steam."*

I drank more white wine. There was an ocean of it.

"I'm sure," said Quint, leaning over the table, "that you're a sensitive person. You're interested in character. So am I—for example, in my family, the women have been stronger than the men. My great-grandfather was the last strong one. He used up all our strength. My great-aunts—both of them—you—"

Oh God, we're both drunk, I thought.

"My Great-Aunt Elizabeth suffered very much, you know. Two world wars."

I thought of Gramps. "Thank God for Veterans Benefits."

"What? All of her staff at Castle Deake were drafted, both times, and her house in London was requisitioned, then bombed, in the Second War. She had a sad life." He poured himself another glass of wine. "But a long one. The women in our family live much longer than the men. They don't drive, so they don't smash up."

"Your Great-Aunt Elizabeth did once. She drove. And smashed up." I hiccoughed. Bubbles in my throat.

"Twice. There was the accident with the servant."

"What? What accident?" I asked.

Quint was looking around for the waiter. "After my great-grandfather was killed. A day or two later."

"No, it was before. In the bubble race."

"Twice. I heard it from my mother. Of course, she would say anything bad about *us*."

"Quint—" I stood up slowly. I walked very steadily, in brightness, caught between one time and another. "What was the accident?"

"They didn't talk about it. But there was one. We're an interesting family, in a way. Perhaps we could have made our way in the world."

I wondered what he meant. No more worlds to conquer?

"I was wondering . . ." He coughed a businesslike cough that I remembered from our labor-management negotiations. It put me on my guard. "I know that Great-Aunt Victoria has offered you a certain sum to write about the family. And perhaps—although she hasn't told me—about her father's death. It's so important to her. I can see that you're the right person to do it. Her notion of a commission is rather old-fashioned, I suppose. Of course, she means to be generous. But I think two or three thousand would be more appropriate— without her knowing, of course. Or five thousand, for a book. Certainly for a book. And articles, of course— very publishable . . . Of course, I'm not a professional, but that is my opinion." He smiled, suddenly shy again.

He was telling me that he could publish me. That is, he would publish an official biography or whitewash or whatever. I believed him. All publishing houses, all magazines were now subsidiaries of subsidiaries of giant companies on whose boards of directors Quint sat. His wishes would trickle down to editors. I realized that this was the important information he had to impart to me.

Would it be wrong to take Wentworth money for a defense of Elizabeth Wentworth—when I wanted to believe in her innocence anyway? All writers had their patrons in the old days. But I wasn't a writer—not a real one, just a daydreamer and paid fact finder.

Confrontation with a moral dilemma—if that's what it was—had a sobering effect.

"Think about it, Penny. I have a high opinion of your judgment."

"Perhaps a women's studies approach," I began.

"Of course."

I doubted Quint understood what I was saying. But I had to put moral judgment aside and concentrate on walking out of the restaurant. *Au revoir. Je reviens.* Ah, that was the name of the boat that was sunk in *Rebecca.* Oh, to be always fourteen and running through the long grass on a summer holiday and reading *Rebecca* for the first time.

As we waited for the car to be brought up, I tried to remember what Quint had talked about while I was daydreaming about the obstacle race. Business? A bit. After two generations of wastrels, the Wentworth money-making gene had popped up again. In this sly—and not bad-looking—throwback.

"Shall we go for a drive along the sea? And then Ocean Drive?"

We did. Bars of gold floated on Narragansett Bay. "There's the Ida Lewis Yacht Club. We'll go there some day. You remind me of Ida Lewis. She saved people. The lighthouse keeper."

"What?" I was confused. I noticed, though, that Quint in liquor was a much more confident driver.

"My great-aunt likes you," Quint said.

"You're the only two left," I said. I was feeling maudlin. "Or aren't you?"

"Yes. We've had so many deaths. Maybe we do have a murderer in the family—in our genes. My ulcers—you know, I've always held them in. My own murderous instincts."

"Everyone has them. Instincts, I mean, not ulcers. Watch out!" I winced as we narrowly missed sideswiping a car.

We sped along the darkening avenues. Quint was shouting in the convertible.

"I can't talk to anybody. I just don't have time to think. Except about money; I'm good at that. But I married Betty because my mother liked her and my great-aunt liked the way she poured tea. They planned it. But we were wretched. I had to get rid of her."

"Get rid of her? Quint, be careful!"

"Why am I telling you this? Betty was my wife, but she had an affair with my man."

"Your man?"

"My man. Valet. So I had to get rid of her."

"Get rid of—? Quint, you don't mean—"

"I don't believe in divorce. I'm High Church. But I did it—"

"You—got rid—"

"It cost me a lot. Annulment."

"Oh—that's a relief."

"I had to let her tell lies about me."

"I didn't know you had an ex-wife," I said.

"There's a lot you don't know about me." said Quint. The round glasses glittered like twin monocles in the murky green light from the dashboard. "We're a crazy family. Obsessed. Luckily, one or two ancestors were obsessed with money-making, so the rest of us can afford *our* obsessions. My Great-Aunt Victoria, for example. She likes attention. She would like to be the Last of the Wentworths. You know, she tried to prove my parents weren't married, so I wouldn't inherit. She never wanted my Great-Aunt Elizabeth to come back to Werthmere and live with her after her divorce. Because Elizabeth had got all the attention so long ago. And Great-Aunt Victoria seems so controlled . . . we all do. . . ."

He was driving erratically. I saw that we were approaching Werthmere.

"Quint, I want to go back to my place—"

"Can't you stay a while? I hate the two weeks I spend up here every summer. I wouldn't have survived this week except for you."

"No, I want to go back to my place—not to Werthmere. Quint—"

He just laughed. That infuriated me. I tried to make him turn. He resisted, and I felt the terror rising in me like a great wave. As we shot through the open gate at Werthmere, I tried to take the wheel from Quint.

"No, you'll kill us!"

The car raced across the open lawn before the house. I thought I had my foot on Quint's on the brake, but— was it the gas—?

An empty stone urn rose up before us—some giant's wine goblet. No, thanks, I've had too much, I thought.

And that was the last I remembered.

Mrs. Wentworth's
Tableaux Vivants

I couldn't have been unconscious very long. I came to in the great hall, in one of the Jacobean sidechairs. Two pale faces were peering at me: Quint and Perry, the old-young and the ageless.

"Give her air."

The faces bobbed away and like clouds before the sun revealed Miss Wentworth in awful grandeur far above, up somewhere among the swirled plaster heaven.

"What is it? What is this commotion?" Miss Wentworth was saying from the floor above.

"A slight accident." It seemed to me that Perry was the speaker. But I could not be sure anymore what happened in the real world and what happened only in my own mind.

"Slight? Well, then, bring her up. Let me see her."

Perry and Quint protested a bit, but I started up the stairs, and they hurried to support me.

"I'm all right. Dizzy."

"People always claim whiplash," Quint said.

"Whiplash is vulgar," I said loudly.

CHAINS OF GOLD

"Shhh. My God, was I thinking out loud?" Quint said.

"Maybe I've got to the point," I said, "where I can read other people's thoughts."

"Oh, God, I did say it. Because that other woman claimed whiplash."

"I'm not that other woman. It was my fault. For a minute you looked crazy, Quint."

"Now, what," said Miss Wentworth, standing above us, leaning on a cane, "what is all this fuss? Perry, you know I never sleep at night. I mean to say, young Harold, are you holdin' a nighttime obstacle race out there?"

"It's not very late, Aunt."

Still supported, I tried to walk. I groaned. My ankle hurt.

"What is it? What have you done with the child?"

"Please, Aunt . . ."

I drooped with shame. The others went into a whispered consultation.

"She ought to stay at Werthmere for the night."

"No, no, no . . . don't want to bother you . . ." I remembered Ingrid or Joan in the movies, led along to bed by a sinister old woman and son. . . .

"Where shall we . . . which way . . ." More whispers along the corridor, unattributable in the shadows.

"In the Newport Maid Room?" I asked. A fitting place to expire. I felt fatalistic. And sleepy.

"Well . . . if you wish." More whispers.

"Whispers, whispers," I said. Let them do what they wanted.

I stepped into the Newport Maid Room and was suddenly overcome with mortification. "Oh, Miss Wentworth, I'm so embarrassed, I—" I could not bring myself to say "I drank too much" in front of Miss Wentworth.

152

A woman in black, with a white starched apron, entered the room. Perry and Quint had vanished. The woman started to help me with my clothes. Miss Wentworth was leaving.

"Oh, Miss Wentworth. I wish I could find out. About your father. Did you dream about him?"

"No, never," said Miss Wentworth. "Never. But after his death I dreamed about the ghost."

"The ghost? Yes, a child would . . ."

"Looking out my window. The ghost all white and shimmery . . . going to the Pavilion." The old woman raised her cane toward the dark row of windows. "And then the ghost leaving the Pavilion, coming back the other way to the house. All shrunken up and skimming along. But on the way there, it had been larger, don't you know. And then . . . the ghost shrank."

I felt something shrink in my mind. A thought? A connection of some kind?

Then I was alone in the Newport Maid Room, in the great canopied bed where Elizabeth Wentworth had been so fearful of the ghost that she had started to write poetry. Was it a shrunken ghost? Had a murderess slept in that very bed? Had a poet-parricide been writing of what happened in the Pompeiian Pavilion in the lines:

> *Destroying Angel*
> *White wingèd Death*
> *You stare at me*
> *You spare me*
> *And destroy me.*
> *Through the mirror youth enters through that door.*
> *My life runs out in fire upon the floor.*

Did they drug my drink? I wondered. That was silly: they hadn't even given me anything to drink. I lay, virtually a prisoner (at least of my own reviving sense of propriety), in the famous ghost chamber. Where Elizabeth Wentworth had waited and wondered what to do. Where she had heard the carriages coming up the drive the night of the great reception for Lord Deake.

It is ten o'clock at night, and Mrs. Wentworth's tableaux vivants in honor of American Progress—and titled alliances—will soon begin. Werthmere is ablaze from top to bottom.

Outside the gate a group of townspeople stand to watch the guests arrive. The Pinkertons before the piked fence seem superfluous; this is not New York with its immigrant radicals, but a resort where the natives find employment in the great cottages. Perhaps that is one reason why Lord Deake's reception is being held here rather than in the Fifth Avenue mansion.

In a steady stream the coaches-and-four pass through the gate and up the graveled drive. The coachmen wear blue or black coats, with high hats and black cockades. The coaches discharge their passengers and continue on in a graceful curve to the stables.

In the great hall footmen in knee breeches (paid extra for tonight's indignity of powdered hair) take the coats of the men who have brought them on this balmy night. The footmen direct the ladies upstairs. In the state bedrooms the maids attend to the ladies' needs. Perhaps thin Mary, promoted upstairs, assists: a wraith amidst the splendid women. To her, their brocades and diamonds, jet and pearls may not be objects of envy—merely proofs of the ephemeral nature of this proud parade. Mary has heard Elizabeth weeping in the Newport Maid Room. The maid's hearing is painfully acute—as is her sense of suffering. She hears Elizabeth crying, as she hears voices, as she hears the children at home; as she heard the walls at Ellis Island, the voices from the tenements all at once. If her sensibility gives her pain, it also provides her with a sense of purpose. Confusing voices! But she must work. . . .

In the Newport Maid Room, Elizabeth is still weeping hysterically. Can she appeal to her father tonight? She hears the laughter and conversation outside in the corridor, but she knows that no one can hear her.

The ladies, refreshed, descend to their hostess in the ballroom-art gallery. Eugenie Wentworth stands with her husband and the guest of honor, Lord Deake, and makes excuses for her daughter Elizabeth—who is, for the moment, indisposed. With her superb properties of glance and inflection, Mrs. Wentworth fashions of her daughter's ailments or vapors a compliment to Lord Deake's slender charm. She is backed up by the Sargent portrait behind her—the triumphant full-length oil painting that would prompt Edith Wharton to observe in later years: "Beside his 'Mrs. Wentworth,' the master's 'Madame X' is a Gibson girl." Alongside the Sargent, a fine old Copley shows a Ritchey merchant in old age—he of the seventy ships in the Triangular Trade: the ancestor is pointing with a hand, and perhaps a leg as well, past a breezy drapery to cockleshell ships adance in a shallow harbor, an eighteenth-century world without shadow.

Mr. Wentworth does not mind the battery of superior in-laws. He is himself no snob. But he knows that these more spiritual values lodged in dead ancestors can be translated into his own terms and be worth a transcendent weight in gold. Next winter at the Court of St. James he means to go to work on his son-in-law's great connections, and let them think they are using the bland American tycoon. The American frontier, even in business, will be closing soon. The next rush in gold, oil, and markets will be in the British Empire. Mr. Wentworth's boiled front, his bare black republican suit, are devoid of medals—equal to an undertaker's best. But beneath a shirt pale and stiff as McKinley's brow beats a heart sure of a future on which the sun will never set.

Now the talk is not of business. The results of Tennis Week last month are discussed again. The Americas Cup trials that were postponed off New York. Court tennis. One sporting subject is studiously avoided—the afternoon's bubble race. The host is one of the few people in the room who has not heard the story.

At one end of the great room, little gold sticks of ballroom chairs face the stage. After being received, the guests find places, lean over to greet friends they haven't seen for five hours, and crane their necks backwards to see who is just entering. Behind a jungle of palms a hired orchestra (the only paid entertainment on this night of well-drilled volunteers) saws away.

Behind the heavy gold draperies too there is great commotion. The temporary stage backs onto the anteroom (or "print room"), which leads to the Werthmere library. In that usually masculine sanctuary of silences and good cigars, young girls in dancing-length white satin run about, prinking the silver gauze overskirts embroidered with rhinestone "foam." They are a collective Niagara. Other amateur performers, Indian maidens with brown satin leggings, practice their steps. The Golden Spike does her twirl, mindful of her enormous spiky gilded crown. The Society dancing master Mr. VanMeer argues with the artist Mr. Barbizon Peale Schmitt. Mr. Schmitt, who has arranged the visual aspects, rushes back and forth, calming cases of the artistic vapors. *He* is in a state. Most of his work has been in landscape—which never gets stage fright. He has set up his easel on precipices and reservations all across the country; he is more at ease with the real Niagara or a herd of bison than with young ladies of good family. But his wife has dragged him back East. She wants to "get into" Society, and so he has accepted Mrs. Wentworth's commission. And a difficult one it is, too. When the cotillion was canceled due to national mourning for the president, the tableaux vivants were expanded and set in motion. This will be a new sort of patriotic entertainment.

All this picturesque scene, a pretty ghost dance of the past, is reflected darkly from casements and glassed-in bookcases.

Next door in the great dining room the activity has reached an even greater pitch, with as large a cast of actors. Maids and footmen set out the buffet. Those who wish to sit for the late supper of eight courses will have that option. The favors to commemorate the evening are being set out: for the ladies, specially ordered French fans with hand-painted American scenes; for the gentlemen, Golden Spike pins of real gold. For everyone, great jeweled mounds of jellied teal and fruits, fishes glittering in aspic, pastries for which a Delmonico chef came up on the Fall River boat—all laid out against the more lasting splendor of massive gold candelabra, gold epergnes, and lengths of embroidered Parisian tablecloth as great and heavy as the stage curtain.

Back in the immense kitchen the beef and mutton and canvasbacks are slowly cooking. The cook, sweating like a pig, frets over the special patriotic entrée of coarse-fibered venison. Jeroboams and smaller bottles all in rank pass muster for the butler. On their errands back and forth, the servants pause briefly to look out the dining room French windows to the great lawn. The thin, dark-haired maid feels strongly pulled toward the windows, almost battered by the sea—which is out of sight, of course, from the main floor windows. It is dark now. But the immensity of the sky, the sea that breathes with her own rhythm, the moon and stars that mock the precious stones on the people inside the house, who pay no heed to the majesty! Though she feels the presence of evil, the phantasmagoria of the coming tableaux vivants makes her feel all the more strongly that this is passing, fleeting, soon . . .

Outside, the flags and dummies of the obstacle race lie in the dark. In the flurry at the end they were left on the lawn. There, the fireworks—also planned by the landscape artist—will entertain the guests during their supper. The supper is in fact the one feature, in this evening devoted to "realistic" triumphs of art, that (being in itself the real thing) must be cooked up or got up to resemble something else: a sherbet Niagara, a bear made of ice.

Back in the ballroom, the expectant guests, having exhausted older news at the afternoon's obstacle race, are telling one another what they had for dinner. Mrs. Wentworth still stands beneath her portrait. Both she and the portrait are in black satin with diamonds sewn into the sleeves, the living figure fiercely corseted and chokered below an unbridled face. Nothing escapes the eyes of the living model. Mentally she checks off the guests as they approach. At the same time she repeats to herself the schedule, which she knows as a devotee knows the rosary: guests arrive ten to ten-thirty, tableaux at eleven, supper and fireworks at midnight. A simple affair, no dancing.

Mrs. Wentworth is more at ease now. She can apologize to new arrivals that her daughter is not receiving because she has a part in the first tableau. Perhaps that's the reason for Elizabeth's sudden urge to be a part of Niagara; she has always been shy meeting people.

Footmen douse the ballroom candles, leaving a few electric lights to shine unobtrusively behind shields of gilded bronze. The gold curtain is parted. The performance begins.

Against a painted sunset and gilded trees of the Hudson River School, the Niagara Falls sparkle—amazingly pure and real. The spectators gasp with satisfaction. Niagara starts to flow, turning into young ladies on ladders who doff their white tulle veils to descend and dance in sedate waves over the stage. It is in some sense a bridal cortège.

"Tableaux vivants?" whispers a dowager.

"Tableaux mouvants," her companion whispers.

The category seems apt. The picture must not only fool the eye—it must become a *moving* picture. The public is greedy for fact without consequence—and, conversely, for illusions galore. Mrs. Wentworth's tableaux offer both. Flattering connections are made, or at least hinted at: the family has participated in the struggles for control of the Great Lakes, railroads, and Indian ore mountains; H. H. Wentworth helped to drive the Golden Spike into Mr. Villard; and so on.

And what of Lord Deake, how is he impressed by these marriage masques? He is safely fortified from immediate harm in a breastworks of dowagers. He doesn't intend to move until the entertainment is ended. The afternoon's shock has stirred him from the inherited boredom of centuries.

Did she mean it? Is she mad?

He stares at his fiancée as she floats about the stage in her white dress—a mute Lucia di Lammermoor. Her still-whiter face is frozen as she falls with neurasthenic grace, surrounded by bridesmaids sinister in their silence. Is this in the act? The gold curtain quickly falls and the audience applauds.

Mr. Wentworth slips out in the interval. He lights a cigar, nods to his son, and goes out quickly through the conservatory. Out on the terrace he breathes the sea air more deeply. The tableaux vivants were all very well. If he had designed the entertainment to show the progress of the nation, the tableaux vivants would have looked very different. The great scenes in which he has partici- pated, the great occasions of progress in his lifetime, could not be danced by young ladies. Progress does not gush forth like Niagara. It is the result of dramatic struggle. . . .

He draws on his cigar. The immensity of the universe is satisfying to him. Especially when seen and savored in the tiny red glow of a good cigar.

But—this business of the marriage. It is somewhat troubling to him. Should he speak to the girl? No, that is women's business. Yet . . . he has no one to speak to, so he contemplates the night. He is, he believes, the only one who would rather see the stars than Society's stage show.

He strolls out across the lawn toward the Pompeiian Pavilion. The night air has a hint of autumn. He feels expansive, generous-minded. We shall see, he says to himself. . . .

Meanwhile, Mrs. Wentworth gives the house and guests a quick survey. Is everyone important there? Yes . . . except for one guest. Which? Ah, her husband, of course. As soon as the lights go down for the Great Divide, she will search him out. This business of Elizabeth's be- havior—where is she?—must be settled now, before there is an incident of real danger or scandal.

And then, what next? What happened in the Pom- peiian Pavilion? Stark awake, I wrestled with the "Destroying Angel" of Elizabeth's poem and of the murder scene. But the light in the Pavilion guttered and went out. Werthmere of old flickered and faded into darkness. I lay awake in the Newport Maid Room.

Anyhow, I told myself, this imaginative reconstruction stuff is good for my head. Cure that stupid city-bred paranoia. For example, at this very moment I can clearly see the ghost of the Newport Maid coming toward me through the door. My imagination is really rusticating on me out here. Here comes the ghost, called forth by my own psyche, poor girl, and I can lie here and lucidly study this approaching figment—I'm even imagining it has footsteps, how literal-minded, but the old brain pan is really fantasizing on all cylinders. It's amusing, or it will be tomorrow. Ad she looks like—could the Newport Maid look like Elizabeth Wentworth—pale and blond . . . ?

The specter laid a hand on my arm. And it was as if the touch made *me* the ghost, for I could not scream.

What Happened in the Pompeiian Pavilion

The ghost put a hand on my breast.

"Hey!" At least I could whisper. "What's the big idea—"

The ghost was trying to get into bed with me. Pale and wan, an astral body with an aura of Scotch and milk, and definitely male.

"Quint—you get away! Get out. You're no gentleman."

I had slipped out the other side of the bed. The ankle I'd hurt ached just a bit. Quint, on the other side of the four-poster, smiled sepulchrally.

"I'll scream. I'll wake Miss Wentworth. . . ." All bravado. To scream in the Newport Maid Room would be unthinkable, like screaming in church. "Quint, you schmuck. Get out of here."

Winking and chuckling like an old man, the poor substitute for a ghost was coming around the foot of the bed, tripping over the chest in which perhaps the real ghost reposed.

"God damn . . ."

"Quint. You don't fool me. You're no Newport Maid.

You twerp . . ." I was tumbling across the wide bed, away from him.

With Quint still on the sea-side of the bed, I hopped across the room and out the door. Could I lock him in? No time for such fancy maneuvers. I crept along in the near-darkness of the hallway and down the broad stairs. Carpeted, thank God. I'd hate to wake the old lady, who claimed never to sleep. ("What's goin' on there? There's been no fornicatin' at Werthmere, don't you know, in my time. If the Stuyvesants can die out, I mean to say, why not the Wentworths?")

I gained the landing, which was eerily lit by an electric candle inside the grill-patterned helmet of a knight in armor. I almost tripped over the knight's pointy toes. Recovering, I hugged the banister (copied from Grinling Gibbons) and made my way trembling to the great hall.

Trembling—for above me I could hear Quint feeling his way toward the stairs. I went to the great front door but could not budge it. The effort brought tears of frustration to my eyes. No doubt it was locked by some devilish Renaissance device.

Above and behind me, the knight creaked. I whirled in time to see the lambent metal figure lurch forward and fall. The crash should have awakened the dead. But Werthmere slept as if under a spell.

"Where's a girl gone?" The faint question reassured me that my pursuer had at least not been killed instantly by the armor. I turned from the hall toward the ballroom and slipped through the opening in the sliding doors.

Moonlight filtered through the conservatory windows and lay in pools on the polished parquet. I ran limping toward the conservatory, but the palms, beckoning in the bluish submarine atmosphere of the hothouse, looked like sea monsters waiting to drown me. That way H. H. Wentworth had gone out to his death.

I ran the other way, through the door where the improvised stage for the tableaux of progress had been, then through the next doorway and into the library.

Suddenly, Quint was in the library behind me. Oh, no, time to run again! But he merely bowed and went over to a glittering sideboard and crashed about amidst cut-glass decanters. Had he forgotten he was chasing me? He seemed to have. No concentration span.

"Women like . . ." Quint was saying with difficulty, "women like men who are forceful. Glam'rous. Dang'rous. How do men ever feel forceful and glamorous? Dangerous?"

"Don't cry, Quint. . . ."

"I have to drink to feel like that." He sloshed brandy into a glass and drank.

"No, Quint, don't. It's bad for your stomach. I ask you, is it good to drink with your history of ulcers? Heartburn? Your nervous constitution? Put it down. I'll tell you what's good. Alka-Seltzer. Every night. And for hangover, the best is Mydol. I'm not kidding. A man told me that."

I sounded to my own ears so much like my own mother that I was reassured enough to forget about Quint. And Quint poured himself another. My head ached. Maybe it was from imagining scenes and trying to force conclusions. Quint and the winking decanters were on the rim of my consciousness. At the whirling center was the crime.

What would help me solve it? Other books? Famous Criminals? No, probably not. That wasn't the right description for the kind of information I thought I needed. . . . I glanced up at the portrait of H. H. Wentworth, and he seemed to be winking too. Famous Criminal, eh? he seemed to say. Who, me?

No, not in this instance. Or perhaps . . . yes?

I peered out the window. Darkness where the folly would be. My mental movies replayed rapidly. Mrs. Wentworth rushing to the Pavilion—to discover what? Elizabeth Wentworth running light-footed to the Pavilion—to see what? The millionaire in boiled shirt strolling with his cigar into the folly—to confront what and whom? Backwards and forwards I ran the scenes. They flickered out. The words and pictures wouldn't synchronize.

"Here, have li'l drink. Make you dangerous."

Quint was lurching toward me, extending a snifter, a demonic look in his glasses. But such an innocent face, poor thing, like a rheumatic child. Maybe it would be best to humor him.

"Oh, thanks. Thanks, Quint, for the nice drink. There, there . . ."

But he was pressing me against the moving book ladder. Drink in hand, I climbed away from him, the drink sloshing. That was one drink I would never drink! Quint started to shake the ladder so that it swayed on the little rail-runner it was attached to far overhead on the shelves. Quint was looking up my nightgown—or his great-aunt's nightgown or the Newport Maid's. He really did change in drink. As I retreated up, Quint started to push the ladder along the wall of books.

"Hey, Quint, stop—"

Why be surprised? Jack the Ripper was probably Queen Victoria's grandson. The last of the Wentworths might be something even worse.

"Hey, hey—stop it, you jerk! I'll fall off the ladder—"

If I can get up to the little mezzanine, I thought, if I can climb to that level, then I can jump off the ladder and be safe up there.

I sprang from the ladder to the mezzanine gallery. The ladder shuddered. I crept along behind the railings of the little gallery while, below me, Quint pushed the ladder along and crooned. Couldn't he tell the difference in the weight he was pushing? Maybe I wasn't as heavy as I thought. I went quietly down the permanent spiral stair in the corner and—once again on the floor—tiptoed, limping, toward the ballroom door.

Quint saw me. I ran around the album table with him after me. He tried to hold me. His glass fell on my foot. But I broke free of his grasp and hobbled to the casement. Throwing open the tall windows, I ran out into the cool night and was awed—almost stopped short—by the presence of great space in darkness. The sky was clouded and mysterious, the grass was richly black. Oh, for the powdered mauve night of the city, with its merely human fears!

I heard a crash behind me. More glass, on the terrace now. Could he be chasing me with drink in hand? Or had he picked up something else? Such as a weapon? Blind childish terror arose to choke me; the sensation was horrible, like running through grass up to my neck. I ran hobbling over grass as trimly clipped as a welcome mat, but I couldn't outrun the fear.

Then I could hear the waves before me. Behind me I heard Quint puffing along like a Baskerville puppy. No light before, only the ancient call of the sea. And only the house behind.

Yes, there *was* a light before me. I ran gimping toward it. Only when I saw the cold stone steps and pillars did I realize—the source of light came from within the Pompeiian Pavilion.

But the folly was never used!

Quint was close behind me, calling some woman's name, not mine. It sounded like Elizabeth.

I turned toward the mysterious light again and ran into the Pavilion for sanctuary, hoping there would be a door to close, although I could not remember.

I saw the dark figure, sensed the odd but familiar odor.

"*Eeeeeek!*"

"Hey. Hi."

"Let me in! Where are you?" Quint cried outside.

I looked wildly around me. The window of the Pompeiian Pavilion was open and moonlight streamed in. A sturdy red-rimmed miner's flashlight sat on the floor—that was the mysterious light that had drawn me there. The flashlight lit up the cavernous ghostly face of a sepulchral figure on the sarcophagus-bench. The cadaverous form rose, glowing red at the mouth.

"Oh, Pierre!" I ran to him and screamed: he had burned me on my cheek as I embraced him.

"Watch it. Cigarette." He smelled of pot.

He dropped the joint and held me.

"He's after me. But what are you doing here?"

"Doing here?" he cried. "Spying on you! Not that I care. You can have your damn Wentworths. I waited on your porch for hours. We had a date, remember? I called here, and they were so mysterious. I don't know why I bothered coming by, but I didn't know what else to do with myself."

"Oh, God, he's after me. Help me shut the door."

But Pierre suddenly slid into philosophic calm. A smoke mood. "I hate these people. I try to be cool, value-free. But I'm not. Smoking helps. . . ."

"Never mind. Help me—"

But it was too late to close the door. Quint stood in the doorway, pale ghost of his great-grandfather.

"Bang, bang." Pierre was pointing a finger at Quint.

167

"Who are you?" Quint asked. "Who is this fella, Penny? This is private property."

"Property is theft, heh, heh. Who are you?"

"I'm . . . oh, I'm sick."

"I know. You're Pint, the Last of the Werewolves," Pierre said, extending his hand and then waving it playfully.

"Who are you? Don't come a step closer."

"I am the ghost of your sinful ancestor. For shooting strikers at the Wentworth Works I am doomed—dooooooomed—to be visited by decadent descendants at midnight."

"Oh, oh . . . I am going to be sick. Sorry."

I had shut the door after him. Quint spun around and went for the large window. He climbed up on the bench and scrambled out, dropped down, and disappeared out the window.

"Hey!"

"Maybe he's fallen into the sea," Pierre said, waving. "Bye-bye."

I opened the door and ran around the Pavilion in time to see Quint walk into the barbed wire on the edge of Werthmere that overhung the Cliff Walk.

"No, Quint! You'll cut yourself."

"No. Sick. Must—mustn't. Aunt Victoria wouldn't like—"

Quint was leaning his head over the barbed wire. I was afraid he'd decapitate himself. He tried to climb up. Or castrate himself.

"If you're going to be sick, be sick, damn it!"

"No, no, not at Werthmere . . . can't get sick at Werthmere."

He pushed me aside and, using the barbed wire as a guide, stumbled along down to where there was a break in the fence. I remembered that that was the place where Pierre and I had climbed up, the time we had trespassed. So Quint wanted to be sick on public property. There he went! The headline flashed into my mind, tomorrow's tabloid treat:

WENTWORTH HEIR DROWNS
AFTER SEX-DRUG PARTY

GIRL REPORTER,
RADICAL INVOLVED

I called out to Pierre for help. I went down the treacherous rocky slope after Quint, grabbed his shirt, trying to hold him back. But he pulled me along.

"What are you doing, Quint? Stop!"

"Clean—be sick, clean—smell ocean—"

He wanted to sniff the ocean, or vomit into it, or perhaps be born again through total immersion. He hung over the cliff. The roar was like a wave up to my feet. And the waves—I could almost *feel* them up to my neck, though I knew the water was far below us. Terror again. Would it be worse to die in the dark? I was terrified that he would pull me in after him if he went, but if I let go . . .

"Here, hold him—"

Pierre was hanging on to Quint. The flashlight, nested now in high grass, sculpted them nobly as they struggled.

At last, Quint was persuaded to be sick on the Cliff Walk.

"Oh, God, all over my shoes." It seemed to sober him up. "I never drink. I've had ulcers since I was thirteen. I started drinking at sixteen. Quit at twenty-three."

169

"That's wonderful, Quint."

"Do I know you?" Quint asked Pierre.

"Not socially. Just a passing beachcomber who heard your cries."

"Weren't you . . . oh, my head."

Lantern swinging in wide swathes over the lawn, we walked Quint back up to the house and through the wide-open window of the library.

Pierre put up a hand to help me through. "Well, good night."

"What?" I was hurt. Then outraged. "I'm not staying."

"Your chosen bridegroom," said Pierre, "awaits you. Within."

"I'm so sick," said Quint.

"Pierre, don't leave me alone in this house of horrors. I'm going too. I have to get my clothes—"

"Oh, your clothes," said Pierre.

"Well, I was in bed."

"I understand," said Pierre. *"Droit du seigneur."*

"Stay here," whined Quint. He sat down on the Bessarabian rug and patted it with bloody hands. "We have room. We put you in the Newport Maid Room. Aunt Tory tucked you in."

"Yes, and you came in after me. When I was asleep. I'll have you up for attempted rape—and whiplash."

"Women like . . . forceful men. . . ." Quint said weakly. "I mean, I'm awfully sorry. 'Pologize."

Pierre was leaving through the window. I grabbed his arm. "You just wait here, Pierre. Don't move. Until I get back."

I made Pierre promise to stay, just outside the window, with an eye on Quint.

"Bye-bye," Quint said, waving weakly, reclining like an Etruscan tomb carving.

I made my way through the ballroom, where the moonlight fell on dancing ghosts, then up the staircase, past the fallen heap of armor—emblem of dead chivalry! —thus to the Newport Maid Room and my clothes on a chair. I made so little noise, I felt like a ghost myself.

When I returned, creeping and fearful, to the library, it was empty. No Quint, no Pierre.

"Pierre!" I whispered.

I went out again through the open window. I ran through the grass. Pierre was down near the Pompeiian Pavilion, cadaverously thin, shivering in the dark.

"Pierre, where are you going? What's wrong?"

"I'm upset." His teeth were chattering, his hair dewy. "You took so long. I thought you decided to stay. Well, who could blame you? Maybe you'll get the chance to join this outfit. The Last of the Werewolves likes you."

"You're raving. Come on, let's beat it."

He retrieved the miner's flashlight from the Pavilion steps and we descended with care to the Cliff Walk.

"Public property! At last. I could kiss the ground," I said.

"Kiss me instead," said Pierre.

I did.

"I'm upset that I'm upset," he said. "I don't know why I was so bothered by the thought of you with that jerk. I just went to the Pavilion to think. I sometimes go there for a smoke or to work. It's my own private writer's colony."

"The Temple of Vesta," I said. I thought of Miss Wentworth tending the flame.

"What?" We were moving hand in hand along the Cliff Walk. No vistas now. The great cottages were dark. "It's none of my business who you spend your

171

nights with. I realize that. I'm not an old-fashioned chauvinist pig. I'm glad if Elizabeth Wentworth struck a blow at the patriarchal system.''

I stopped and dropped his hand. ''Pierre, how can you be so dumb? People in families don't kill one another for ideological reasons.''

''They do for economic reasons. She was economically dependent.''

I felt suddenly shaky. To be attacked first by Quint and now—verbally—by Pierre was more than I could bear.

''If you're one of those people who thinks that a battered wife who chops up the brute while he's asleep is a feminist heroine—if you see Elizabeth as a domestic Charlotte Corday—'' I swayed above the waves and almost tripped.

''Powerless people may have to take extreme measures—''

''Pierre, how can you talk like that *now?* You haven't even asked me what happened. Here I'm so upset—so glad to see you—it was really a nightmare. . . .'' I started to shake, then to laugh.

''A funny nightmare?''

''It's still a nightmare. Are we going to argue about politics, or what?''

''Or what, that's my vote,'' he said.

All the long walk back to my place, I thought about an old murder, Quint's reversion to his grandfather's type, Pierre's stubborn refusal to consider the night's events from *my* point-of-view.

I wouldn't let Pierre come in. Like Sherlock Holmes, the true sleuth must be celibate.

Back in the narrow maid's bed—a ghostproof bed—I slept. My dreams starred me running away through ticklish long grass from wolves with human heads and careening pilotless ancient automobiles. The second dream-feature had me explaining the dream in my shrink's terms to Pierre, who just laughed.

THREE

"*Newport is damp, and cold, and windy and excessively disagreeable,*" said the daughter, "*but it is very select. One cannot be fastidious about minor matters when one has no choice.*"

—MARK TWAIN, *The Gilded Age*

Newport, Farewell
and Hail

Next morning, Sunday, I slept late, dreamed of reluctant brides, and awoke now and then to church bells. When I went downstairs at high noon there was a formal letter waiting for me in the hallway. The landlady was fluttering about it.

"The chauffeur from Werthmere brought it. I didn't want to wake you, since you got back rather late. . . ."

Rather late. So she'd noticed. If I'd let Pierre come up, would she have objected?

A creamy rag envelope and fine, spidered Spencerian hand. I wondered if Miss Wentworth had heard the goings on in the night; if she was banishing me.

Miss Wentworth
presents her compliments to
Miss Miller
and requests the honor of her presence
for tea
four-thirty o'clock on Saturday next
in the Newport Maid Room, Werthmere.

(On the day of the Annual Open House

*of the Werthmere State Apartments,
the Eugenie Wentworth Police Widows'
and Orphans' Fund Benefit Fund
established in nineteen hundred and one.)*

R.S.V.P.

I called Werthmere at once, afraid of losing my nerve if I delayed. Imperturbable Perry was summoned at the other end.

"I have to go to New York next week for my magazine, but I'm sure I can get back here on Saturday." I didn't want to lose the Werthmere connection by refusing the invitation to tea on the great occasion of the public invasion of the cottage and its grounds. I hoped I had better reasons than Ward Dart for wanting to keep my entrée.

"Very good, miss. Miss Wentworth will be pleased, I'm sure. And she wondered if you might have an outline of the research you have done thus far. Perhaps sample pages of the monograph. If anything appropriate can be prepared."

"Of course," I said. "I'll have something."

So that was how Miss Wentworth welshed on the "research" commissions she proffered every year. She demanded instant results. In a week! Not even a week. Now I had to go back to *Pleasures and Palaces:* the brownstone debunker was claiming to have been misquoted or misunderstood, and I had to spend time on that at the magazine. Why didn't I just tell Great-Aunt Victoria to take her thousand dollars and throw it into the sea?

No, I promised myself, I'll do it—though what "it" might be, I did not know.

I called Pierre's number to tell him the happy news, that I'd be back in a week.

"Oh, I'm afraid . . . I'd rather not wake him. He got back rather late and tired," said an apologetic motherly voice.

I left a message and called Ward. He too had been invited to Miss Wentworth's little tea party. It was, it seemed, an exclusive annual affair to help Miss Wentworth bear the onslaught of the barbarian hordes upon Werthmere, which was entirely private the rest of the year.

"Yeah, but did you know Miss Wentworth wants results by then?" I told him. "You got me into this, Ward. Now I have to look at Newport city records here tomorrow. And luckily I've sprained—well, strained—my ankle. So I'll call up the magazine tomorrow and say I can't hobble into work until Tuesday. Back me up."

"You're leading me into crime . . . white-collar crime."

"You've led me into crime. Up to my neck."

I put an ace bandage around the slightly swollen ankle. That relieved the pressure on the working girl's conscience. I sat in one of the airy twin parlors of the boardinghouse and read over notes and copies of journal entries after the fatal day. The maid's journal stopped the day before the crime:

> *I am almost too weary to write. So many dishes—and only the family, only those of us in the hall. Think of tomorrow and dishes for 200, says Cook. Yes, think!*
>
> *I think always of You. Hear your voices in the sea. Unending. Never satisfied, never stopped. So much is invisible.*
>
> *Today Mr. W. followed me and clocked my moves. I saw his eyes. Perhaps he means to reduce wages here. It is strange: he alone of all these people is aware that we think. He sees that we study and clock him as well, I see it.*
>
> *I am so tired, but I write. I cannot tell what is important, what not, that is not for me to decide. I posted a letter to Mother E. in New York—it seems a small thing, but perhaps not. A window to You. Exhilarated today—feverish. I am*

*only a wave of many that break—to ebb back and join in the
flow. Break, break, break!*

Little Victoria Wentworth wrote of her grief after the
murder:

> *Poor Papa was buried today. I cried and cried at the
> funeral. No one else cried. They were happy because he
> was a Christen, the minister said so. We are all wearing
> black.*
>
> *We are in New York but I am writing about dear Werth-
> mere. On the fatel night. He died during the party. I looked
> out. I saw the ghost. I told Mlle. later. She said, Do not tell
> lies. I did not tell.*
>
> *I did not even talk with Papa on his last day. I watched
> the obstacle race. Poor Lizzy and Lord Deake (Reggie, but I
> do not want to say it) were almost killed. It is like a curs in a
> story. Hallie won the race. But they should not hit the maids
> and babies and policemen made of cloth. It is like hitting
> dolls. Sickning.*
>
> *After the accidents I will never travel. I will never drive.
> The real maid was sickning too—when it hit. I will never
> tell.*
>
> *Hallie said it was his fault. He was telling me a story. He
> and I would run away.*
>
> *Remember Papa. I will talk to him in my prayers.*
>
> *We are in morning. We cannot go to the horse Show next
> month. Mama cannot go to the opera. Lizzy can still get
> married.*

Hallie's entries after the murder were few but full of
anger directed toward someone unnamed:

> *Today, with the police here, we went and picked up the
> dummies and flags from the obstacle race. The dummies
> made me sick. I can do nothing—cannot ask. This family is
> damned. Tell no one. Both are crazy. I did not mean to use
> the bubble—I would not—with Father just killed—mad, mad,
> mad!!*

She said: "Father's Bridget."
Why?

Mother and elder daughter were much more circumspect, even in their expressions of grief. And after the daughter left the country as a married woman, there was apparently never any further direct communication between Mrs. Wentworth and Lady Deake—not even by letter. Mrs. Wentworth never saw Castle Deake, never lent St. James her bustling presence. What were those lines of the daughter's?

> *The sea keeps its secrets*
> *They say.*
> *The waves though still whisper*
> Speak speak.

In the afternoon, I was in a blurry romantic Sunday mood. I wandered around the old colonial center of the city, along Farewell Street with its graveyards of weather-pitted slabs and into Trinity Church. Beautiful twisted balusters, wineglass pulpit. Then houses with fanlights and gambrel roofs.

I went to sleep early, slept heavily, and heard in the morning that Pierre had called. The landlady hadn't wanted to wake me.

Monday's streets were very different from Sunday's. At City Hall, when I mentioned Miss Wentworth, these civil servants of the 1980s presented me with the Record of Deaths, but they made faces at the name or pretended to draw a blank.

I knew a great deal about H. H. Wentworth's death, almost nothing about Mary Smith's. Deaths were entered by successive numbers on city forms. The maid's death was the next after Wentworth's. Age, twenty-six.

No children, no known relatives. Occupation, domestic service. Birthplace, not known. Surely they should have known at least whether Mary Smith was born in America or elsewhere. (I remembered the Gaelic slogan in the journal.) Cause of death—and here the doctor had started to write one word, but had blacked it out heavily and written *accident*. The other false start had been blotted out so I couldn't read it.

The place of burial was a local cemetery, with the Wentworths paying costs. There was no record of a funeral.

I thought of the Wentworth funerary rites, with the president of the New Haven lending the bereaved family his private railroad car. With the body packed in ice from the feast—the sculptured bear chopped up, and the swan—and the doors to the private parlor car festooned in swags of purple and black, the Wentworths had fled Newport. After the New York funeral, heavily attended by the public and police, the coffin had gone on West, alone (except for some Pinkertons) for burial in a mountain mausoleum. The widow was too distracted by shock, continued police badgering, and plans for her daughter's wedding to go along.

The servant's death record seemed to lead to no line of further inquiry—except, possibly, the doctor who had signed the certificate. On an impulse, I looked up the doctor's cranky-sounding Yankee name in the current Newport directory. Sure enough, there was the name.

My girl-reporter image always went scattering when I was absorbed in research. But perhaps my diffidence on the telephone helped me to gain entry. So did the mention of Miss Wentworth.

"Why, yes, I know that my grandfather did attend at Werthmere. I'll see what I have. . . . Local history is my passion.

"Could I come over this afternoon? I have to go back to New York tonight."

Hesitation. "Oh, yes, do."

She was in her fifties. The curios surrounding her made her look startlingly young. There were photos and mementos and seashells and, upstairs—I gathered—a few discreetly chosen summer boarders. It was just the kind of house I liked.

"You see," I heard myself saying, "what we like to do now is a kind of social history. Not only the family and the house, but the people they were associated with."

"Yes. You mean Society. Oh, we're used to them here. You see, Miss Miller, my family has been here since the eighteenth century. I'm directly descended from—oh, it doesn't matter. I don't want to talk like that. But Quakers and, if you please, some of the old Jewish families, though the name doesn't show it. We've seen the summer people come and go. Some of us older Newporters won't admit to it, but I say the cottage people have kept Newport alive. Especially now that the destroyers and the Navy are going. We all play our part. There's bad and good in Society."

"Yes, that's quite true. But by 'social history' I meant everyone *around* the summer people. Staff. Servants. The family's relations with everyone."

"Oh, I see. You know, I've felt guilty ever since you called. My grandfather didn't attend the family at Werthmere. But he was sometimes called in for the staff."

"Yes. I've been looking up records for Miss Wentworth. Your grandfather signed a death certificate for a maid at Werthmere."

"Well, we'll see. . . . Here are his diaries. He was very conscientious. Also very interested in the flora and the varieties of seashell. I've meant to give these to the Historical Society some day when I'm gone. For now, I like to hang on to them, for some reason. But of course, for a scholar . . . you're welcome to browse. Would you like a drink? Tea? Something stronger? Sherry?''

''Thank you. Sherry would be lovely.''

''Well, I usually have a stiff Scotch about this time myself.''

''Oh, thank you.''

My hostess went out and I turned to the doctor's medical diaries. Everyone in Newport, I thought, must have something destined eventually for the Historical Society.

The doctor had been meticulous about everything: dosages, dates, comments. He had a nice collection of patients' last words, as I noticed when I paged through the 1901 record.

> *Called to Werthmere. Still the uproar over the murder. A reporter arrested for trying to come up from the Cliff Walk. The police care more for that than for this poor woman. Very bad accident. Those infernal machines—playthings for the wealthy! Bleeding internally. Mary Smith, 26. Hysterical, raving with pain, talked of newspapers. Of the murder? Spoke of the sun. Poor creature, in that cramped attic! Begged me to keep her journal. Gave me a ticket which she seemed to think was money—or worth money. Religious— spoke of Paradise. I took the ticket. Morphine. She died at 8:34 in the evening.*

A numbered ticket with the words GRAND CENTRAL STATION printed on it was pressed into the crease of the record book.

Scarcely thinking, I dropped the ticket into my pocket. A moment later, my hostess returned with two Scotch-and-sodas and some fancy crackers on a plate.

I drank my Scotch quickly and looked through the volume. There were no other references to Werthmere in the little book.

My hostess began to glance furtively at her watch and the television set. "I hope you found some useful information."

"Yes, your grandfather was very careful in his descriptions. Helps establish the atmosphere." I told her that if I published my "study," I would note my thanks to her for her grandfather's contribution. Leaving the house, I realized that I was beginning to think of writing it up for publication. Pierre Rose, look out!

I ran to the library and got there just before closing. There in the 1901 volume of the local newspaper, in the back, among the obituaries, was the notice:

Deaths: Mary Smith, 26, servant, of injuries suffered in an accident, yesterday.

It didn't even say she had been at Werthmere.

Back at the rooming house, I found two notes saying that Pierre had called and one saying that Quint had called. I called Pierre's number, but he was out.

Ward came by to give me some copy for the magazine and to take me to dinner. I didn't mention the stolen Grand Central ticket, but I did tell him I wanted to do more research on the journal-keeping maid.

"Ummm? The religious fanatic."

"For one thing . . . doesn't it seem strange that she's so literate? The maid?"

"Ummm. She *wasn't* the governess. I've got it! What if Elizabeth Wentworth really wrote it? She was schizo, you know. In England she thought she was back here, pacing up and down the Cliff Walk—using different voices.

I remember hearing that she'd go very far into herself sometimes. Talk in different voices." He was animated; he'd had several drinks.

"A lot of writers do that," I said.

"What is your hypothesis, if you have one? And what is it based on?" Ward's face wobbled, but his eyes were steady. He was a good old Front Pager.

"My own studies. Serendipity. Hunches. There are things I half remember reading." I felt stupid. I still had nothing to go on.

"You're doing what the old Commodore always did. In his own immortal words: 'Never tell nobody what yer goin' ter do 'til ye do it.' Well. You've been out of New York for a whole week. You ought to see it now in a fresh light. Newport is not for everyone." He sighed. "Newport and *I* are not, evidently, for everyone. But consider the possibility of Elizabeth Wentworth forging a servant's diary. Perhaps it's connected with an alibi. And a message. She *posed* for the rest of her life, you know. Everyone from Sargent to Augustus John painted her. Otherwise she wrote poetry and went bonkers."

"Oh, of course Elizabeth Deake had a couple of break-downs. But from what I've read, she seems to have been quite gallant about her periods of instability."

"What fascinates me about that world is that it's so perfectly neat and sealed off. Like Racine. Like Henry James. The outside world does not impinge." And Ward looked very smug.

"Not so," I said. "The outside world did impinge." I quoted:

> *"H. H. Wentworth hardly bled*
> *Couldn't tell if he was dead*
> *Thought his furnaces were swell*
> *'Til he cooled off stoking hell."*

"What's that?" Ward asked.

"Popular jingle, circa 1900. Before the murder."

Ward called the waiter. "Go ahead then, think of a solution that satisfies you. Involve the 'larger world,' if you despise us.

" 'Us'! Oy, oy! Ward, come off it."

On the plane, passively cocooned like a space traveler, I thought alternately of the heiress and the maid. A young woman in 1980s America was part American Princess, part upstairs or kitchen maid. I identified with both of these women from the past—as I had always identified all over the place. My old history advisor, the one who galloped about in front of the blackboard, had once barked, "You take the part of both Mary Stuart *and* Queen Elizabeth? *Both* right? Who do you think you are, Everywoman? You must take a responsible point of view."

I tried to take the heiress's point of view. It was difficult for me to see public commitment as the iron fate it had been eighty years back. I saw Elizabeth Wentworth, pale, scarcely able to walk, leaving as a bride the church where her father's funeral had been held a month earlier. The platoon of police outside restraining a crowd even larger—and much more vociferous—than had attended the earlier event. A mob of hysterical women breaking through the line to touch the white satin, tear pieces off the point-lace veil, and scramble with mad cries for the exploding bouquet of white orchids, lilies of the valley, orange blossoms. The broken string of matched pearls—touted by the *New York Herald* as a gift chosen by the murdered father—had bounced along the Fifth Avenue gutter, into quick hands, under horses' hooves. The police with their nightsticks had beaten back thousands. There had been several arrests. Some of the pearls had never been recovered. Two men in the crowd had unfurled a banner proclaiming that Elizabeth was a murderess, the *Press* and the *Sun* reported. According to the *Press*, she had fainted when she saw it. At any rate, the bride had been too upset to proceed to Sherry's for the wedding breakfast.

This scene had followed a month of seclusion and secret wedding preparations. All this time, Elizabeth had been kept closely guarded by her mother—and by the police? The mother had moved up the wedding date and severely toned down the lavish display. The ceremony was, by Wentworth standards, hugger-mugger. Yet the thousands at the church had been succeeded by the disappointed hundreds milling outside Sherry's, and another thousand at the pier when the young couple sailed on the *Boadicea*. The Chief Inspector of the New York Police Department had seen fit to release to the newspapers a statement that he had cleared the Deakes' departure from the country. The implication was plain in the official refutation of it.

Press and public had hated Mrs. Wentworth passionately for forcing the marriage on her daughter. Yet when an Anarchist speaker in Union Square had suggested that H. H. Wentworth was much more a killer than his unknown assassin, and hinted that Wentworth's children had callously killed a servant, the speaker was mobbed and beaten. The police, always in attendance at radical meetings, had had to save the speaker by using night-sticks on the crowd. This incident occurred in a week when strikebreakers and militia killed four strikers in an attempted takeover of a Wentworth Works in Colorado. In Pennsylvania, the hired Pinkertons and Wentworth Works strikers were shooting at one another.

I wondered why people could see justice so much more clearly in a private situation. Perhaps because it was not so immense—everything could be tidied up in a final chapter. How soothing to read for two hours about a poisoning at the vicarage and forget for a time the wars that killed millions, the corruption in high places where everybody knew who-done-it but no one told!

After only a week away, the city made me nervous. The New York air was slightly acrid on the roof of my mouth. I had to refocus constantly to understand spaces and faces. I had slowed down, and could not get to the head of a line. The brownstone controversy (an article on the darkness, boring layout, and inconveniences of that type of residence) seemed less than compelling. After work, I wandered uptown on the West Side, warmed by the tropical sounds and faces, the heat rising from the cement. On Broadway, a man in a raincoat passed saying in a singsong *sotto voce* (and lurching in my direction as he spoke, as if he intended to mutter an obscenity), "Eighteen-carat gold chains, eighteen-carat gold chains." He was certainly not the man who had snatched mine two weeks earlier.

At lunch hour on Wednesday I hurried to Grand Central. There I heard "you got to be kidding" four times.

"Lady, that building was torn down in 1910. Whatever it was is long gone. We have auctions for unclaimed articles."

"Lady, you got to be kidding. Was it a relative's?"

"Yes, I guess . . ."

It was no use. After work, I walked over to the Public Library to do some research on criminal cases, Americana, the Wentworths, and politics. Looking around me in the vast reading room with the peeling ceiling, I wondered if any of those bent heads could be a new Karl Marx scribbling away. At the library in Newport, that thought would not have occurred to me. Descending the great marble staircase, I saw the name WENT-WORTH chiseled into a list of library benefactors.

Next day, while I was supposed to be doing research on furniture at the Cooper-Hewitt Museum, I went again to the Forty-Second Street Library, and then to the Newspaper Library.

In the evening I wandered downtown from my East Village apartment to the neighborhood where my great-grandparents had lived. At the turn of the century, the Lower East Side had had the most densely populated blocks in the world. I looked for faces like those in Jacob Riis's photographs. The faces were no longer there. Or perhaps only the clothing had changed, the race, religion, and language. Now on Orchard Street the street vendors cried, "Peso, peso."

They speak my language, I thought.

I decided not to go back to Newport until Saturday morning. I wanted to go along Canal Street and the Chinatown Bowery to see the vegetables and fish for sale on Friday evening, the crowds, the families full of purpose, the sea of life. Yet I was still full of a story more than eighty years old. I didn't call friends; I refused invitations. I wanted to think it out, play the mystery over in my head. I passed the rest of the New York workweek in a dream.

"Penny, are you in love?" asked Flora MacIsaac.

"Hmmm? Oh, no. Just thinking. Research."

"You take the job too seriously. Go see a movie or something."

Once I walked up Fifth Avenue. The church where Elizabeth had been married—and from which her father had been buried—still stood. Over the bridal entrance the sculptor had carved a dollar sign—intricately worked, yet recognizable—into the decoration. Farther up Fifth, the old Wentworth mansion had long ago been replaced by a hotel that was in turn being replaced by some-body's corporate headquarters. Bulldozers waddled over the muddy hills and vales of the construction site, as dinosaurs had once done.

I was cooking. I called Pierre in Newport, asked him to look up a few things.

"Pierre, I think I have the answer now. I know what happened."

"Oh? What?"

"I'll tell you when I see you."

The pieces, as they say, were falling into place.

And I noticed that I seemed to be changing. I wasn't wondering all the time whether I was being followed. For the moment, at least, only one problem had the power to fret and worry me: an old mystery. Was that healthy?

By lunchtime Friday I knew what I wanted to say. But I couldn't get a word of it down on paper. In desperation, I called Dr. Geldohr's office. An answering service answered.

"I'm *sor*-ry The *sec*-re-*tar*-y is also on her va-*ca*-tion. The girl who usually answers for our service is out to lunch. I can't tell you anything. May I help you?"

"Then why did you answer Dr. Geldohr's phone? Damn it, suppose I have a real problem? Talk what way? *You* talk that way, that's why. I have a problem I have to talk to him about right now. A block. A phobia. When is he coming back? Can't I get an appointment before September? I have lots to tell."

"We can't—"

"Well, forget it, then. Tell Dr. Geldohr I'm paying him off, and I won't be back. I'm coming into money." I slammed down the receiver.

Saturday morning I took a plane back to Newport. As the plane started down toward the hilltop airport, I had a

beautiful sunlit view of the city. The clear view stopped
right at the harbor. As if by magic, the pearly fog stood
straight up out of the bay and continued out to sea. The
old resort was like a castle that had slept a hundred
years or more, enchanted, surrounded by an impenetra-
ble wall of fog.

A Gathering in the
Newport Maid Room

So near the end, I somehow still managed to feel defeated. While I was gone, Pierre had not found any police records on the maid's death beyond the first bare entry: "Accident." Had there been no inquiry?

We walked along the Cliff Walk. This time, I was too troubled to admire the great cottages. Twenty, thirty feet below, the waves danced. I felt dazzled, dizzy; I was afraid of heights.

"I have a solution. I'm sure I'm right. And right on the second killing, as well. The problem is—I can't write it. So I can't do a presentation for Miss Wentworth. I have writer's block. I have notes, but I can't get them together. I was up all last night, but I felt as if the back of my brain was dissolving. Don't laugh."

"Maybe you could talk it out. To me," said Pierre.

"Right now? I can't. I guess I'm a researcher, not a writer. Let's face it. A lot of women—especially women—have this problem of not being able to write. We're not brought up to see ourselves as writers—"

"Balls," said Pierre. "What a stupid argument. You

can do it." He laughed. "Cheer up. If your solution is better than mine, I'll help you write it up. Ghostwrite it."

"Thanks." I wondered why I had to tell him my troubles. "Why am I so dependent? Neurotic."

"Don't talk that way. That's another kind of fantasizing."

"I promised I'd have something for her today. Even if you help, it's too late. We couldn't get anything ready for this afternoon."

"Could you talk it out? To Miss Wentworth, I mean? Gather everyone at the scene of the crime and . . ."

"Maybe. I can usually give a performance, when I work myself up to it. But I think I'm more interested in what you think of my theory than I am in what Miss Wentworth thinks. For all her thousand dollars." I didn't mention Quint's offer of more money, of possible publication. After all, Pierre was also the competition.

"I missed you a lot," Pierre said. "I was jealous of New York. As I am of Werthmere. . . . Miss Wentworth doesn't know me by sight," he said. "No one would know me from when I worked at Werthmere as a kid. It's just a thought, but . . . could I go along with you to the—the denouement or whatever it is? As—"

"As my secretary?"

"Sure." He shrugged. I wondered if he had meant to suggest some grander role. "Your male secretary. And take down what you say, in squiggles. I'll be very self-effacing. And give moral encouragement. I'd be able to get down the main points and reconstruct it all later, if . . ."

"If you think it's worth it."

"Well, yes. I'd love to get into the place. I've been wildly envious because you saw the old girl up close. I'll

put on my academic threads. I can look quite respect-
able when I have to."

"What have we got to lose?"

We parted, arranging to meet at Werthmere just before four-thirty. Long ago, Pierre had interviewed a social secretary, since dismissed, at Werthmere; otherwise
Perry, with his professional memory for faces, was the
only person who might recognize him.

I was happy with this arrangement. I didn't want
Pierre to meet Ward too early. Ward might smell a rat.

Feeling a bit more hopeful, I rang up Ward to say I
would meet him at Werthmere.

"Why don't you have lunch with me?"

"I'd like to go over there early," I said.

"Whatever for?"

"I'd like to see something in the attic. A possible
Exhibit A."

But when I rang Werthmere, I could not get Perry,
who was busy with the head of the Gardens Group and
the Historical Dwelling Places Committee.

I thought of asking Miss Wentworth if I could see the
attic. I didn't particularly want to ask a favor of her. Or
Quint. I was still a bit afraid of Miss Wentworth. I didn't
ask.

"Could I leave a message for Perry—or Miss Wentworth? I'd like to bring someone to tea. My secretary."

There seemed to be no objection to that.

"And I'd like to have some old records I've been
working on made available to me this afternoon." I
described the family diaries. "Perry will know where
they are. It's for Miss Wentworth."

I went over to the restaurant where Ward was lunch-
ing. I wanted to prepare him for Pierre's presence at tea.
As we walked out to Ward's car, I said casually that I

had arranged for a friend to make notes from my "oral presentation of the monograph."

"Oh? I hope it's not too long. What do you have to say?"

"I have a theory. . . ."

"So have I. I could have another before we get to Werthmere—if that would help."

"Mine can't be refuted. It may not be true. But it fits the existing facts. And I've added some facts of my own."

"Is that fair?"

"Yes, because in the real world facts always connect with other outside facts. Anyway, I made use of my learning."

Ward drove through the open main gate of Werthmere. I was shocked to see the crowds of people in summer suits and dresses, children in blue jeans, all grazing on these opulent, hitherto private, pastures. I was even more shocked to realize that I had a proprietary attitude toward Werthmere. The acquisitory spirit dwelt within me. And the exclusionary spirit, too?

"I'll garage the car. Don't want to lose the hubcaps to the hoi polloi," said Ward.

"Don't be nasty."

"Why not? People pinch things at Werthmere, I'm sure. Or try to."

"You're—"

"Oh, I'm not prejudiced. Rich people take things, too. From restaurants and hotels. These people just think Werthmere is a hotel."

As we sauntered back from the stables to the house, I sensed that Ward too had a faint air of hereditary ownership. It was in the way he walked and casually glanced up at the windows, ignoring the tourists. Perhaps most of the visitors shared the same temporary fantasy. The feeling wasn't after all, so different from the illusion that had caused such palaces to be built in the first place.

A young man in a white summer suit was standing on the terrace. He too had taken on the hereditary slouch. As he came toward us, he looked vaguely familiar; a Fitzgerald character.

"Oh, my God, it's—" I checked myself before I said "Pierre." I murmured a name, a Henry James character's, to Ward. "We studied this period together. Merton—Ward." Luckily Ward had never met the scourge of the Wentworths.

"I'm a whiz at shorthand," Pierre said. "Men make better secretaries, don't you know." Pierre fanned himself swishily with a conspicuous new stenographer's notebook.

A footman ushered us upstairs. Ascending, I caught a glimpse of Perry in the ballroom, surrounded by women in pantsuits and shorts.

Miss Wentworth was at her post near the fireplace in the Newport Maid Room. Deep in cushions, she took my hand and gripped it tightly for a moment.

"Well, young lady, do you have anything for me?"

"Well . . . I have notes. . . ." I saw the family diaries on a table.

"Does that mean yes or no? Do you have anything for me?"

"Yes." I took a deep breath. "I brought my . . . uh, secretary. He works with me on, uh, such occasions." When I solve old murders.

In the background Pierre half bowed, and opened his notebook.

"My father," said Miss Wentworth, "always had a male secretary. Now, Harold, what are you doing?"

The old woman nodded toward Quint, who was at the oriel window, opening it wider. Quint turned and saw

Pierre. He was about to say something when Ward rushed over to introduce himself to young Wentworth.

After this little flurry, there was a sudden silence in the Newport Maid Room. Everyone studiously watched a parlor maid who brought in the tea things.

Voices floated up through the open windows.

"Hey, Jerry—look at the playhouse."

"Nah, it's a mausoleum. Hey, c'mon."

Miss Wentworth surveyed the group: Quint, Ward, the "secretary," me. "Now we can get down to business. Young lady, do you have anything that's worth my printing it up? Do you? Speak up."

I felt faint. I began my peroration with the curious dreamlike sensation that I would have to speak in French or Latin, that my clothes were somehow slipping off—or that the tourists downstairs might be revolutionaries in disguise, storming and sacking Werthmere. I had one hand on the diaries on the table.

"Well. I'd rather speak than read. . . . In doing research on Mr. Wentworth—the Second—and his family and work, I kept returning to one point. I kept finding particular points of interest and even some fresh information on the circumstances of his—of his death."

I whispered the last word. I saw Miss Wentworth stiffen and grow steely-eyed.

"Go on," said Miss Wentworth.

"It was an important death because he was an important figure of the time. It was not a classic puzzle any more than it was an open-and-shut case. First, there were a great many people here on the night he was killed. The five family members and their guest, Lord Deake. Perhaps two hundred guests. An interesting feature of all the testimony is that no one made a statement suggesting that any of the guests had gone out on the lawn during the entertainment, before Mr. Wentworth was found killed.''

"In those days," said Miss Wentworth, "People were well bred. If they accepted entertainment and hospitality, they responded with their attention. Oh, they would sometimes talk and gossip, but they wouldn't go running about the place like a pack of hunting dogs. Not in my mother's time. We had the tableaux vivants and our guests gave their full attention.''

"Then there were the servants at Werthmere. A huge staff. Perhaps a nursemaid as well as a governess. An English butler, a cook—''

"A French chef, if you please,'' said Miss Wentworth.

"A French chef, parlor maid, upstairs maids, scullery maids, pantry man, brass cleaner, footmen, laundresses, coachman and chauffeur, gardeners, stableboys—''

"Yes, yes. I knew 'em all as a child, knew their names, no matter how fast they'd come and go. I made a game of it," said Miss Wentworth. "I kept track of 'em. Where'd they all go?''

Voices floated up through the oriel window: "We're over here!'' The crowd below had gone onto the terrace. They gasped and cried in admiration of the view. "They still *live* here!'' "Imagine the upkeep!'' They fell silent as the guide began to tell the dimensions of the house, the size of the staff, then and now. . . .

"So," I continued, "despite the presence that night of local police and employed Pinkerton agents at the front gate and on the Cliff Walk—despite the high walls on three sides of the estate—access was not really limited. One of the Pinkertons on the cliffside might even have been involved in the murder. The point is that the possibilities are—from a purely technical point of view—open-ended.''

In a painful moment of silence, I realized why professors went in for tedious humor and big words: such stuff could glue up the pauses when the mind went blank. I was talking the way Pierre wrote.

"So we go to motive, and to questions that may or may not be related to the murder. What happened to the murder weapon? Why was it not found? Why did Mrs. Wentworth and Elizabeth Wentworth each claim—in their first, separately taken testimony—to have found the body first? Why, conversely, did they agree that they had seen someone go over the cliff, when the Pinkertons stationed there testified that they had seen no one?

"This is all police evidence. Other questions involve the later actions of family members. Was there a reason for Mrs. Wentworth to move the Deake marriage *forward* rather than *back* in time after a period of mourning? Any reason for Elizabeth's strict seclusion both before and after the marriage?"

"There was the reason . . ." Miss Wentworth began.

"No. Go on."

"—That the mother desired this marriage no matter what. And feared that to delay, in view of the public interest and speculation, would be to court doubt and disaster. Perhaps that is a strong enough motive. But it does not explain why Lady Deake and her mother never again met—particularly when the mother had meant to carry her social campaign to England. And it does not explain why the son became estranged from his mother.

"These are the questions most frequently asked. They are the basis for the theory, advanced most recently by a young professor in a curious article, that Elizabeth killed her father in what he describes as 'a fit of near-insanity.' The writer, however, did not have access to the Wentworth private papers. And in my view his conclusions were wrong." With some satisfaction I watched Pierre as he pretended to take this down in shorthand.

"There are other questions that the private sources pose. From the contemporary journals of Mrs. Wentworth, Elizabeth, and a maid—as well as from veiled references in Lady Elizabeth Deake's published memoir —we know that Mrs. Wentworth told her daughter something that quite shocked the daughter. Something about men, with particular examples. This occurred during the two days before the murder, and was part of the campaign to promote a marriage of interest. Other questions involve the servants. One, a maid, died shortly after the murder, and her death was not explained on the death certificate. Miss Wentworth, do you remember Mary Smith? Twenty-six years old. She worked at Werthmere only that one summer and was killed in an accident two days after your father's death."

Miss Wentworth's face was fierce, then bland, then fierce again. I thought, this was what her father was like when crushing competitors or strikers.

"No. I'm old. I don't remember. There were so many servants."

I knew she was lying. Miss Wentworth had forgotten nothing. But perhaps that meant she *knew* something I hadn't counted on. All that time with records, and I had forgotten there might be a living witness.

"I found Mary Smith's diary in a little room in the attic," I said. "A locked room."

"What's locked should stay locked," said Miss Wentworth. "Who gave you permission? Perry?"

"Uh . . . no."

"Who gave you leave?"

"Please, Aunt Tory," said Quint. He stood behind her chair. Miss Wentworth's hands gripped the chair arm, hard as two carved wooden claws, digging into the crewelwork.

201

"Is it the maid's death that's important, or the diary?" Ward asked.

"Both," I said. "But to get on. Instead of trying to imagine the moment of the crime itself, I started to go backwards. Like running a movie backwards in my mind. The actions and statements of the family members were so confusing. I had to try to take them one at a time, working from the outside.

"Mr. Wentworth Junior, for example. Taking him as the outermost circle—before the police came in to widen it—and imagining him as he approached the Pompeiian Pavilion. What did he see? His mother and elder sister standing over the body of his father. That's agreed on. But what did he *think?*

"In the police testimony the son is quoted as saying, 'I'd like to kill the b-blank.' Then, 'My God, if I could do something.' And again. 'I wish I could kill the b-blank.' "

"I think you might say the word," Miss Wentworth said drily, "in this day and age."

"Which word?"

"Now, now, young lady. It's not my language, don't you know. But a gentleman was entitled to use strong language to express strong feeling. My brother's sentiments did him proud."

"The word," said Ward, "is *bastard*."

"No," I said. "One might think so at first. But notice that the young man says '*if* I could do something.' 'I *wish* I could kill.' A young man eager to avenge his father ought to say, 'I'm *going* to do something.' 'I'm *going* to find and kill the bastard.' In his diary after the murder, Hallie wrote: 'What can I do? I can't tell anyone. I can't ask anyone for help.' That leads me to believe that the word he used—which was suppressed by the prudish police-recording practice—was *bitch*. 'I'd like to kill the bitch.' He believed that his mother was the killer."

"No more," said Miss Wentworth. She was rising to her feet, her own claws clutching the arms of the chair. "My mother did not kill my father, and I thought you would have more sense than to say that."

"But I didn't say that, Miss Wentworth."

"That happens, of course. In café society—or whatever they call it now. People ruled by their passions. But we do not kill our own nearest kin—we do not—*that* was what I hired you to prove."

"Aunt Tory—"

"Miss Wentworth"—and I tried to stave off the Curse of the Wentworths (which I saw on her trembling lips) by waving Eugenie Wentworth's diary—"Miss Wentworth, I know she didn't do it. But your brother *thought* she did. That caused their estrangement all those years."

All the ferocity went out of her. She sat down again. "Then tell me. All those years . . ."

"Mrs. Wentworth was known to be a woman with a ferocious temper. She made threats. In her appointments diary Mrs. Wentworth mentioned telling her husband she 'could kill' a maid—Bridget, who had had an affair with the son, and . . . well, there was more. What's important is that the son entered the library just as the mother was telling the father how she felt about the servant girl." I opened the diary, found the passage and read it: " 'Told Mr. W. about the girl. Told him I could have killed her—I am so helpless, everyone crosses me—and just then Junior came in for his "few words" from father. I hope Hallie heard what I said. He should know what suffering he causes his mother.'

"Now suppose Mrs. Wentworth was quoting to her husband the exact words she had used to the girl. Suppose she is saying, 'I'd like to kill you,' quoting herself, and the son comes in at that moment. The young man might have thought his mother was threatening to kill the person she was addressing: his father.

"Hallie was already feeling pretty bitter about his mother. Earlier that day, according to her appointments diary, she had slapped him. Then, later, on the day of his precious obstacle race, she insulted him in front of his friends by ordering a fire engine in attendance. The race came two days after. On the day of the murder.

"With this immediate background of strong negative feeling about his mother"—I paused, struck by strong negative feelings about my language, the fruits of my golden hours with Dr. Geldohr—"such feelings, he immediately jumped to the conclusion that his mother had killed his father in a fit of anger. His sister's shock, and her later reluctance to talk, would have deepened his conviction."

"But his mother bullied him just as much after the murder as she had before," Pierre objected. "And if she was the killer, he could have blackmailed her. Or, of course, accused her."

"My mother," said Miss Wentworth, "never changed. She went straight ahead."

"Yes. Hallie was wrong. He had to wait four years to come into his inheritance. Then he left his mother as fast as he could. He was always running away. Fast cars, fast—uh, so let us leave young Mr. Wentworth for the moment. If he had ever confronted his mother, made a Greek tragedy scene—'You did it, you killed Papa'—then he might have learned he was wrong. But perhaps Hallie Wentworth was . . . a docile sort of man."

"Alcoholics," croaked Miss Wentworth, "are docile men. A man should not be too nice." She looked at Quint, who shriveled up before her glance.

"And then," I continued, "remember, the code worked

against him. A gentleman owed a great deal to his mother. He was told how to treat a lady. A lady, of course, was never wrong. So he never spoke up. So he kept running. He never escaped his mother."

"And the ladies?" Ward asked. "Which one arrived on the scene first?"

"In the police testimony, each claimed to have arrived first. Suppose that Elizabeth, having crossed the lawn from the library, finds her mother in the Pavilion, bending over the body of her father. What then? She might suspect her mother of having murdered the one person who might have stopped the marriage—her dear father. If so, what would the young woman have done?

"Would she have defended her mother by telling the police that she herself had come onto the scene first? Would she have meekly surrendered to a marriage that she found abhorrent? Could it be that she was in complete terror that her mother would next murder *her?*"

"No, no . . ." said Miss Wentworth. This time she was not objecting, simply shaking her head. "No. I know you don't believe that, child. My poor sister. She told me later, at the funeral—and she wrote me later, from England—that she had wanted to die then. She was not frightened. She was . . . worse."

"She was in despair," I said. "She was more in her mother's power than ever. And I don't believe that even a very traumatized and impractical young woman could have failed to realize that she had powerful means of blackmail: if Mrs. Wentworth was the killer, Elizabeth could have freed herself from the marriage.

"After the murder, remember, Elizabeth *did* have access to outside powers. Police, the press. If she had accused her mother, there would have been a terrible scandal—but the marriage need not have taken place.

But she did not take this course. She acted the part of a beaten creature.

"And the mother? More than ever, she takes matters into her own hands. She tyrannizes the girl—and at the same time shelters her. From what? I believe that Mrs. Wentworth reached the Pavilion *after* the daughter. She saw Elizabeth with Mr. Wentworth's body—and leaped to conclusions. She thought that Elizabeth had appealed to her father. The father had said that the marriage must take place. In a fit of near-insanity the daughter had killed him."

"You say Mrs. Wentworth only *thought* this?" Pierre asked.

"Yes. Earlier that day, there had been a near-accident in the obstacle race. Elizabeth may have provoked the accident."

"The obstacle race?" said Miss Wentworth, squinting. "Oh, d'you mean when they lost control?"

"What happened?" I asked. "Do you remember, Miss Wentworth?"

"I was there. They let me attend, with Nanny. There were other children, too. I saw it happen. They almost went over the cliff. It was Reggie—Lord Deake's—fault. He was driving, and my sister had gone along with him. I remember I thought it was exciting, although the grown-ups were nervous. But my sister . . . she told me later she thought it was exciting, too. She laughed and told me a secret. She said, 'I'll try it again, Tory. Just you wait.' I missed my sister later on. She wasn't like a grown-up."

"But Penny," Ward said. "You're only bringing us back to the fellow who wrote the article about Elizabeth Wentworth. And if it's 'a fit of near-insanity,' as *he* said, what about the gun? Having a gun makes it first degree."

"No, no, she could not have done it," said Miss

Wentworth. "Not my poor sister. She could have done—certain things. But she would not have killed my father."

"Yes, the theory that Elizabeth Wentworth killed her father on the spur of the moment is ridiculous on the face of it, because—where's the gun? We would have to assume that the starting revolver for the obstacle race had been left in or near the Pavilion, so that Elizabeth could discover it conveniently, at the critical moment. *And* assume that she fired it accurately: no mean feat for someone who has never intended to use firearms until she has 'a fit of near-insanity.' The starting revolver, by the way, belonged to Hallie. He kept real bullets, probably in his automobile. Hallie was known to have threatened angry farmers with a loaded revolver during some of his automobile jaunts through the countryside.

"But no weapon was ever found. And there were no ballistics tests made. Anyone might have picked up that revolver on the lawn that afternoon. Or it might have been another gun after all. If Hallie Wentworth missed his revolver later he wouldn't have mentioned it—*if* he suspected his mother of having used it."

"Nobody tells anything, according to you," Ward said.

"True. One of the curious points of this case is that no one tells anyone else what suspicions he has. It's a curious code. Hear no evil, see no, speak no. In this respect Society follows the strict code of *omertà*.

"Mr. Wentworth Junior does not tell his mother that he suspects her of murder even though his future relations to her are colored by this suspicion. Mrs. Wentworth does not tell her daughter that she suspects her of murder—is indeed convinced of it. No. The mother believes that the daughter's balance is very delicate indeed; more than anything else, the mother wants the marriage to take place. Perhaps her main fear is that the

207

daughter will confess. She gave the girl a sedative at once and insisted to the police that she herself had discovered the body. Maybe it never occurred to Mrs. Wentworth, with her immense social self-assurance, that anyone could suspect *her*. The police records, though, show Mrs. Wentworth in a very damaging light. She tried to manipulate the police. And she succeeded. She squashed the inquiry. Perhaps she felt"—and I realized it was bad history to speculate on motivations in that way—"that if the marriage took place her husband's death would be in a way avenged. The daughter would have been sufficiently punished. And the Eugenie Wentworth Police Widows' and Orphans' Fund was immediately established. It poured immense funds into the police treasury. Insuring *omertà*. It still pays—contributes to— the police. You have been careful to keep up this eleemosynary work, Miss Wentworth. It is the only social fund to which the Wentworth family contributes."

"But you don't believe Elizabeth did it," Pierre said.

"No. She did not do it."

"Who then? Who did it?"

Deed and Motive

I looked at Miss Wentworth. The old woman looked very much shrunken up. Her eyes were closed. For a moment I thought she might have dozed off.

"You're lookin' at me, young lady," said Miss Wentworth. She had not opened her eyes.

It seemed to me that she was willing me to pull out of her what she knew of the story, to draw from the living witness—what?

"Yes, Miss Wentworth. I was wondering . . . That summer when you were ten years old you sometimes got out of bed at night to look out on the lawn for the ghost. The ghost of the Newport Maid."

Miss Wentworth opened her eyes. "Did I?"

"It's in your old diary, Miss Wentworth. And you saw the Newport Maid some nights. I believe that you saw her going across the lawn to the folly. Earlier, that summer."

"I was a child. But I knew no ghost killed my father."

"No. The ghost you saw earlier that summer was a woman from the house who was meeting someone in the folly late at night. Until she was dismissed from service. But the point is, having seen the ghost a few times, did you stay up on the night of the murder? Were you looking out your window toward the Pavilion? Watching for the ghost?''

All eyes turned toward Miss Wentworth. She broke the spell. She snorted indignantly. ''Ghost, fiddlesticks. On that night I stayed up to see the fireworks.'' She nodded around to all. ''Oh, yes. We were goin' to have fireworks. *They* were—the grown-ups. I had wheedled and begged to stay up, but no. Well, never you mind; my poor old nanny always dropped right off, and I crept out of bed. I watched for hours. I was afraid I'd fall asleep and not wake up at midnight for the fireworks. So I sat by the window all evening.''

''And then?''

''And then? Nothing. Of course, they didn't have the fireworks after all.''

''But didn't you see people go out to the Pavilion?'' I wanted her to say what she had told me the night I had stayed in the Newport Maid Room. ''First your father . . . and then others?''

''It's such a long time ago . . .'' said the old child's voice. ''Such a long time . . . I had nightmares. Oh, they were quiet about it after they found him there . . . there was no general cry. I must have fallen asleep at the window. In the morning they told me I'd never see Papa again.''

''Did you hear the shots, Miss Wentworth?''

''I thought the fireworks were starting. I looked . . . but there were no lights in the sky. Only the moon. I only saw—I imagined I saw a ghost.''

''What kind of ghost? Remember: you told me the dream.''

''Oh, I had nightmares for a long time. The ghost

going away from the house, below me. White and shimmery. Toward the Pavilion. I saw the light there. That's when I decided to stay up—I thought the light in the folly meant the fireworks would start. But I didn't see my father go out there."

"Because he wore black. His white shirtfront would have been going away from you, or too small to show him off. . . ."

"This white shimmery ghost . . . up to the folly. Fireworks. Then . . . coming back . . ." Her eyes were closed. "The ghost was all shrunken up and skimming along. The dress was smaller. It went back the other way. . . ."

"It went from the library side out to the folly, and then came back almost immediately toward the other wing."

"Yes, but that's nothing. A child's picture of it. I didn't imagine it though. I never imagined like most children. I never believed in the Newport Maid story until I saw her that summer, don't you know."

"You saw what you saw. Not Mrs. Wentworth, who wore black that night. Neither your father nor your brother, who wore black. But you had an impression of your sister Elizabeth in her Niagara costume with the rhinestones sewn in. She reached the Pavilion, you have just said, before the 'fireworks.' Before the shots were fired."

"Oh, no. Then it wasn't that way," said Miss Wentworth.

"Picture," I said, "Elizabeth Wentworth. Picture her running up the steps of the Pompeiian Pavilion—eager to talk to her father alone, when for once she is not being watched."

"No, no," said Miss Wentworth. "Not like that. Whatever you mean to say about my sister, I never believed that she went out of the house that night to look for my father. My poor sister. No. Not 'eager.' '' She shook her head.

"No?" I was shaken, afraid my picture was about to be shattered. "Why, then? Why do you think she went out?"

"She never told me. But I always thought . . . You spoke, child, of her 'despair.' Don't you know, with all your research, that my sister could *never* have appealed to my father as you think? Oh, perhaps another daughter and another father. Even in those days. And, to be sure, my poor sister *wanted* to speak to him. But she was so terribly shy. The shyest person I ever knew. I was the only one in all that household she could really talk to. No. After that first—the accident with the automobile— she went out that night meaning to die."

"To die?"

"To go down to the sea. Oh, she was drawn to the sea. But she had the strength not to do it. My beautiful sister. She knew her duty. She never disgraced us." Miss Wentworth closed her eyes. "Not once. Never."

"But . . . well, perhaps—if she wanted to die—in that case . . .'' I tried to redirect the scene. "Yes. Picture Elizabeth running down the greensward toward the cliff. To the death she'd failed to achieve that afternoon. What stops her?

"She sees a light in the Pompeiian Pavilion. And something more? Something happening? She goes to the folly, and sees—by the light of the Egyptian oil lamp— what? Only her father's body on the ground? Mrs. Wentworth, when she first told the police that *she* had discovered the body, she said she entered right after hearing two shots. And that she saw someone go over the cliff. Now we are—for the moment—assuming that she has fabricated testimony to protect her daughter.

But, unconsciously, she has synchronized the sounds as she really heard them. So she reached the Pavilion a minute or less after the shots were fired.

"Elizabeth, in her police testimony, did not mention shots. She told the police chief the next morning: 'I saw a light in the Pavilion and went toward it. I looked in. There was Papa.' I think that she actually entered the Pavilion just before the shots were fired. She stood paralyzed in the entrance and actually witnessed her father's murder."

"By whom?" Ward asked.

"By a servant from the house. A maid."

If I expected an electric silence, I didn't get it. Pierre objected at once: "But Elizabeth didn't go into a catatonic shock. She would have reported a maid."

"Mmm. There are hints as to why she might not have reported the maid. Her mother's appointment journal, the maid's diary, her own published and private writings all indicate that the mother—by way of convincing her to marry Lord Deake—had been giving her some very nasty propaganda about men. Miss Wentworth had heard rumors of Lord Deake's 'cure' at Baden; no doubt for a venereal disease. If she argued that he was not morally fit, her mother countered that *all* men were swine. Her mother told her, during the two days before the murder, dirty stories both true and untrue. Her brother's affair with a servant girl, Bridget, who almost died from a self-induced abortion with lye. Elizabeth's American ex-fiancé's affair with a married woman—for which Mrs. Wentworth furnished letters. No doubt Mrs. Wentworth talked about other men in her own family. She strongly implied that her own husband was a complete libertine."

"My father—"

"—Was a model of virtue in that respect."

"He was. In every respect," said Miss Wentworth.

"But Eugenie Wentworth never cared what she said. For her, truth was whatever brought about the end she wanted. If she could reduce all men to nothing, the point of marriage might be clear to her daughter: it could only be an arrangement for security, power, and the larger exercise of personal freedom. It was also—although she never quite said so to Elizabeth—a kind of revenge.

"The daughter was of course overwhelmed by the visceral shock of these revelations—and the general blackening of the other sex. She had no experience, no other source of knowledge, in that time, with her upbringing. So Elizabeth could not fight back. The very fact that her mother could bring herself to speak of 'such matters' might seem to Elizabeth proof that they were true.

"Mrs. Wentworth was the kind of person whose efficiency and success resulted from a flattening of the spiritual landscape. Like some others who tear people down psychologically to reconstruct them in their own later plans, the mother underestimated the power, even in defeat, of those larger, better feelings. Elizabeth confided in some measure to a servant, she was so overwhelmed with disgust. It's in the maid's diary. The maid overheard the argument. To the police chief Elizabeth later said, 'Oh, it's terrible. So disgusting.' An odd word in the context, 'disgusting.' From Elizabeth Wentworth's later poetry, we know that that shock—the murder and her interpretation of it, coming so soon after her mother's revelations—that shock lasted her all her life.

"In a way, perhaps, she never got beyond that moment: running into the Pompeiian Pavilion to see her father in close embrace, or struggle, with a young woman, a servant. For a moment, Elizabeth watched in horror. What she saw seemed to confirm the repellent picture of men her mother had presented. Her brother Hallie had

had assignations with a servant in the Pavilion. And now—her father. But the maid was resisting.

"The daughter stood there; she saw the maid struggle, pull free, and shoot twice—pointblank—at her father.

"Wentworth fell. He died instantly. The maid looked at the daughter for a moment—or I imagine she did. . . ."

And I saw their confrontation vividly: the dark young woman and the blonde, the maid and the heiress, almost strangers, now tied so intimately, fatefully, by what had just happened. Had the maid raised the gun for a moment to point it at Elizabeth's breast? Had any words passed between them? Probably none.

"And then what happened?" To my surprise, it was Miss Wentworth who asked.

"The servant turned. She may have heard Mrs. Wentworth coming. She climbed up on a bench and went out the window opposite the only door to the Pavilion. It's possible to exit very quickly that way."

I looked at Quint. Did he remember taking that route the night he'd been drinking and chasing me?

"Yes," said Quint. "You tested it out. Or I did. I didn't know it was a test."

"You see, the killer leaves by the window just before Mrs. Wentworth enters the Pavilion. The maid runs back toward the kitchen end of the house. Remember that on this occasion the servants had more freedom of movement than the guests. The guests had to stay inside and watch the tableaux vivants. The maid wears a white apron over her black uniform. The white provides the 'shrunken' ghost seen returning by the child—by Miss Wentworth. Going toward the Pavilion, the maid wouldn't have shown all that white, not from the back."

"Is that what I saw?" Miss Wentworth asked. "My sister going out to the Pavilion . . . and then the maid coming back? I told you. I never imagined things, even then. I saw what I saw. I was a witness." She seemed satisfied.

"But why," Ward asked, "why on earth didn't the maid shoot Elizabeth?"

"Yes. Why not?" Quint asked.

"Well, some people won't kill a second person when they've meant to kill only one. In fact, for this particular killer it would have been fatal—in a certain sense—to kill Elizabeth.

"This has to do with the killer's motive. Elizabeth saw the deed but mistook the motive. The motive was fairly rare. Or perhaps the instances where the deed was done are fairly rare, in comparison with the domestic killings that go on all the time. But the motive is a famous one, nevertheless. Americans are sometimes accused of imagining tragedy only in domestic terms. But a family like the Wentworths does not exist only in domestic terms. Hence—motive."

I went to my ratty straw handbag. I pulled out the maid's journal and held it up.

"What? The religious fanatic?" said Ward.

"This is a journal I found in the attic. It belongs to a woman who worked here at Werthmere that summer." I opened the book and read:

" 'I have thought whether it is right to keep this record. Only as a footnote to the other. Because I sense so strongly the evil at Werthmere. I have lain awake all night and wondered if it is right to write this. It is right, for I do it for You. All for You.'

"And the diarist goes on to speak of 'the Deed.' The expectation of Paradise. 'What a dawn we shall see together.' She speaks of sacrifice. Over and over."

I closed the book.

"Do you mean to tell me," said Miss Wentworth, "that my father was killed by a religious maniac?"

"No," I said. I realized I was pacing up and down, like my favorite history teacher, who had always galloped in her moments of transport. "It was a political assassination. That is, it was political in the ideological sense. The language like 'dawn' and 'paradise': words of faith used by radical visionaries. Rosa Luxemburg spoke of knocking on the gates of Paradise. Here is another section." I read: " 'We must build in the hearts of men. We must establish a kingdom of God.' That is a quote from the anarchist philosopher Prince Kropotkin. And she paraphrases Marx, with 'spectres haunting' such a place as Werthmere. The 'You' she invokes is not God. 'You' is the People, or History. History will judge. Political radicals of the time were always waiting for a Day of Judgment. The language was often very Old Testament.

"But this little journal is not specific. No doubt she was afraid to write particulars in this house, before she had accomplished her mission. But she was full of it and she had to let it out in some disguised fashion. So she wrote. . . . She had managed to get taken on as a summer domestic—Mrs. Wentworth, after all, had a hard time keeping servants. It was advertised well in advance that Mr. Wentworth was to come here for the Deake reception. As he did. I believe there was another—much more specific—journal detailing 'Mary Smith's' political activities and beliefs; her history. In fact, I have a receipt for that journal, which she left in Grand Central. She had written out plan and motive in detail. But her confession is lost forever."

"Is everything lost forever?" Pierre asked. "What else do you have to go on?"

"Do you remember reading the passages about 'G.'? Her going to see and hear G.? The raptures? The quotations. We thought this was a housemaid gushing over an actress. No. The dates she mentions correspond to Emma Goldman's public speeches in New York. So does some of the language. Mary Smith—if that was her real name—had evidently spent some time in New York. At one point, she quotes the *Fas a Bealàc*—'Clear the Way'—of the Irish Socialists. But I doubt she belonged to them. Or to any party. I believe she worked alone."

"Why?" Ward asked.

"Because her journal is so lonely. Also, it's in the nature of Anarchists of the Deed to work alone. In 1892 Alexander Berkman acted alone, except for Emma Goldman, when he shot Henry Clay Frick. The president of France, the Spanish premier, the Empress Elisabeth and King Humbert of Italy had all been assassinated in the six or seven years before Wentworth. The address on a strongbox in the attic room was 'Mary Smith, Paterson.' Paterson was a center of anarchism, with a newspaper. It was from Paterson that the assassin of King Humbert had gone to Italy to do the deed."

"But those anarchists were Italians. This Mary Smith wasn't, was she? And all the other Anarchists of the Deed were men."

"We don't know who she was. Maybe this is, among other things, a bit of important lost history for women. Mary Smith may have started to form her plan in the early summer, when the labor troubles in the Wentworth Works started to get very bad. She applied at Werthmere and was hired. She had no guarantee of success with the Deed. Remember, there were cases where servants worked for years at Newport without ever seeing their employers."

"My mother," said Miss Wentworth, "never entered the kitchen. In her life."

"And it may be," I continued, "that Mary Smith had a good record of domestic service. Despite her raptures

—political, but semidisguised—she was calm enough otherwise to notice and jot down her observations about life here. And she was not one of those 'Ego Anarchists' who would throw a bomb into a theater or a crowded café. Her refusal to shoot Elizabeth Wentworth shows this. Elizabeth wrote a poem about that shattering moment:

> *"Destroying Angel*
> *White winged Death*
> *You stare at me*
> *You spare me*
> *And destroy me.*
> *Through the mirror youth enters*
> *through that door.*
> *My life runs out in fire upon the floor.*

"Maid's uniforms of the time often had stiff white apron-shoulders springing up. So—'White winged Death.' Maybe she saw the maid as a mirror of herself. The oil lamp—the fire—tipped over and ran out on the floor of the Pavilion."

For me, this seemed to be the moment most important of all. It was important to respect and understand both women, and the terrible connection between them through the Deed.

"You lost your train of thought," Ward said.

"Anyway . . . Mary didn't shoot Elizabeth. The maid's journal shows a sense of mission and balance. With patience—and some luck—she did manage to become an Anarchist of the Deed. She did shoot H. H. Wentworth. Yet, in the larger sense, Mary Smith was a dismal failure. She accomplished only half—or perhaps less than half—of her terrible errand."

"But what else did she want?" Ward asked. "She did what she wanted."

"It's very plain from the journal. Partly it's in the style. Remember, you remarked that it was too well-written to be the work of a servant. You suggested another possible author. And remember what everyone has remarked: People wrote so much in those days. People are self-consciously eloquent when they *want* to publish. The maid is literate. Her education, for a domestic, is in itself suspect. Factory workers of the time were more likely than domestics to educate themselves or to become political. This woman may have been anything. She is bursting to speak. She writes too well. The fact is, no mystery was ever intended. *The murder would never have taken place if the murderer had not intended to confess.*"

"Not confess," Pierre cried, "but declare!" He jumped up. He paced excitedly, waving the notebook. "The country was still shocked by McKinley's assassination by the Anarchist Czolgosz. McKinley had died only two—three?—weeks earlier. I bet the Werthmere maid hoped, if she wasn't caught at once, to let suspense build for a day or so and then declare herself. Yes! First, she would make sure that the press got her story. Someone at Werthmere, obviously a servant, did tell a reporter that there would be a big break in the case soon. Mary Smith told the police she 'knew' something. She probably thought about Berkman's attempt on Frick. Berkman had had his jaw broken. He hadn't been allowed to speak his piece during his trial. Maybe Mary Smith meant to write a letter first, tell the public that this assassination was complementary to—or even more important than—McKinley's."

"Not a letter," I corrected Pierre. "Her manifesto would have been in the other diary, the one that she left in the locker room of the old Grand Central Station—to be picked up later by a reporter."

"Well, whatever. The point is, a multimillionaire industrialist was more important than the President of the United States."

"Oh, really," Ward objected to Pierre. "That's typical sixties rhetoric."

I tried to speak, but Pierre had jumped up and was waving his hands. Miss Wentworth had fixed him with her owlish glare—undoubtedly wondering what this ersatz secretary was up to—but Pierre was oblivious to her disapproval. "Not at all," he said. "Marc Hanna believed that the problems of government had become the problems of money. McKinley believed he served the public best by serving through the big financial and industrial powers. And a man like Wentworth was served by senators as he was served by the police. Imagine the sensation an Anarchist assassination would have made at such a moment: when Wentworth's hired thugs were shooting strikers with the aid of state militias; when his daughter was about to be sacrificed at the altar for the sake of a titled alliance. The Anarchists had a theory that the Deed, coming at the right moment, would ignite the imagination of the public. The people—Americans, in this case—would become dramatically aware of the injustice of those who had power and money."

"And the assassin meant to declare herself—through the newspapers."

"But do you think the public would believe this? Do *you* think so, Penny?" Quint looked very uncomfortable.

"I? No," I said slowly. "I don't think it would have worked here. The American public had by and large been conservative. When Anarchists were executed in Chicago in the eighties—the Haymarket Affair—the public was aroused, but not radicalized. When Alexander Berkman shot Henry Clay Frick during the Homestead Strike, the Deed was supposed to jolt the country into political consciousness and revolution. But it backfired. People were horrified. The Molly McGuires failed in the coalfields. The Wentworth Deed might have had more effect—*if* it had become known. There was the additional tabloid interest of the cruel marriage. But generally, the idea of the Deed has not worked in this country. Multiple assassinations—we know from more recent times—have a numbing effect.

"So the two women stared at each other for a moment." I could not get that moment out of my mind: I was certain that it had existed once, in the unwritten history I was claiming for the future. I could see the two women, and their burning eyes. "For an instant, Mary the housemaid held the life of the heiress in her hands."

"My sister would have thanked her," said Miss Wentworth, "for taking her life."

"But the world would not have thanked Mary Smith. It was important that the world see Elizabeth as a victim of capitalism and the greed of aristocrats. Not as the victim of an Anarchist of the Deed. And perhaps, to give Mary credit, she did see Elizabeth as a fellow victim."

"Or maybe," Ward said, "she was frightened, and just bolted. She could just as well have put down the gun and declared herself right there."

"Perhaps she couldn't bear to face Elizabeth," I said, "and the horror that she saw in Elizabeth's eyes."

"So, after killing Wentworth," said Pierre, "Mary Smith goes back to the house. All the servants are running back and forth at the time."

"Yes. And remember, going out to kill him, it would have been easy for her to slip out the pantry door at the right moment. Remember, Gramps—a former footman for the big parties at Werthmere—said it was like a battle. Mary may have meant to make the attempt after the party. But from the dining room she could easily have seen Mr. Wentworth on the terrace, strolling out to enjoy his cigar in the Pavilion. So Mary, who has the weapon with her—concealed in the voluminous uniform and apron—goes out to meet him.

"After she returns to the house, Mary Smith must expect to be arrested at any moment. But then, Elizabeth unaccountably shields her father's killer. When the industrialist's daughter fails to accuse her—what must the servant think?

"And what does Eugenie Wentworth think? When she enters the Pavilion, sees Elizabeth standing over the dead man, what are her first words to her daughter?"

" 'Be quiet. Say nothing,' " offered Pierre. "Because the mother immediately assumes the daughter has killed the father. And the daughter is in shock. Her words and actions are consistent with what the mother thinks."

"And," I said, "the daughter has no time to explain— for Hallie comes in and sees *both* women, his mother and sister, standing over his father's body. The alarm is sounded. Elizabeth, fainting—and perhaps drugged, to make sure—is carried upstairs and locked in her room. The police chief keeps vigil, despite Mrs. Wentworth's protests. Next day he gets a statement from the girl.

"And next day, Elizabeth may think that an accusation against the maid will drag her father in the mud. He has been killed for what seems to her a sordid sexual reason. After making an assignation with a housemaid—or luring her to the Pompeiian Pavilion. Where Hallie met the other maid, Bridget. Like father, like son. There is a fight—perhaps the maid resists his advances—the father's. The daughter has been brought up to see public respectability as an absolute standard. And now—scandal."

"And then, two days after that," said Pierre, "the

maid is dead. There is no question of Elizabeth's letting a killer go free through her silence.''

"Yes, but that death is pretty fishy," said Ward.

"Tragic," said Pierre. "Mary is killed in an accident—knowing that she must speak, must tell the word about the Deed. Imagine her dying, losing consciousness just when she has something to say to the world.''

"She *did* try to tell someone," I said. "The doctor who was called in. She tried to give the ticket to the doctor—I mean the receipt for the other, more political diary she had left for posterity in the locker room at the old Grand Central. She wanted the doctor to give the receipt to a reporter for the *New York Sun*. He didn't understand—he thought she was out of her head. But he was a very methodical man and he kept the ticket. And so she died.''

"Dead and be damned," said Miss Wentworth from the depths of her crewelwork chair. Her eyes had been shut for a long time; now they were open. "She ruined my life. Cut down my father in his prime. If what you say is true, she ruined all our lives. My sister's, too. My brother's. My mother's. Planting nasty evil suspicions of murder among us. And she even made my sister . . . well, it's over. She cursed us. Now it's lifted.''

It was over. Almost. I felt exhausted where before I had been exhilarated.

"Miss Wentworth," I said. "Can you tell us what else happened? The second accident?"

"Everything ended that night," she said. "The night of the tableaux vivants.''

"But you wrote something in your diary, about 'the accidents.' '' I took the faded old report book from the table and opened it. "You were ten years old. Here: 'After the accidents I will never travel. I will never drive. The real maid was sickning too—when it hit. *I will never tell.'* You underlined that." I handed her the book.

Miss Wentworth held the child's diary in her hands without looking at it. She was looking at me. "Then I can say it now? It's not a secret anymore?"

"No, it doesn't have to be."

"Child, are you sure now that the servant woman did it? Skinny Mary?"

"I don't know if it can be proved. But neither can your story."

"I can see it now," the old lady said, "as clear as clear. It was after they—she—killed him. Two days, did you say? I was in the library. I wasn't allowed there, but I went. No one paid any attention to me. Oh, what terrible days! Hallie came in and saw me crying. He took me in his lap and petted me. Why, I'd forgotten! Usually Hallie didn't pay much attention. 'Poor baby, poor baby,' he said. He said he wanted to kill someone but he could never do it—he said it was the worst thing that could ever happen to a man, that he could only run away. . . ." The old lady broke off. "You mean to say, young lady," she said, after a moment, "that he was talking about wanting to kill my mother? That my brother could think she had done . . ."

I said to myself: You know it, old woman. You know that's what Hallie thought. But I was afraid to speak, afraid she'd give up on that day long past when her father's killer had been killed.

"No. My brother, whatever his faults, was a gentleman. He could never have believed such foolishness as you said he did. He said that we'd go away, the two of us, away from Werthmere where bad things happened. I said I wanted to stay here, because it made me think of Papa. But Hallie said we'd run away. It was just as if he was telling me a children's story. And it was comforting.

225

"Then he said, 'Come on! I'll show you how we'll run away.' And he took me out to the terrace. The automobiles had all been taken away, of course, since the race. All but the one he kept by the terrace. 'Hallie's beloved Stanley.' That's what my sister called it.

"Hallie started up the boiler, and he ran around the 'bubble.' And he kept telling me how we would run away in the steamer, go right away from Werthmere. I suppose he meant to take me for a drive. He was like a child himself, with his car. Of course, he wasn't very old. But I thought he was, then.

"Then my sister came running out on the terrace, through the French doors. As if she were running away, too. She was as pale as could be, with her long hair down. She had stayed in her room since my father was killed. Overcome by grief, that's what they kept saying. I hadn't seen her. Mama wanted her to stay in her room. The servants shouldn't see us cry. But now my sister came running out.

"I ran over to her and said, 'Oh, Lizzie, they killed Papa.' She held me and we cried but then she stiffened up—she was looking at someone else, and she let go of me. It was a maid coming around from the kitchen side. Oh, if I had known that wicked creature had killed my father!

"The maid saw my sister, and they went to meet each other. Oh, so slowly. I thought it was naughty of the maid to come outside when we were playing unless she had a message for us. I ran over after Lizzie. They looked at each other, my sister and the maid, for the longest time. The one so beautiful and the other just a dark little stick of a thing. Then someone said—the maid?—not to worry, that she would tell everything to someone. Then I looked where they were looking. Out

226

over the lawn, past the folly, there was a man coming up from the Cliff Walk.

"Then my sister told her not to. Lizzie tried to make the maid obey, but Mary paid no attention to her—she just started down across the lawn. Lizzie ran over to Hallie, asking him to help. Hallie had the car all ready and a-tremble—once he started on his cars he wouldn't pay attention to anyone else. And way down across the lawn a man was sitting at the top of the steps and fixing his shoelace."

"The reporter from the *Sun*," I said. "With whom Mary had made an appointment. To whom she meant to confess. Declare the Deed."

"Then I saw the automobile shoot right across the lawn. Hallie was shouting. Elizabeth was standing right beside him. The maid looked back. And the man coming up from the Cliff Walk—he yelled and fell down out of sight. But the skinny maid just stood there. The automobile hit her. It knocked her over and stopped. I remember she just lay there like a rag doll. I never played with dolls after that. An accident. That's what it was."

Her statement was a plea. Why should I tell the old lady that her brother had said her sister and mother were both crazy? Why should I insist on the version that I had constructed from the family diaries, from random comments of Quint's and Gramps'? When Mary had assured Elizabeth that she meant to tell the story, she was assuring the daughter that the father's assassination would not go unpunished. But for Elizabeth, the threat of a sordid sex story, revealed in the tabloids, was the ultimate horror.

Elizabeth had gone over to the Stanley, and had said to Hallie, "She is Father's Bridget." And—while her bewildered brother watched—she had sent the car careening down upon the maid like (as she later wrote in a

227

poem) a "juggernaut of steam"—one that was "driving women to their deaths." Thus in the poem she wrote did Elizabeth Wentworth identify with her victim.

"It was an accident," said Miss Wentworth. "I am the only living witness to that accident." She glared at me.

An accident only in that it succeeded in killing Mary, I thought. No accident that Elizabeth sent the steamer shooting down over the lawn. Hallie had known that Elizabeth had done it deliberately. So, I was sure, did Victoria Wentworth.

But she would never admit it.

I was tired of explanations. There was a stale dry feeling in my lungs, my eyes, my brain. My mind was running down. On the edge of my consciousness, I could hear again the crowd who had come for the Werthmere open house. They were running wild in the library and the ballroom. Open houses and lotteries and tabloid scandals would keep the revolution away. The shades of Werthmere would not be polluted.

"I thank God for the accident that killed that wicked woman," said Miss Wentworth. "Indeed I do."

I didn't want to argue with her. I was feeling a kind of postpartum depression. To think that Mrs. Wentworth had believed her daughter guilty of killing twice—and yet had married her off anyway. And Lord Deake must have thought the same. Had he kept Elizabeth locked up in the castle, a prisoner writing her poetry?

"But the gun?" asked Quint.

"It could have gone into the sea, of course. Though the police searched the sand and the Cliff Walk. It wasn't found in the Pavilion or on the lawn. The house was searched. A big house, but the search was thorough. What was still out on the lawn and picked up later? According to Hallie's diary, the flags and dummies on the lawn had been left after the obstacle race. Perhaps they were meant to provide a conversation piece during the fireworks, a kind of sporting still life.''

''The dummies,'' said Quint.

''Skinny Mary went out the Pavilion window. Behind or near it was one of the dummies from the obstacle race. She thrust the gun into it; perhaps its head was closest. To retrieve it later? Or to thrust away temptation to shoot again? Or out of a wild—but natural and nonpolitical—impulse to escape the consequences of the Deed? Mrs. Wentworth told the police that she had seen something go over the cliff. This may have been true. The dummy landed on the Cliff Walk and was picked up the next day, along with the other 'obstacles.' That's in one of the journals. Some of those dummies are still in the attic.''

''Yes, I was just going to say—'' Quint was standing. His face was flushed, he was so eager. ''I'll look—''

He went out the door. Without thinking, I followed him. I too remembered the dummy with the heavy head that went *thunk*. Downstairs I could hear a great roar of voices, tourists shouting. Was Werthmere that exciting? But I pounded up the front stairs after Quint, and up into the attic.

We searched in the dusty gloom, bending over to avoid hitting the peaked roof, the screens, the crazy jumble of discarded possessions.

''There's one here.'' Quint indecently frisked a sailor-boy dummy. ''No, not here—but the head is a harder material, you can get your hand into it.'' His rare energy gave him an almost demonic glow. ''No, try the maid there.''

It was the dummy that had so frightened me the day I searched the attic. We made our way through piles of expensive rubbish to where she lay. Downstairs people were shouting, slamming doors. Grown-ups not wanting the children to play dolls in the attic. Secret games. Dust made me cough as we picked up the dummy of the maid. The dust was terribly thick; I could breathe only with difficulty.

Quint turned over the lifesize doll. A rusty stain ran along the featureless face. It was an ugly scar, as insulting as the maid's uniform, as the original game. Quint was thrusting his hand up the back of the head.

"Here!"

He was snaking something out, rusty and caked. Something metal?

"What?"

"Fire!"

"What did you say?"

"Here it is," Quint said. But his hand had stopped moving in the dummy's head.

"Fire! Fire!" we heard people cry.

We looked at each other. Then we sprang up, choking, and ran toward the stairway, down to the door at the bottom of the attic stair. Quint put his hand on the door.

"It feels hot."

We ran up again, found the service stairs, and tumbled down the steep-pitched narrow airless flights.

The Last of the
Wentworths

We came out at last through the pantry door to the terrace, and ran to join the crowd on the greensward. Hundreds of people in sportsclothes stood snapping pictures and pointing out the various features—flame magnified in the mullions, smoke sailing ghostlike from one oriel window to the next. I thought I saw smoke on the second floor, too, in the Newport Maid Room; but perhaps it was only the reflection on the casement of dark clouds billowing up from below.

Quint and I searched the holiday crowd. Some ecstatic little boys kept jumping up and down, obscuring the faces behind them.

"I don't see Aunt Victoria," Quint cried.

"Ooooooh," the paying guests cooed as a window drapery in the dining room became a pillar of flame.

We ran around to the west side of the house. My heart clanged in time with the fire engines that were just entering the gate. The witnesses on the avenue side were a smaller group, more somberly appreciative of the scene. The shrunken staff—reduced to ten or so in these

latter days—stood in a half-circle behind Miss Wentworth and Ward. Miss Wentworth was sitting, stiff with
indignation, in a Queen Anne tapestry chair from the
great hall. Her own glare was almost matched by the
sunset on the west façade of Werthmere: the hundreds
of small panes of glass made a fierce waving pattern of
red and black flags—shades of the revolution at Werthmere!

Miss Wentworth looked almost relieved to see us. A
softened expression splintered her identity. Only for a
moment. Then she nodded, as if any acknowledgment of
apprehension would be a breach of the Wentworth faith.

"Where's Pierre?" I cried.

"Who?" Ward asked.

"My friend."

I couldn't see him. So much was happening. There
were hoarse confusing shouts about the private water
supply and deficient pressure. Men with axes raised
rushed in through the main door. With the fountains of
crossing sprays Werthmere was a spectacle worthy of
Versailles.

I ran up to the front door. Two firemen were just
emerging with a swearing, water-soaked man. It was
Pierre, filthy but safe.

"Penny! I was looking for you. How'd you get out?"

"Service stairs."

I took his arm—he was shaking like a wet dog—and
we returned to our tea-party group. Miss Wentworth sat
and watched steadily. Quint and Ward stood to one side,
Pierre and I on the other. When Miss Wentworth spoke
to her grand-nephew, I strained to hear:

"Mother always thought . . . if we ever rebuilt . . . a
porte-cochère would be . . . a practical addition."

As Miss Wentworth insisted on staying at the scene,
her court felt obliged to stay, too. The open house

paying guests would not leave for anything. After sunset, police beams and loudspeakers made it an impromptu *son-et-lumière* event. Spectators kept arriving with hot dogs, soft drinks, and clam fries; entrepreneurs were evidently pitching their tents without the gates. Perry presided over a sumptuous cold buffet sent over by a famous club. By that time the fire was out, and fire inspectors were assessing the damage.

Quint and Perry returned from a tour to announce that heavy fire damage had been confined to the older, partly wood-constructed dining room and hall. Smoke damage to the library was in some ways more serious because of the books and paintings. Worst of all was the water and axe damage. The fire captain believed that a visitor must have left the guided tour to sneak a smoke in the dining room. The great lace tablecloth, the draperies, and a little jungle of palms had gone up before anyone noticed.

"And upstairs . . ."

We spoke in bedside whispers, away from Miss Wentworth. Wordlessly Quint handed me a book. It was Mary Smith's journal. The pages were soggy and ink-blurred. In the harsh searchlight I could decipher very little.

Miss Wentworth refused the many invitations that came in from other cottage dwellers. She declared she would sleep in the stables.

"I haven't slept away from Werthmere since they tore down Papa's house in New York. Now, you know that, Perry."

Maids went into the house with firemen escorts, to fetch Miss Wentworth's necessaries for the night. Other servants rushed off to ready the extra guestrooms in the converted stables. Miss Wentworth's entourage rallied with a new sense of energy and purpose.

Miss Wentworth stood up and wagged a finger at me.

233

"I'll say good night to you now, child. But you write it all down, just as you said. I knew it all along. It was those wicked, wicked men who killed my father. Wicked people. No one in the family. I told you at the first. Did you take it down, young man?"

"Yes, every word," said Pierre.

I felt so euphoric—I saw my feeling reflected in Quint's face—I heard Pierre's acknowledgment: I was ready to tell Miss Wentworth that Pierre was her old nemesis. But a sixth sense warned me not to.

Miss Wentworth insisted she would walk to the stables. Her entourage started a stately progress past dying elms, away from the light. Ward hesitated, then followed Miss Wentworth and Quint. Pierre and I, the outsiders, turned toward Werthmere gate.

"Penny! Wait for me!" A voice out of the darkness.

Quint was coming after us in his spry old man's walk. He stopped, confused, when he saw Pierre standing next to me.

"Penny," Quint said. "May I talk to you a minute? It doesn't have to be tonight—but I'd much rather—"

"Of course." My heart beat faster: I thought of the money. How much would it be? I stepped toward him, then remembered Pierre. "Do you mind—"

"I'll go," said Pierre.

"No, wait for me—just here, at the gate." I could tell that Pierre was hurt. He didn't understand.

I walked eagerly to Quint. Embarrassed, he ducked his head to Pierre, then turned toward the house. I walked alongside him.

Except for broken windows and wet glistening stones, Werthmere looked as always. Scores of tourists were coming around from the cliffside on their way home. I caught their voices, exhausted happy murmurs:

"I can't wait to develop my pictures."

"Maybe it'll be on the late news."

"Penny, I feel so happy," Quint was saying. "Released. And you've done it." He laughed shyly, said hastily, "Aunt Victoria is livid. First, at the visitors starting the fire. The firemen's vandalism, too."

"Only one visitor started the fire, I suppose."

"Well, you see, Aunt Victoria lumps them all together. And she thinks the firemen smashed things on purpose. She thinks it's all on account of this new liberal attitude toward the townspeople, you know . . . the natives."

"What attitude?"

"Well, you know. Accepting them."

He was hurrying me along. I could feel the excitement in his arm, hear it in his voice. Was he happy that Werthmere had burned?

We had come around the house to the great east lawn. It was like a dark rolling sea. With no lights from the house, it was almost frightening.

"What? I think that's—"

"What? What's wrong?" He caught and held me to prevent me from pitching forward.

"I tripped on something," I said.

"I have a light. Stupid of me to forget." He flashed the pencil-light on a soft drink bottle, then on a used disposable baby diaper, then on a jagged piece from a whiskey bottle.

"How awful."

"Don't mind," said Quint. "They only get in once a year."

I wondered if, now that I'd proved a Wentworth had not murdered a Wentworth, the Police Widows' and Orphans' Fund benefit would continue to get an annual Open House at Werthmere. As for the bubble killing of the maid—the police had not investigated that. Why would they be interested now in an "accident" with such a victim?

"The gardeners will pick up all that in the morning," said Quint. "Do you know the kind of things the fire has turned up? The firemen broke through a wall in the map room and found a skeleton."

"A skeleton? Of what?"

"Of a man, of course. I mean, of a person."

"Who was it?"

"Well, no one knows. It's certainly old. I suppose the police will find out. That's their business."

He talked on, but I was plunged in puzzlement, even gloom. Would this new-old skeleton knock my theory into a cocked hat? How could I fit it in . . . ?

"Aunt Victoria is so angry about the fire, she's going to change her will. You know, she meant to leave Werthmere to the public. Now she says she wants to give the estate to me."

"To you." I turned in surprise. Quint—the heir to Werthmere. Well, why not?

"You know, I'm good at business, but not at—not at what Werthmere was built for. I could see rebuilding it. The fire wasn't *that* bad, after all. But I could never *run* the place. I'm not social or artistic. Or imaginative— except about money."

"Oh, don't worry about it, Quint."

"I feel a responsibility toward Werthmere, but it'll be so draining. I can't do it alone."

He smiled nervously. For a moment I wondered if he needed a loan. No, not from me, it wasn't possible. More likely a social secretary.

"You were wonderful today, Penny. The way you defended Great-Aunt Elizabeth. The reconstruction of it all. Aunt Victoria, too: she said you were a—a Porsche."

"What? Like the car?"

"A *Portia*. In Shakespeare. Defending us against the little Jew fellow who wrote that article—the one who threatened to write a book. It was quite clever the way Aunt Tory said it."

"Ay-yi-yi. Didn't I tell you I'm Jewish?"

"Doesn't matter. Aunt Victoria believes in an aristocracy of the spirit."

"What does she mean by that?"

"I think she means people she can stand to have in the same room with her."

Quint's essay at humor kept me from exploding. "That's select company. Very restricted, I suppose. But I have to get back. My friend is waiting—my secretary-friend."

I turned, but Quint caught me again, his hands on my shoulders. He seemed changed—confident, happy. And in charge, as he had been during the *Clio* labor-management negotiations.

"Listen to me, Penny," he said. "I have to speak now, while I have the confidence. I'm changed. I always secretly thought we *did* have a murderer in the family."

"Well, maybe you do. Depends how you define it."

"Oh, what Aunt Elizabeth did—that's revenge. If she did it. But I thought the Wentworths were strange, somehow warped."

"Oh, how could you think that?"

"After all, if my Great-Grandmother Eugenie or my Great-Aunt Elizabeth had—well, done it . . . I thought it might be better if we just died out. Now—you've made me so happy. Vindicated us. You were splendid. I've never met anyone like you. I love you. Will you marry me? Wait, Penny! It's really right. You've given me a new faith . . . Penny, wait . . ."

"Thanks—I'm sure—I can't—"

I started walking back across the lawn, with Quint baying after me. Temptations flashed by, ghosts in the

237

dark. A gay rock festival on the Werthmere grounds, the American Communist Party convention at Werthmere, the history magazine *Clio* revived with me as editor-in-chief.

Ah, but people changed! What about Penny Wentworth descending the great staircase, receiving the remains of Newport society under her portrait painted by Gloria Vanderbilt—no, no, no: Penelope Wentworth growing fat on champagne and *foie gras*, growing thin dancing the newest dances until dawn?

I couldn't trust a Penny Wentworth.

"Penny, I can't keep up—"

I realized I was trying to outrun my fantasies. Werthmere itself and all it stood for; that was the evil I was running away from in the night. But a modern young woman didn't have to run away from terrors known or unknown in a big old house. Not when she could cope with life in New York City, thank you. And knew when to say no.

I imagined my mother having tea in the library with Miss Wentworth. That stopped me dead.

"I'm sorry. I didn't realize I was running. I just couldn't, Quint."

"Oh. Why not, Penny?"

"Well, for starters—I don't love you. No, don't interrupt me! Why shouldn't you deserve to be loved? And politically—oh, but why go into it?" As Quint started to argue, I cut him off sharp. "How could I marry into a family with such a past? Your great-grandfather may have been a great man, by his code. But he killed hundreds. Maimed the lives of thousands. Cheated millions!"

He gasped. "That's rather cheap."

"I'm sorry. I just wanted to convince you. It's no good."

I extended my hand, and we shook. Management and Labor.

Quint looked hurt. He looked handsome. He spoke stiffly. Something about a check.

"No—I couldn't take it. I'd tear it up and send it back. I *like* your Great-Aunt Elizabeth, you know." Noblesse oblige. The code was rubbing off on me. "I wish I'd known her." I liked Mary Smith, too.

And I could never tell my mother about Quint's proposal. She wouldn't believe it.

Pierre was waiting outside the gate. We walked along the avenue hand in hand.

"You were pretty good," Pierre said. "I can make your hypothesis an appendix to my book. Crediting you throughout, of course."

"Pierre, I don't want to be your appendix. Or anybody's. I'll write my own book. From a women's studies approach. On Mary and Elizabeth. And Eugenie. But thanks, anyway."

We quarreled. We enjoyed it. It was a beautiful romantic night in Newport. Ghosts of drunken women in white evening dresses lay in the grass and lifted champagne glasses. An ancient roadster, soundless and without lights, almost ran us down.

EPILOGUE:
The Faux Pas
of the Century

It was all over. The day after the fire.

I was relaxing with Ward at the club where he had promised to take me. We sat in one of the club rooms, having drinks while waiting for our dinner to be announced. It was just about the most exclusive place in Newport, and Ward had been flaunting his membership since my arrival. The club was, for all that, surprisingly comfortable and pleasant. A butler, not a maître d', had met us at the door.

"Now, isn't it nice to be here?"

"Yes, it's a very relaxing place."

"When we get back to New York," Ward said, "we'll have to see more of each other."

It was, I thought, the statement of a man who had lost interest. He had taken on an avuncular tone in speaking to me. Just as well. This dinner was a sort of good-bye to Ward and all that.

I had dined once already that day, a Sunday afternoon dinner with Pierre and his mother and Gramps. I wished I could have stayed longer with them, or brought Pierre along. But Ward liked his little treats and he liked them to be exclusive.

"Are you really interested in this muckraker fellow?" he began. Ward went into his slippery version of wise old uncle. "And what sort of family does he have?"

"By pedigree, you mean? Part French-Canadian. But mostly English. Seven American generations of poor farmers and fishermen. I didn't know there were such people. He's the first to go to college."

"Fascinating, I'm sure. At least it's picturesque . . . isn't it?"

"There is nothing wrong with flowered linoleum on the living-room floor. I just realized that today." I wanted to discuss this new discovery, one that somehow linked politics and aesthetics. But Ward played doggo. He was not going to help me any longer with my sentimental education.

"That was fascinating, their discovering those skeletons last night in the fire," he said, sipping his Scotch. "Wasn't it?"

"Skeletons? You mean there was more than one?"

I was sure he would tell me next that all bets were off—that Elizabeth or someone had murdered several people, that the pattern had to be seen differently—

"Well, of course they knew they were there. When Werthmere was built, there were all these Italian workmen camping on the lawn. Stone masons, plasterers, fancy cabinetmakers—even gilders. The first time they built the roof it collapsed, you know. Something about the way Eugenie Wentworth wanted it done. Several workmen were buried in the rubble, and some couldn't be dug out in time. And two, apparently, were never found. Until now."

"And no one inquired?"

"Well, they were temporary workers, weren't they? Just recruited for that job. I'm not sure they kept very good track of those people then. There were no passports, of course." He added gloomily, "And no income tax."

"So at least no one is blaming Elizabeth for that one. Or Mary." And it *didn't* knock my hypothesis into a cocked hat.

"No, no one at all is to blame. It's just life," said Ward.

I let it pass. "Maybe I should go into detective work," I said. "What do you think?"

That afternoon Pierre had told me where he had found the Wentworth murder police records that had been missing so long. In 1930, they had been sent down to Carribua: The commissioner there had been looking for a possible link to Lord Deake's murder in that year. The onionskin transcripts I had seen that day when I met Pierre had been sent up from the island.

"I almost feel now like taking a crack at the Lord Deake murder mystery. What do you say, Ward? An assignment in Carribua. British stately plantations. You know all the nobs down there. I'll go down and solve that one."

"I don't think that will be necessary, my dear. Just rest on your laurels and have another drink." He kept looking around, as if worried that other members of the club would raise their eyebrows at his raucous dinner partner. But we had arrived early. There was no one else in the room. "Anyway, I must say I was aesthetically disturbed by that Wentworth solution of yours. So untidy. So many elements coming in from outside."

"That's what you get in life."

"Yes. Well. But not *here*." He looked around with satisfaction.

"Well . . . I'd like to earn money *some* way." The Wentworth Commission sank like lost pirate bullion. I'd refused Quint's check. Now there was no way of getting the money and satisfaction too.

Again, Elizabeth and Mary flashed through my mind. Their two meetings. They should have had something to say to each other.

"I'd like to go away, maybe to Vermont. A fall vacation." I thought I might look for a new job.

My mention of vacation was Ward's cue. *He* didn't know where *he* could spend *his* vacation. What with the bad news from his broker and his ex-wives.

"—And the hurricane that's absolutely smashed my boat down in Carribua. If I want to repair the boat—and I must, it's an investment, I can't be irresponsible about it—I'll have to give up my pied-à-terre in Paris. If I could sell the condominium in New York, I would. Never get one. It's cheaper to pay rent. . . ."

I kept nodding and sympathizing and wondering if I should have another drink. Ward looked around as if for a waiter and immediately stood up, his face aglow with happy recognition.

An elderly couple were approaching us. The man had a dapper, dessicated look. The woman was augustly dowdy.

Somehow a rather attractive couple, I thought.

And then it happened. One of those common synapse-breaks, especially common after a few cocktails: Ward forgot the couple's names, my name, probably even his own name. The elderly man and woman stood smiling with benign anticipation.

"Ah, Penny, uh," said Ward, "uh . . . Lord and Lady Deake."

My jaw dropped. I knew the title was extinct.

There was the merest pause.

"Cyril and Beatrice Rattan-Roger," the woman murmured with well-bred ease.

" 'Course, of course, Sir Cyril and Lady Beatrice . . ."

Ward tried desperately to recover his fumble as Sir Cyril and Lady Beatrice spoke calmly of Carribua and London and Aiken, and whom they had seen most recently, and where. They had just dropped anchor at Newport.

Our dinner was announced. We took leave of the elderly couple and hurried into the dining room.

"Oh, my God, oh, my God," Ward mumbled. "Oh, how could I? I've made the faux pas of the century. I'll never dare show my face in Carribua again. Or here. Or anywhere."

"Oh, it's not that bad," I said as I was seated opposite him. "I often make mistakes in introductions."

"No, no, you don't understand. . . ." He kept mumbling and shuddering until the waiter went away. Ward looked quite green around the gills. "You see, everyone *knows* that Sir Cyril killed Lord Deake."

"*He . . .?* In 1930?"

"Yes. My train of thought was quite apparent, I'm afraid." Ward was fish-eyed with horror, crumbling oyster crackers and strewing them with abandon over the snowy table linen.

"I don't see . . ."

"You see, Deake was Lady Rattan-Roger's lover. Don't sit there and look stupid. Of course everyone knows about it; everyone knew *then*, on the island. But one doesn't *say* . . . Oh, my head . . . I'm finished. Finished. You don't know Society, how cruel and implacable . . . oh, my God, the faux pas of the century!"